# MAGIC IN THE MARSH

# MAGIC IN THE MARSH

## ACADEMY OF NECESSARY MAGIC™ BOOK TWO

MARTHA CARR

MICHAEL ANDERLE

DISRUPTIVE IMAGINATION®

Copyright © 2021 LMBPN Publishing
Cover Art by Jake @ J Caleb Design
http://jcalebdesign.com / jcalebdesign@gmail.com
Cover copyright © LMBPN Publishing
A Michael Anderle Production

LMBPN Publishing
PMB 196, 2540 South Maryland Pkwy
Las Vegas, NV 89109

First Version, February 2021
Version 1.01, May 2021
eBook ISBN: 978-1-64971-571-5
Print ISBN: 978-1-64971-572-2

***From Martha***

*To everyone who still believes in magic and all the possibilities that holds.*

*To all the readers who make this entire ride so much fun.*

*To Louie, Jackie, and so many wonderful friends who remind me all the time of what really matters and how wonderful life can be in any given moment.*

***From Michael***

*To Family, Friends and*
*Those Who Love*
*To Read.*
*May We All Enjoy Grace*
*To Live The Life We Are*
*Called.*

# THE MAGIC IN THE MARSH TEAM

## JIT Readers

Dave Hicks
Diane L. Smith
Thomas Ogden
Dorothy Lloyd
Daniel Weigert

*If I missed anyone, please let me know!*

## Editor

Skyhunter Editing Team

# CHAPTER ONE

Amanda Coulier watched the thick underbrush of the Everglades swamp rush by through the sky-blue sedan's window. A small smile played on her lips even before the front gates of the Academy came into view.

"You ready?" Lisa Breyer shot the young shifter girl a sidelong glance as they bumped over the uneven dirt road heading straight for the school.

"Even more ready than the first day." Amanda turned to flash the half-Light Elf a winning grin. "At least now I know what I'm getting into."

Lisa chuckled. "There's something to be said for that, sure."

A faint purple light flickered into existence as the car passed through the wards around the Academy. Lisa blinked and glanced at the disappearing light through the rearview mirror. "I hope they got a better handle on those wards this time."

Cringing, Amanda sank a little lower in the passenger seat. "You know about that?"

"Johnny told me. I'm pretty sure he didn't have to threaten the information out of anyone this time."

"Okay, to be clear, it wasn't my fault."

"Oh, I know. Most places don't have to amp up their wards against vengeful spirits. Though I can't in good conscience say it was a good idea to try using someone else's soul stone for your gain."

"I was only trying to pass my classes," the girl muttered. "Especially the one where they expected a shifter to be able to cast illusion spells."

Lisa slowly nodded as she pulled the car to a stop in the wide dirt lot at the end of the road. "Another oversight on their part. Seems to be a theme here."

"Yeah, or *I'm* the problem."

"Hey." After shifting into park, Lisa turned toward the girl and laid a hand on her shoulder. "Listen to me. You belong here, like the rest of these kids. Maybe even more, in some ways."

"I know that." Amanda stared at the steering wheel until the silence drew out so long, she had to look up at the half-Light Elf. Lisa might as well be as much of a parent to her now as the bounty hunter who'd taken her in. "I'll do better this semester."

"I know you will. No time like the present, right?"

Forcing a small, weak smile, Amanda turned to grab her duffel bag from the back seat. "Yeah, I'm gonna kick ass this time."

"Okay." Lisa smirked as the girl opened her door and practically leapt out of the car. Then she followed and walked around the hood, spreading her arms for a hug. "You know if you need help with anything, you can always call one of us."

"I won't have to." Amanda slung the strap of the bag over her shoulder. "Plus, you guys are busy with the whole small business thing. I get it."

They hugged each other, then Lisa stepped back and wrinkled her nose. "He did want to be here to see you off."

"Yeah, I know. But come on. If *I* had to choose between a convention for cutting-edge weapons tech and dropping a kid off at school, I would've made the same choice."

Lisa laughed. "I think he might be regretting that right now. When I talked to him this morning, it kind of sounded like the 'borgs were driving him up the wall."

Amanda rolled her eyes. "Everything drives him up the wall. They were getting a little antsy anyway, cooped up in the houseboat."

"They were?" The half-Light Elf cocked her head with a small frown. "What makes you think that?"

"Oh, I don't know. Maybe it was the explosion that knocked out the entire starboard-side wall at the fore. Or that June told me she was going crazy."

"Okay, well, they'll be fixing that hole as soon as they get back."

The shifter laughed. "I'm surprised he hasn't built *you* an extra room off the side of the cabin or something."

Lisa's eyes widened, and a light flush crept up her cheeks. "No. Where I sleep is—"

"Yeah, I get it. It's none of my business." With a coy smile, Amanda shrugged. *Johnny would freak out right now if he heard us talking about him. And them.*

Lisa recovered quickly and shook her head. "We'll let you know when they're back in town. I'm always here. If you need anything."

"Thanks. See ya." The shifter girl headed toward the main field in the center of the Academy's campus, then turned back as Lisa opened the driver's side door. "Hey, Lisa."

"Yeah?"

"Why didn't he say anything?"

"You're gonna have to be a little more specific than that, kiddo."

Amanda wrinkled her nose and gestured vaguely toward the campus. "You know, the whole *vengeful spirit* thing. And the stone. If he already knew…"

"Johnny doesn't blame you for any of it." Lisa glanced at the rise of school buildings on the other side of a stand of cattails partially blocking the view from the dirt lot. "Don't get me wrong. He was pissed, but not at you. Don't worry about that Illusions class, okay? If they took his advice, you'll be doing something a little different in classes that require magic."

"Meaning?"

"Meaning you're back at school, Amanda." Lisa nodded toward the campus. "Time to focus on that, so get outta here."

The shifter girl grinned, spun, and headed quickly toward the central field where some of the older students who lived at the Academy year-round were lounging around in the grass, soaking up the Florida sunshine at the beginning of January without all the muggy heat and humidity.

Her shifter hearing picked up Lisa muttering under her breath, "They better have taken his advice."

Then the car door shut, the engine started, and the crunch of tires across gravel faded away down the road.

Amanda smirked but didn't turn around to watch the half-Light Elf drive away.

*I'm back at school. Back where I belong. This time, I'm way more prepared.*

Some of the upperclassmen jerked their chins up at her or raised hands in greeting as she hurried across the central field with her duffel bag slung over her shoulder and thumping against her hip.

"Hey, Amanda." Margaret propped herself up on her elbows and smirked. "Enjoy your vacation?"

"You mean break? Yeah. You?"

"Same old, same old."

"Would've been better if *we* could get outta here," Kurt added. "You should take us with you next time. Show us around the middle of nowhere."

"Nah, you wouldn't like it." Amanda gestured at the swamp all around them. "It's more of this. No cities. Plus, the locals aren't exactly what you'd call normal."

The upperclassmen chuckled. "Fine. You keep the whole podunk town to yourself."

She shot them a crooked smile and trudged toward the girls' dorm on the other side of the main buildings where they held their classes. *Pretty sure if they knew how Johnny felt about a bunch of LA kids running around in the Everglades, they wouldn't even joke about leaving campus.*

The common room of the girls' dorm was fuller than usual, but then again, it was the last Saturday of winter break before the spring semester started. The students still had a little of their freedom left before classes resumed on Monday. Amanda nodded and gave vague hellos to the other girls who greeted her. Most of them were too caught up in their small groups and private conversations to notice another student at the Academy showing up after two weeks off.

Amanda made her way up the empty, echoing staircase to the third floor. The hallway was empty when she emerged, but more random, carefree conversations from the other girls' open rooms greeted her as she headed down toward room 228C on the left—her home for the next five months.

She pulled her room key from her pocket, and the familiar buzz of the magic set to respond only to her skittered up her hand when she unlocked her door. A door opened behind her across the hall as she stepped into her room.

"Hey, shifter girl."

With a grin, Amanda tossed her duffel bag onto the floor and turned. "Hey, Sum—whoa."

Summer Flannerty stood in her room's entrance across the hall, one arm propped against the frame as she gave Amanda a lazy smirk. "What? Didn't expect me to be here still when you got back from Fun Time with your bounty hunter?"

"He's not my—whatever. What did you do to your hair?"

"Whatever the hell I feel like." Summer stalked across the hallway and folded her arms. "I needed a change, that's all."

"Yeah. Definitely a change." Amanda pressed her lips together and fought back a laugh.

The witch had shaved one side of her head entirely although the line wasn't exactly straight, and there were still patches of longer hair along the edge where Summer hadn't quite been able to double-check her work.

"Did you do that yourself?"

"Duh. I'm not gonna let someone else touch my hair."

"Right. You know, if you need an extra mirror, I have one right—"

"Nah, I don't use mirrors." Summer stopped right outside Amanda's room and peered inside. "I go with the flow. Whatever feels good."

"Yeah, that's...definitely what it looks like."

"Good. So what did *you* do for two weeks without boring classes and teachers breathing down your neck?"

"Um...not a lot, really." Amanda grabbed her duffel bag and took it to her bed, where she unzipped it to pull out her clothes. "You know, hanging out in the swamp with Johnny and the hounds." *And Lisa and four cyborgs trying to figure out how not to break everything they touch.* "Pretty normal. What about you?"

Summer sniffed and shrugged. "Just about clawed my eyes out cooped up in this place with nothing to do. And no one to break the rules with me."

Amanda cast a glance into the hallway. "Maybe keep it down about that, huh?"

"Oh, come on, shifter girl. It's not like anyone cares. We already outed ourselves the first week of last semester."

"That doesn't mean we have to make it a pattern."

Summer chuckled. "Aw, did you get in *trouble*?"

"No." She took her folded clothes to the dresser and tossed

them inside. "Which was kinda weird. Seriously, if we're gonna keep doing what we were doing, we have to be more careful."

"Yeah, yeah, I know. If we don't get caught, they can't stop us." Summer scratched the poorly shaved side of her head. "We're still going, right?"

"Totally." Amanda glanced at her duffel bag. "Not now, though."

"Clearly." With a deep breath and a heavy sigh, Summer turned away from the shifter girl's room and tossed a hand in the air. "Get all *settled* in your room. I'll see you when I see you."

"Okay."

The black-haired witch returned to her room and shut the door behind her.

Amanda frowned across the hall, then snorted and shook her head. *Yeah, she'll see me at every meal and in every class. Whatever.*

Before unpacking anything else from her bag, she closed her door and tried not to look suspicious doing so. Still, she couldn't help her excitement when she returned to her bed and rummaged around in the bag for what she'd been thinking about using since she'd found it in Johnny's workshop, and he'd explained what the device was for.

She bit her bottom lip as she pulled out an object sized somewhere between a smartphone and a small tablet. The screen was chalky, and the black and silver components bulky and heavy in her hand. When she turned it on to double-check, the screen flickered with a soft backlight before illuminating with an orange glow. She grinned and shut it off immediately.

*Yeah. This is gonna be a game-changer for sure. Hopefully, Johnny has his hands full enough with the 'borgs that he doesn't notice it's missing.*

# CHAPTER TWO

Principal Glasket called all the Academy's students down to the central field before dinner for an announcement. Amanda was one of the last to make it out after fully unpacking her bag and settling back into her room. The other students shouted at each other, joking around and jostling one another as the principal stepped up onto the stage. One of Mr. LeFor's new microphones hovered in midair above the witch's head. She swiped at it three times before she managed to grab it and pull it down to face-level because the thing kept floating out of her reach.

Glasket shot Mr. LeFor a condescending frown, and the redheaded Augmented Technology teacher shrugged and readjusted his glasses. Then the principal cleared her throat and spoke. "Welcome back to your—"

The mic squealed in protest, followed by the students' protests as they clapped their hands over their ears and leaned away from the stage, laughing.

The principal leaned away from the microphone and glared at the teachers gathered beside the stage. "If I'd wanted feedback like this, I would've used a regular mic."

"It's a prototype." Mr. LeFor shrugged. "Still has a few bugs."

Glasket straightened the front of her light cardigan, swatted the floating mic away from her face—ignoring LeFor's anxious groan at the treatment of his tech—and snapped her fingers. This time, when she spoke, her voice projected across the field by her spell instead of an enchanted microphone.

"Welcome back for your second semester, students."

The laughing and jostling died down for the most part as the kids realized they weren't getting out of this announcement.

"You've made it through your first, and now you've had the opportunity to decompress over the winter break," Glasket continued.

"Hard to believe this place is still here, right?" Rob shouted, which brought a round of laughter from the other students.

"*You* won't be, Mr. Mackey, if you insist on starting your semester by interrupting me with lame jokes."

Rob's friends jeered and shoved him around, and even Principal Glasket allowed herself a small smile at the student's expense.

She cleared her throat and continued. "Now, before this gets more out of hand than we intend, allow me to remind you all that the freedom you've enjoyed over the last two weeks is quickly coming to an end. Once Monday arrives, you'll be back to your regular schedule to continue the second half of the school year. I also feel that a reminder is in order after the winter break. Skinny-dipping is strictly prohibited, at any hour of the day, whether class is in session or not. I don't care how warm the water is. Yes, Mr. Brunsen, I'm looking specifically at you."

The students replied with laughter and shouts of encouragement as the kid in question got jostled around and thumped on the back.

"The kitchens have cooked up something a little more celebratory than usual to welcome you all back to the structure of the school year. Enjoy the rest of your weekend. Curfew and Lights Out return tomorrow night at ten o'clock." Glasket snapped her fingers beside her throat again, and her projection spell cut off before she shot a disapproving glance at the floating microphone. It was now attempting to follow her off the stage, and she batted it aside as she stepped down.

Mr. LeFor looked horrified by the treatment of his newest invention.

Amanda fought back her laugh and turned to head toward the outdoor cafeteria, where the smell of shrimp and corn on the cob and biscuits had been making her mouth water for the last five minutes. The other students rushed past her to get to their dinner, and a hand clapped down on her shoulder from behind.

"Look who decided to show up." Jackson Pris grinned at the shifter girl, glanced at his hand on her shoulder, and immediately removed it. "I thought you would've for sure decided not to come back to *this* awesome place."

Amanda grinned at the wizard. "How many times do I have to tell people I wanna be here?"

"Aw, I know. Just checking. How was your break?"

"Two weeks at home. Pretty uneventful."

"Uh-huh. I bet. Shifter in the swamp and everything." He hissed out a laugh and shook his head. "You look different."

"Um…"

"I don't know what it is, but something's—"

"Amanda!" Grace hurried to join them, offering them both a wide smile. "Good to see you."

"Yeah, you too."

"So what'd you get for Christmas?"

"What?"

"You know…" Grace wiggled her eyebrows. "Christmas. That happened over break. Don't tell me that bounty hunter you're living with doesn't do Christmas."

"I mean, he doesn't *not* do it." Amanda shrugged. "I only wanted one thing, so…"

"Well, spit it out, Coulier." Jackson gestured to the crowd of students milling toward the outdoor cafeteria for dinner. "We're living vicariously through you. You know that, right? You have somewhere to go over the break, you're not cooped up here on campus, and you *had* to have gotten something for Christmas."

"You guys didn't?"

Grace gave a mocking grimace. "I mean, if you count fifteen pies from the kitchen pixies an actual *present*."

"Yeah, I didn't even get to taste 'em all," Jackson added.

"Because you ate half the cookies."

"And they were *so* good. Even worth lying in bed Christmas Day without being able to move." Jackson grinned and bumped Amanda with his shoulder. "So? What was that *one thing*?"

Amanda scanned the outdoor kitchen with a tiny smile. "Johnny built me something."

"What, like a sweet gun or something? Or a treehouse?"

Grace snorted and elbowed the wizard in the side. "You think one of the bounty hunters that set up this school would build her a treehouse?"

"I don't know. She's not saying anything." He spread his arms. "Either spit it out, or I'll keep throwing out guesses. Was it a motorcycle?"

Amanda shot him a playful frown. "I'm pretty sure I'd need a driver's license for that."

"Not out here in the middle of nowhere."

"You're ridiculous," Grace muttered.

"Well, I wouldn't have to be if Coulier would quit being all secretive and answer the question. Hey, remember what happened last semester when you kept secrets from the *whole school*—"

"Jackson." Grace glared at him and shook her head. "Why would you say something like that?"

"What?" His eyes widened, and he glanced back and forth between the girls staring at him. "I mean, it *did* happen."

"It's okay." Amanda shrugged off the minor awkwardness

11

and brushed past her friends to get in the already long line trailing away from the banquet tables. "I got an obstacle course."

Jackson and Grace stared at each other, and the wizard wrinkled his nose before spinning around to hurry after the shifter girl. "Wait, wait, wait. You got *what*?"

"You heard me." She stuck her hands into the pockets of her light hoodie and shrugged.

"That doesn't sound like a Christmas present," Grace added as she stepped in line behind Jackson. "That sounds like torture."

"Yeah, the kinda torture we're about to be reliving every other morning with Mr. Petrov."

Amanda couldn't hold back the grin that felt like it would split her face in half. "That was kinda the point."

"Okay, wait. My brain's exploding, Coulier." Jackson ran a hand through his shaggy blond hair, then pointed at her. "Are you saying what I think you're saying?"

"I can't even *pretend* to know what you're thinking."

"Amanda." Grace leaned forward past the wizard and widened her eyes. "The *same* obstacle course?"

"Yep. Or at least as close as I could remember it, but I'm pretty sure it was close enough."

Jackson puffed out a heavy sigh through loose lips. "I could run that course in my sleep at this point. And fall off at the same place every time."

Grace's mouth fell open in an incredulous smile. "Like with the stupid magical pea-shooters and everything?"

Amanda shrugged. "Yeah. Johnny's good at building things. I wanted to come back here and finally make it to the end of the course. So…"

"So you got two extra weeks of getting your ass kicked on a deadly playground." Jackson blinked. "For Christmas."

"Yeah, plus some tips. It's no big deal."

"No big deal. You hear that?" He turned toward Grace and

shook his head. "This shifter's gonna show us all up in front of Petrov on the *first day*."

The blonde witch smirked. "She's already been showing us up on that thing. In case you haven't noticed."

They moved up the line and reached the end of the banquet table, where they grabbed their plates and waited to get to the actual food.

"Except for the sergeant's gonna notice even *more*, and the rest of us are gonna end up running extra laps or doing pushups until our arms fall off."

Amanda shrugged. "I mean, it's better than scrubbing walls without magic for an entire weekend."

"Huh. Maybe."

"That's the *only* thing you wanted for Christmas?" Grace asked as she slapped a heaping pile of buttered and cheese-covered mashed potatoes on her plate. "For real?"

"Yep." Amanda didn't exactly feel like expanding on it. Her first Christmas without her family had been a hard one, and building that obstacle course in Johnny Walker's back yard so she could run herself through it a few times a day had seemed like the best way to deal with it.

*No way am I gonna be able to explain four cyborgs camped out in his giant houseboat. That was weird enough to come home to in the first place.*

They finished piling their plates high with food, then turned to look for an empty picnic table under the pavilion.

"So what about you guys?" she asked. "Don't tell me you sat around for two weeks and didn't do *anything* exciting."

"I mean, Mark almost got eaten by a giant bird."

"*What?*" They sat down at an empty picnic table, and Amanda stared back and forth between them. "That can't be right."

"It was a heron," Grace muttered. "I think."

"Well, whatever it was, it chased him out of the swamp and tried to pull his hair out. Or maybe make a nest there. I don't know." Jackson crammed a huge bite of food into his mouth and shrugged.

"Oh, Annabelle cast an enchantment on all the mirrors in the girls' dorm," Grace added. "Most of us already knew what was happening, but Candace freaked *out*."

Amanda smirked. "What was the enchantment?"

"It made everyone see themselves with giant breakouts." The witch managed to hold back a laugh as she took a long sip of water. "Yeah, it was only on the mirrors. She was convinced her other yes-girls were lying to her just to make her feel better. So she kept…putting on more makeup, and it didn't do anything."

Grace and Amanda stared at each other, then cracked up laughing.

Jackson chewed silently and shook his head. "Dumbest thing I've ever heard."

"Hey, Amanda." Alex Montoya sat next to her and leaned over the table as he tossed his long brown ponytail over his shoulder. "What's dumb?"

"Playing zit pranks on each other?" Jackson shrugged. "I don't know, man. Chicks."

"It's funny if you're a girl who gets picked on for every little thing by Candace Jones, okay?"

"She picks on you guys?" Alex picked up his fork and stabbed up a huge bite without looking at anyone.

"Not explicitly." Grace shrugged. "But she sure has it out for anyone who even *acts* like they're not afraid of her when she walks by."

The half-Wood Elf looked up at Jackson and raised his eyebrows. "Maybe someone should say something."

Jackson cleared his throat before shoveling more food in his mouth and didn't say a word.

*What's* that *about?*

Amanda shook her head. "It's fine. Some people have a hard

time figuring out who they wanna be. I think Candace is behind on that a little."

Alex leaned away from her and grinned. "Listen to you. The youngest freshman at the Academy has it all figured out, huh?"

"Amanda might as well be as old as the rest of us," Grace added with a smirk. "She's gonna kick our asses on that obstacle course on Monday."

"You mean more than usual?" Alex shoveled more food into his mouth.

"Dude, she built a freakin' copy of it to practice over break and called it a *Christmas present*." Jackson wouldn't look at her and went right back to eating.

"Huh." Alex shrugged. "Merry Christmas."

Grace burst out laughing, and Amanda smiled at her plate. "It's good to be back."

*Didn't think I'd miss being here that much, but two weeks of weird at Johnny's cabin was more than enough. I have a whole semester to look forward to now.*

# CHAPTER THREE

Even though the curfew and Lights Out had apparently been lifted for the other students who'd spent the break on campus and was still lifted tonight, Amanda felt like she had to sneak back to the girls' dorm at 10:00 p.m. on her return from the kitchens. There was no hole in the security enchantments to slip through tonight and no repercussions for getting caught walking across the field this late. She wasn't even the only student outside. Still, she padded across the grass and entered the dorm through the back door where the hole in the wards usually was.

*Hopefully, it's still there once classes start. Guess I'll have to wait and find out.*

Laughter and light-hearted shouts greeted her from the common room as she headed down the hallway with the large basket from the kitchen pixies in her arms. Almost half of the girls at the Academy had gathered here tonight, and now the tables and chairs set up in the room were all shoved haphazardly against the wall to make room for pillows and blankets and a few folding lawn chairs Jasmine had pilfered from the broom closet by the back door.

"Hey, *there* she is," Annabelle called when she saw Amanda

walking across the common room. "Jeeze. You needed to steal *all* of that?"

"I didn't steal it."

The other girls on the floor turned to see the basket of snacks in her arms and cheered.

"No way did they simply *give* you all that," Margaret said with a laugh. "What'd you do? Knock all the pixies out first before you ransacked the pantry?"

"Amanda doesn't have to steal from the pixies." Grace laughed with the other girls and motioned for the shifter to sit beside her. "They like her."

"Oh, sure." Jasmine rolled her eyes. "Because she's the one eating them out of food for the rest of us—hey!" She glared at Grace and leaned away. "What was that for?"

"For being a brat."

Amanda set the basket of snacks down on the table and tossed aside the cloth covering the top. "Anyone else ever stop to talk to them?"

"The pixies?" Leah Morton snorted. "Why? They don't leave the kitchen."

"Maybe that's why they like me." She grinned at the girl. "And give me free snacks I don't have to steal."

Some girls laughed as they rushed to the table to grab cookies, popcorn, crackers and cheese, and bits of fudge from the basket. One sophomore girl Amanda didn't know that well took a bite of fudge and frowned. "This better not be left over from New Year's."

"Oh, yeah? You have something better to share with the rest of us?"

"Fudge keeps forever."

"Yeah, like Annabelle's hair!"

They cracked up laughing, and Annabelle threw a handful of popcorn at the elf girl who'd thrown out the mock insult. "It's my hairspray, thank you very much."

"Where's Tenney?" someone else asked. "She was supposed to be here with the—"

The front door burst open, and Tenney raised a large tablet in both hands in a show of victory. The other girls cheered. "Aw, you waited for me?"

"Not with the snacks." Havalah crammed two cookies into her mouth. "Hurry up."

Amanda had grabbed four giant chocolate chip cookies and brought them with her to sit beside Grace on the floor. She handed two of them to her friend and couldn't help but smile at the other girls—most of them sophomores and juniors—shuffling around to grab their snacks from the basket and get comfortable. "So I know I offered to get food, but for what, exactly?"

The blonde witch grinned at her. "Movie night."

"If Tenney can get that thing to work." Annabelle tossed another handful of popcorn at the half-witch stepping carefully around the others with the giant tablet in her hands.

"I'll get it to work. LeFor thinks I spent his entire class last semester helping him fix the power breaker in his workshop."

"You did."

Tenney smirked. "Yeah. *And* I managed to reroute some of the wi-fi signal from the teachers' building."

The other girls cheered and laughed and tossed bits of snacks at her as she pulled a table front and center and propped the tablet on it.

"You know it's not gonna last, right?"

"You're getting *so* busted for this!"

"Yeah, but not *tonight!*" The girl snatched up a bit of cookie that landed on the table and popped it into her mouth. "So now we have to pick something. Make it good. I already did my part."

Amanda ducked a flying brownie bite and laughed. *At least I'm not the only one breaking rules and getting in trouble for it later.*

Havalah shook out her bedsheets she'd brought downstairs

with her and cast a quick spell. The sheets whipped around, ruffling the other girls' hair as they ducked out of the way and groaned in complaint. When the spell finished, the girl climbed into a hammock suspended by nothing but thin air and folded her arms behind her head with a sigh.

"Showoff."

"Hey, do one for me."

"You can't even cast a spell to make your handwriting legible. Figure it out yourself."

"Pick the movie!" another girl shouted, and the course of their conversations switched immediately.

"*Dirty Dancing!*"

"What? Ew. Sounds like something my grandma would watch."

"*Harry Potter.*"

"Yeah, because we all know how real *that* is."

"*Twilight!*"

Most of the girls broke out in shrieking laughter and tossed food and the odd pillow at the cackling half-Crystal who'd made the suggestion.

"Jesus, you guys are impossible." Tenney went back to the tablet and blocked the view while she poked around to find a good place to start. "No one gets to argue with me on this. Because no one has decent taste in movies."

"Oh, yeah? And you do?"

"Hey, I spent six months sneaking into the movie theater before we got shipped out here. I know what's good."

Amanda leaned toward Grace. "Did she really?"

"I don't know. Probably. It's not like we had a curfew and checked in with everybody all the time. Perks of living under-ground, right?"

"Yeah, I guess." The shifter girl watched Tenney stab the tablet's screen one final time before she turned and swept her arms wide, showing off with a deep bow.

"You can thank me later, ladies."

More popcorn flew at her face, and she jumped to catch the stray kernels in her mouth before sitting down with the rest of the group.

Amanda crunched on another cookie and watched the opening credits scroll across the tablet's screen. Tenney had the volume turned up incredibly loud. "This is nuts."

"What?" Grace sucked chocolate off her fingers. "You've never had a movie night before?"

"Not like this. I mean, my sister and I used to build forts and watch the R-rated movies our parents wouldn't let us see."

The witch raised an eyebrow. "Like, *how* R-rated?"

"Like *007*."

Grace elbowed her in the side. "Ha! Okay. Good luck trying to get the rest of these nutjobs to agree on something like *that*."

"I don't mind." Amanda's smile faded a little at the memory of her and her twin sister Claire, of those nights when the only thing they had to worry about was how loud they could play those movies so their parents didn't hear.

"Hey." Grace turned to look at her head-on. "That's a big step, right?"

"What?"

"I mean, you usually shut down when stuff comes up about… you know. Family."

"Yeah. Well, I figure it's probably better to talk about it at some point." *Now that everyone saw their ghosts. Can't keep that secret in the bag anymore.*

"I think it's cool." Grace shrugged. "That's all."

"*And*…here we go!" Tenney shouted and pointed at the tablet. The title credit for *Queen of the Damned* appeared, and half of the girls groaned.

"Are you kidding me?"

"You picked *this*?"

"What? He's hot! Complain all you want. You know I'm right."

The laughter died as the movie started, and the sound of two dozen girls munching on midnight snacks from the kitchen pixies and whispering to each other about anything related to the movie—or not—filled the common room.

Amanda grimaced at the opening scene and whispered to Grace, "Have you seen this?"

"Nope. It looks really old."

"Yeah. And weird."

Amanda could barely pay attention to the movie, which served as a background for whatever the other girls wanted to discuss. They focused most of their attention on practicing spells that weren't teacher sanctioned—like Havalah's floating hammock or Annabelle's attempt to restock the snacks with a copy spell—the cookie copies tasted like cardboard after that one—or gossiping in hushed tones.

When the first attempt at a romantic scene showed up on the screen, a handful of girls broke out in exaggerated squeals, falling over laughing and pointing at Tenney.

"*This* is what you thought was so hot, Tenney?"

"You have the *worst* taste in…everything."

"Hey." Tenney crammed a handful of popcorn into her mouth and smirked. "I can dream, right? Vampires aren't real."

"You sure about that?"

"They *might* be."

"You all can shut up. I'm trying to watch this."

"Oh, come on. That's not hot. That's desperation."

"Hey, kinda reminds me of someone we know on campus. Right, Amanda?" Margaret turned over her shoulder to grin at the shifter girl.

Amanda straightened where she sat and frowned at the half-witch. A confused chuckle escaped her. "Uh...I have no idea what you're talking about."

"Right..." Someone tossed a cracker at her, followed by a floppy pillow. "Like you haven't seen the way Jackson Pris has been running around shouting your name to the empty swamp!"

"Whoa, hey. She hasn't. She left for break, remember?"

Amanda picked up the pillow and whacked Margaret with it in the back of the head. The girl shouted in surprise and fell forward onto her face. The other girls cracked up laughing. "Crap. Sorry."

Margaret picked herself back up with a chuckle and snatched the pillow away. "Maybe tone it down a little on the shifter strength, huh? Don't blame *me* for the truth."

"You guys are making that up."

"No way." Tenney placed a hand over her heart and closed her eyes in mock seriousness. "On my honor as a student of the Academy—"

"You don't have any honor!" someone shouted.

"Not any more than the rest of us!"

More laughter and shouts and bits of food were tossed across the common room.

"Fine." Tenney pointed at Amanda. "Still, I'm not lying to you. That wizard has it bad for you, *Coulier*. He spent the whole break running around asking everyone about you. I heard he got kicked out of Glasket's office for telling her it was an emergency and trying to interrogate her about *you* instead."

"That's ridiculous. No way." Amanda shook her head and brushed them all off. "He's a friend. Grace knows."

When she looked at the blonde witch sitting beside her, Grace had her lips tightly pressed together to hide a smirk and stared straight ahead at the practically forgotten movie on the tablet.

"What?" Amanda shoved her friend lightly in the shoulder. Everyone was laughing now. "You don't agree with them?"

"I'm not saying anything." Grace mimed zipping her lips and

shrugged, then shot the shifter girl a sidelong glance. "Not a thing. So don't even ask."

"Oh, jeeze." She snatched up the second giant cookie Grace hadn't gotten around to eating yet and took a large bite before shaking the cookie in the witch's face. "I don't believe anything any of you are saying right now. I thought we were supposed to be watching a movie."

"You wanna watch *this* train wreck?" Jasmine shouted.

"No, not really."

They all fell into another round of laughter, and Grace stared at her second cookie quickly growing smaller in the shifter girl's possession. "I'll remember that, cookie thief."

"Good. *I'll* remember you trying to convince me that Jackson's...whatever." Amanda crammed another bite into her mouth and smirked as she chewed.

*There's no way. Only a bunch of high school girls with nothing else to do but gossip about what doesn't even exist.*

Still, every time she returned her attention to the movie, she kept seeing Jackson Pris' face instead of the actors, and it made her wrinkle her nose every time.

*I should've asked the pixies for more cookies.*

## CHAPTER FOUR

The "movie night" lasted another hour past the end of the actual movie, even through the chain reaction of yawning and exhausted stretching among the group of girls camped out in the common room. Blake Cameron had already fallen asleep on the mattress she'd brought from her room, and the other girls jokingly tried to tickle her awake through her snores. They gave up when Blake grunted and rolled over in her sleep.

"Are you passing out here or going back to your room?" Grace asked as she cracked open a bottle of water.

"I'm gonna go upstairs."

"Yeah, better get some sleep." That coy, secretive smile returned to the witch's lips, and Amanda shook her head.

"Whatever game this is, I'm not buying it."

"Okay. Suit yourself. Good *night...*" Grace pulled a face at her, and Amanda playfully rolled her eyes before heading to the back of the dorm where the second staircase was.

"Sleep tight, shifter girl," Tenney called after her. "Whatever *you're* dreaming about tonight, I'm pretty sure somebody in the building next door's gonna be dreaming about *you*."

The other girls let out tired chuckles interspersed with more yawns, and Amanda tossed them all a flippant wave without saying anything else as she headed toward the staircase in the back hallway.

*If this is what movie nights are like all the time, I'll skip on the next one.*

She climbed the staircase as quickly as she could and raced toward her room. Not because she was tired, but because she didn't think she could handle all the jokes and the laughter and the absurd claims about Jackson. Not to mention the fact that the eighteen girls who thought it was fun to sleep all together in the same room on the first floor would sound like a freight train, thanks to Amanda's shifter hearing.

*If Blake snores like that, everyone else has gotta be way louder.*

Summer's door swung open, and the black-haired witch leaned sideways against the doorframe again. "Christ, they're loud. Even if I were trying to get to sleep right now, I wouldn't be able to."

"I heard earplugs work." Amanda unlocked her door and shrugged. "You know, for magicals with normal hearing."

"Hardy-har." Summer glanced up and down the empty hall, then crossed it to join her friend. "You did bring *something*, though, right?"

"Earplugs?"

"You're *so* funny." The witch rolled her eyes and leaned against the doorway of Amanda's room instead. "You know what I mean."

"Yeah, I brought something." Amanda slid her duffel bag out from under her bed, which held only the small, bulky device she'd taken from Johnny's workshop along with a few other... inventions she figured he wouldn't miss anytime soon. When she stood, she wiggled the thing at her friend. "This."

"Looks like my grandpa's pager."

"What's that?"

"I don't know. A stupid excuse for a one-way phone or something. You sure it works?"

"Oh, yeah. I even know *how* it works."

Summer snorted. "Okay, smartass. So let's go."

Amanda tossed the borrowed device in her hand. "You know half the girls at this school are still down there, right?"

"So? They're too busy braiding each other's hair and talking about boys. They don't care." After studying her friend's face, the black-haired witch narrowed her eyes. "They watched some kinda gross chick flick with magic, didn't they?"

"Vampires. I think. I don't even know if there was a story."

Summer wrinkled her nose. "That's why I don't do movie nights. Come on. You made me wait two weeks for this, and I'm about to explode if I have to wait any longer."

"Yeah, okay." Amanda shoved the device into the pocket of her zip-up hoodie and followed the witch into the hall, softly pulling her door shut behind her. It wasn't exactly against the rules to be out and walking around campus at almost 1:00 a.m. At least, not tonight. However, it was definitely against the rules to be doing what they were heading out to do, hands down.

*As long as nobody asks what we're up to, we'll be fine.*

They snuck around the corner of the back staircase and headed for the dorm's back door without any of the other girls noticing. The raucous conversation had died down, now joined by light snoring and the occasional whispered giggle and aggravated hiss of, "Shut up. I'm trying to sleep."

Summer silently pulled open the back door and grinned as she held it and gestured for Amanda to step outside first. No need to prop it open with the bucket from the broom closet tonight. Not with the security enchantments down on their last night of freedom before classes started.

They hurried past the small pockets of students still hanging around the campus this late at night. Someone was butchering whatever they attempted to play on a harmonica. A larger group of upperclassmen sat around a floating fire pit, laughing and joking.

*At least we're in the swamp and not a forest.*

Amanda eyed them carefully, able to see well enough in the dark to know that none of them paid any attention to a pair of freshmen girls heading out this late and making their way toward the northern edge of campus, far beyond the edge of the main buildings. It wouldn't matter if they had. The whole school had seen Amanda Coulier and Summer Flannerty walking the perimeter of the Academy three times a day for the last few weeks of the fall semester, cleaning up the large, weirdly polka-dotted grubs the reinforced wards attracted.

One of the grubs popped beneath Summer's boot when they reached the edge of the school grounds, throwing off an orange spark when its neon-glowing guts sprayed across the ferns.

"Oh, ugh." The witch studied the underside of her boot, then wiped it off on the waterlogged grass. "I had no idea they did that."

"At least we don't have to keep dropping them in buckets." Amanda stepped carefully along the edge of the reeds until they found the small break in the wards where the teachers had cast an illusion of nothing but swamp instead. "You should probably make sure it's all off your shoe before we go back. I don't think Glasket's done watching us."

Summer scoffed. "Please. If she'd been watching us as closely as she wants us to think, she would've figured out what we're doing a long time ago."

"Yeah, I guess." Amanda stepped through the illusion first, and the thick swamp underbrush shrouded by overhanging tree branches draped with moss gave way to a clear pathway. The trail led to the long dock stretching out into the waterways of the Everglades.

"Hurry up, huh? You took long enough watching a stupid

movie you didn't even enjoy." Summer brushed past her and practically jogged down the dock.

"Hey, if you don't think we have enough time, we can try again tomorrow—"

"And waste a perfectly good night of *not* having to sneak past the enchantments? Are you crazy?"

"Maybe, if I'm coming out here with you."

"You're all talk, shifter girl." Summer hopped onto one of the three airboats tied to the dock and rubbed her hands together. "I know you wanna find this place as much as I do. *If* that fancy thing you brought does what you think it does."

"I said it'll work, okay?" Amanda stopped to untie the rope from the dock, then hopped up onto the airboat with her friend and smirked. "Guess you're gonna have to trust me."

"Right. 'Cause we've been through so much together already and now we're best friends, blah, blah, blah."

Amanda flipped on the airboat's control throttle and gently cranked up the giant fan at the back of the boat. "I didn't say *that...*"

"Whatever. Take us to the kemana, Captain. For the fifty-thousandth time." Summer stood in the center of the deck and pointed straight ahead as though she knew where they were headed.

The truth was that neither one of them knew where the kemana was, and after the last few weeks spent looking for it at night before winter break, they still hadn't managed to find it. It didn't matter where the signs on the dock pointed or how many different routes Amanda had steered them down along the maze of rivers cutting through the swamp.

*Not this time.* She pulled the device from her pocket and cranked up the throttle now that they were far enough away from the school. *This thing is better than a map.*

"You know what I don't get?" Summer walked carefully back to the stern and stopped to throw her hands on her hips.

"That's probably a fairly long list."

The witch wrinkled her nose and shot Amanda a haughty scowl.

"What? You left yourself wide open for that one."

"Yeah, whatever. *I'm* talking about the fact that they leave the keys in here all the time. Like, they *want* us to steal a boat and head out into the swamp by ourselves."

"They probably assume none of us know how to drive one of these things."

"True." Summer turned toward the front of the boat and tossed half of her un-shaved hair into the wind blasting them in the face. "Good thing you know the swamp like the back of your hand, huh?"

"I don't. I only know how to use an airboat." Amanda powered on the device and smiled at the weak orange glow coming from behind the screen. "But I *do* know somebody who could probably map out half of the Everglades if he had to. And *this* thing'll get us there."

"You sound sure about that."

"That's because I am." Amanda pulled the control throttle toward her to take them around the gentle left-hand bend in the river before it widened and the trees didn't hang over them so closely like a mossy tunnel. "This thing tracks high levels of magical activity. Or something."

"Uh-huh. The bounty hunter simply gave it to you?"

"No." She wrinkled her nose and had to laugh. "It's not a problem. He'll get it back. He won't miss it, anyway. Johnny's out of town with the 'borgs for like...I don't know. Another week."

"Wait, wait, wait. The *what?*"

"Huh?"

Summer lifted her gaze from the orange-glowing device and frowned at her friend. "What the hell are the 'borgs?"

"Oh. Uh..." She scrunched up her face. "He adopted some cyborgs a few months ago. Doesn't matter."

Hissing out a laugh, the witch shook her head. "You got some of the weirdest stories, shifter girl. Part of me wants to figure out how many of them are true, and the rest of me doesn't want anything to do with it."

"Right. Just like I don't want to have anything to do with you blowing up old temple crypts and getting both of us in serious trouble again. Not *this* semester."

"Hey, what happened with that stone was as much your fault as it was mine, okay?" Summer shrugged and smirked at the dark water of the slightly salty river ahead of them. "But yeah, I take full responsibility for the explosions. So how does this thing work, anyway?"

Keeping half her attention on steering them safely down the river, Amanda focused the other half on studying the device in her hand. "I told you. It picks up on high concentrations of magic. Like some kind of radar. Except—"

"Not for sniffing out ships or planes or other machines wherever we are. I get that part. What's the point of using one of these anyway? I mean, besides using it to find a kemana I'm starting to think doesn't exist in the middle of all this…swamp."

"Johnny makes a lot of things most people don't think are all that useful. He finds a use for them, though." *So do I, apparently. I'll have to make this one up to him somehow.*

"Okay, fine. So your bounty hunter has his reasons, and you—"

"Stop calling him that."

"What?" Summer looked clueless.

"He's not *my* bounty hunter."

"So…what is he, then?"

Amanda blinked and steered them around another bend in the river. "He's…I mean, he's pretty much the only family I have right now. Him and Lisa. But if you have to call him *something*, call him Johnny, okay?"

"Oh." Summer lifted both hands in mock surrender. "*Some-body's* touchy about ownership."

"Yeah, well, I was almost somebody else's toy shifter. And not the fun kind. So maybe I still have issues."

"Damn." All traces of levity disappeared from Summer's face in an instant. "Sorry."

"No, it's fine. Let's focus on—oh. Hey! There it is!" Grinning, Amanda shoved the magical radar device under her friend's nose and shook it. "You see that dot?"

"The big green one in at the top of the screen? Yeah, it's kinda hard to miss."

"That's where we're going. Here." She shoved the device into Summer's hands and gripped the airboat's control throttle with both hands, her eyes widening under the sliver of moonlight spilling down on the open river. "You navigate."

"Oh, joy. I've always wanted to be a back-seat driver on a boat with no actual seats."

"Tell me where we are compared to that dot, okay?" Playfully rolling her eyes, Amanda drew a deep breath of the briny night air and nodded. "There's no way that's *not* the kemana. The Academy doesn't show up with that big a dot, and we're all there to learn magic, right?"

"Most of us, sure." Summer slowly lowered herself to the deck of the airboat and crossed her legs beneath her, staring intently at the green blip on the device they now had to follow.

*Yeah. Most of us. Because shifters can't do magic without the soul stone of some dead guy to power them up. Doesn't mean I'm useless. I still belong here.*

"So…we might have a little problem." Summer extended her arm over the starboard side and pointed without looking up from the device. "I can't exactly tell you to turn right at the next intersection, but we're about to go right past this place."

"Okay, fine. We'll find the next branch in the river and head back upstream a little. No big deal."

"You're sure there *will* be a branch in the river?"

Amanda smirked and turned up the throttle so the fan whirred louder and faster behind them. "There's always another route through the swamp. Trust me."

Summer snorted. "Hey, you've proven your ability to get completely lost and smell your way back to the dock off-campus. I can suspend disbelief a little longer."

"Yeah, thanks a lot." She glanced down at the device in her friend's hand and didn't say a word. They'd get to the kemana. Maybe letting Summer believe she was navigating would keep her from asking more questions Amanda didn't want to answer.

# CHAPTER FIVE

"We're so close." Summer shot to her feet ten minutes later and pointed straight ahead. "Right there. That little island. It *has* to be there, right?"

"That's what it says on the radar." Amanda turned down the throttle and squinted into the darkness. The island was small, splitting the river in half before the tributaries joined on the other side. Half a dozen watercraft were moored to stands of trees or two-foot poles sticking up out of the ground—fishing boats, two small airboats, and a jet ski. The last one made her frown.

"Wait a minute. Shouldn't this be, like, an actual city?" Summer scratched the shaved side of her head. "It looks like an abandoned camp spot."

Amanda grimaced. "Definitely wouldn't wanna camp out here. The island's too small."

"What, it'll flood or something?"

"No, it's that much easier for gators and snakes to come slithering up and *bite* you in your sleep." She jabbed Summer's arm like a striking snake, and the witch jumped before punching Amanda's shoulder in response.

"Cut it out. You want me to drop this thing in the river, or what?"

Amanda laughed and pulled back on the throttle control as they approached the island. "Relax. We're not camping out here overnight."

"Yeah, like all that crap is even a thing."

The shifter girl gave her friend a deadpan stare. "It's definitely a thing."

Summer zipped it after that.

After easily maneuvering the airboat along the bank of the island, Amanda hopped off to tie the rope to a thick tree stump that had been cut perfectly level and polished with some kind of extra-glossy finish. The image of what she guessed was supposed to be a crystal had been carved into the top of the stump. "Looks like this is it."

"You gotta be shitting me." Summer stepped sloppily off the airboat and gestured at the single wooden building in the center of the island. "There's no way *that's* the kemana."

"You've never been to one before either, huh?"

"Like it matters."

Amanda held her hand out for the magical radar, which Summer slapped down into her palm so she could pocket it before they moved slowly toward the building. It wasn't very large—seven feet tall and maybe three and a half feet across, with a single door set in the center that took up almost the whole wall. The whole thing was made of warped, peeling, aged wood and looked like it had been out here in the middle of nowhere for decades.

"What the hell *is* this?" Summer peered around the back of the building, then returned to the front and scowled. "I thought the kemana was supposed to be an underground *city*."

"I think this is the entrance." Fighting back a laugh, Amanda grabbed the worn, semi-decayed handle of the door and pulled it open.

Both girls froze.

"Okay, let me rephrase." Summer slowly shook her head. "Hell no."

Amanda barked out a laugh and quickly cut it off before looking over her shoulder. No one was there. The swamp was empty and quiet except for the Florida nightlife and the thin, almost nonexistent hum of insects that stuck around during the warm winter.

Her friend shot her a disbelieving glare. "You think this is funny?"

"Uh, yeah."

"It's a damn porta-potty, shifter girl. No way in hell am I walking into this thing. It looks like it'll fall apart if I blow on it."

Amanda chuckled again and fought to wipe the smile off her face. "I guess it's probably local humor."

"You weren't kidding when you said the magicals around here were a little off."

"They're not off. Just...eccentric. Sometimes. Come on." She stepped into the old-fashioned wooden outhouse, smirking at the immense toilet seat and lid mounted on a wooden box that stretched from wall to wall at the back.

"Yeah, no thanks. I'm not about to step into the john with you. We're not *that* good of friends."

Amanda turned and raised an eyebrow. "So you're chickening out?"

Summer clicked her tongue. "Screw you."

She stepped up into the outhouse anyway, and the girls stood side by side in front of the giant toilet seat. "There's no way this is real. Look, there isn't even toilet paper."

"Yeah, because it's a giant hole in the ground, and anyone who comes all the way out here to use the crapper doesn't have enough sanity to need toilet paper."

Amanda rolled her eyes, lifted the lid, and the bright yellow glow of the kemana's ceaseless magical light filled the outhouse. She laughed again. "This is too good."

"I think it's shit." Summer stiffened, then they both cracked up laughing. "Okay, fine. I'll climb down the can. Are you happy now?"

"Not until I see your head go under."

The witch made a mocking imitation of her friend in an indiscernible voice and climbed up onto the wooden box. She had to turn and face Amanda before stepping one foot down on the first rung of the ladder, then the other.

"Hey." Amanda sniggered. "Bottoms up."

"Shut up." Summer's crooked smile betrayed her amusement with the unexpected entrance to the kemana, and her voice trailed after her as she descended. "So wait. All not-freshmen kids who got to come out here last semester just…stood in line and waited for the next—" She barked out a laugh. "For the next kid to disappear into the toilet, or what?"

Amanda climbed up onto the box to follow her friend down. "I can't *wait* to see Glasket do this. You know, when we officially get to go with everyone else. That's next year, right?"

"Only if we *prove our ability to handle our magic.*" Summer shrugged on the ladder that stretched another twenty feet down onto the first platform built along the kemana's outer wall. "No idea what that means for *you.*"

"Maybe if I fight off another pack of wild boars, she'll let me go early."

"Ha. Oh, man. Can you imagine Petrov's face if he ever has to chaperone a trip here?" Summer dropped from the last rung onto the platform and absently wiped her palms on her jeans. "I can't believe I'm saying this, but I really hope he chaperones us."

Amanda jumped down beside her friend, and with a snort, turned to look over the platform's edge. "Whoa."

"Uh-huh."

The kemana stretched out for miles below them. Some

sections of it were blocked from view by the walls jutting out toward the center, where the massive crystal powering the underground city and even more magic on Earth stood straight, rising high overhead. Concentric circles of glowing runes the same yellow-white color as the crystal were etched into the floor, which could have been concrete or stone or something else entirely.

"Come on, shifter girl." Summer smacked Amanda's arm with the back of a hand. "We made it. Time to make this place our bitch."

The witch strutted toward the open staircase that turned back on itself three times before meeting the floor another thirty feet below them.

Amanda cleared her throat and took off after her. "That's not why we're here."

"Is it not? I mean, really. Is it not?" Spreading her arms, Summer walked backward down the stairs before she reached the first landing and only had to step forward down the next flight. "Look at us. Two baby bounty hunters in the middle of the swamp with no one to tell us where to go or what to do. The night's ours."

"Yeah, not the whole kemana, though."

"Loosen up. Jeeze. I thought you'd already learned a thing or two with the temple."

Amanda shook her head and slowly descended, unable to look away from the sprawling expanse of the kemana with its magical glowing lights overhead, the crystal in the center, the rows of storefronts and bars and magicals-only shops. She hadn't seen anything like this anywhere else in her life.

"I *did* learn a thing or two," she muttered. "Like how not to trust you when you say you know what you're doing."

"Yeah, yeah, yeah. Hurry up, huh? I can't wait to see what they have down here."

They finally reached the bottom of the platform's staircase, and Amanda shoved her hands into her pockets to reassure herself that Johnny's device was still there. "Any idea where to go first?"

"Nope." Summer grinned and stuck her tongue out slightly between her teeth. "That's the fun part."

For almost 2:00 a.m., the kemana was surprisingly busy. Most of the magicals still down here in the middle of the night were gathered in groups around the bars and small restaurants and food trucks dotting the main thoroughfare.

*How the heck did they get food trucks down here?*

"Hey, check it out." Summer pointed at a bar with a neon sign declaring it as The Front Porch. "Looks like these guys don't give a shit about after-hours public drinking laws, right? Hey, maybe they feel the same way about the legal drinking age. Or lack thereof..."

"Wait, wait. *Summer...*" Amanda huffed out a sigh, her shoulders sagging as her troublemaker witch friend strode purposefully toward the establishment. Summer's arms swung loosely at her sides, and she swaggered more than she ever did on campus.

*She's gonna get us thrown out of here before we have a chance to see everything.*

Amanda took off after her friend. "I'm not drinking with you."

"You don't have to."

"No, I mean *we* shouldn't be drinking here. Or at all."

"Stop being such a prude. Let me do all the talking and follow my lead, huh?"

Scowling, Amanda zipped her lips and hurried after Summer, her hands thrust deep in the pockets of her hoodie because she had no idea what else to do with them.

They approached the front door of The Front Porch, where a Kilomea sat with only half of his backside on a stool beside the door. The guy's black suit looked a little too tight on him, and without a human illusion, it also looked ridiculous with all that thick hair sprouting from beneath the neckline of his undershirt and the cuffs of the jacket. His huge eyeteeth protruded at least two inches from his upper and lower jaws, bending his lips around a crooked smile as he chatted up a group of two Wood Elves, a gnome, and a witch standing right outside the entrance.

Summer jerked her chin up at the Kilomea and headed past the group of adult magicals who were old enough to be standing here without drawing suspicion.

"Hold up now. Just a minute." The Kilomea didn't have to move much to lift himself off the stool. He towered over Summer as he extended one long thick arm out in front of her to block her path. His hand was loosely open as he winked at the group he'd been entertaining, then he shot the teenage witch a sidelong glance. "I need to see some ID."

"Yeah, yeah. Sure." Summer patted down her hoodie pockets, then the back pockets of her jeans. "Oh, damn. Guess I left my wallet back at the office. Rough day, know what I mean?"

"I hear ya."

The magicals stepped aside, smirking at Summer's attempts to play it cool.

Amanda had stayed back, her eyes wide as she watched the humiliating exchange. *Great. First place we go, she has to get into it with a Kilomea bouncer. This is gonna suck.*

"Unfortunately," the guy continued, "no ID, no entry. Sorry."

"Naw, it's all good. I know you've seen me before." Summer tossed her black hair over her shoulder and pointed to the shaved side of her head. "Maybe it's the hair. I like to change it up. Sometimes I'm even unrecognizable."

"Maybe." A low chuckle escaped the bouncer. "But the drinks inside ain't free. And you forgot your wallet."

"Oh. No, it's all on my friend tonight." With an achingly wide grin, the witch turned and gestured toward Amanda. "She's taking care of it."

Amanda froze. *Come on...*

One prompting look from her friend overrode all the ideas

she'd had in her head about leaving Summer to fend for herself, and she pulled a credit card from her back pocket to flash it at the bouncer. Her smile felt way too forced.

"Does your friend have an ID?"

"Crap," Amanda muttered.

Summer glared at her as though all their plans were now ruined and it was all the shifter girl's fault.

"Looks like it was a rough day all around." The Kilomea chuckled, and the group of magicals beside the door joined him. "Sorry, ladies. Rules are rules."

The tall witch standing beside the Wood Elves cast the girls a sympathetic smile. "Do your parents know you're out here this late?"

Summer scoffed. "Not since we started college and stopped having to get permission."

"Oh, yeah?" One of the Elves folded his arms and jerked his chin up at her. "Where do you go?"

The young witch's mouth popped open, and Amanda stepped forward with the answer at the tip of her tongue. "Everglades University."

"Huh. Good school."

"Yeah, it's *okay*…" Summer replied flippantly.

"You might not need permission to be down here," the Kilomea added in amusement. A hint of warning laced his words. "You do need *my* permission to step inside this bar. If you're freshmen at Everglades University, you still ain't gettin' my permission."

"This is ridiculous." Summer gestured toward the open door. "I was held back in eighth grade, and I took two gap years. Come on. I'm twenty-one."

Amanda stared at her friend and took a step back, her face flushing hot. *Holy crap, how much longer is she gonna keep dragging this out?*

"Go on, now." The Kilomea pointed down the line of storefronts on this side of the kemana. "There are still a few restaurants open. Y'all can find something down that way if you really need something. Won't be hard liquor, though."

The gnome sniggered. "I think SweetPops is still operating twenty-four-seven too. You know, kids love candy."

The other magicals chuckled, and the Kilomea stepped in front of Summer to block her path to the door.

"You'll be hearing from my lawyer," Summer spat before spinning smartly on her heel and stomping off down the row of storefronts. She didn't bother to wait for Amanda, who stared at the Kilomea in dumb fascination.

He folded his arms and slowly sat halfway back on the stool again as Summer disappeared from his view. Then he smirked at Amanda and nodded for her to get lost too.

She scurried after the young witch, grateful he hadn't tossed them out of the kemana for trying to put one over on a bouncer. *Not sure even I could take him as a wolf. Why would I even wanna try?*

# CHAPTER SIX

"Summer. Hey." She jogged to catch up with her friend. "Okay, can we not, like, *ever* try that again?"

"Are you kidding? I'll find a way into that bar eventually. It'll take a little more time."

"Why? What's so great about getting alcohol when we have this entire place to look through?"

Summer stopped, and a slow smile spread across her face. "You've obviously never gotten drunk, have you?"

Amanda stared right back at her. There was no point in telling her friend she'd already gotten into Johnny's ridiculously large store of whiskey the dwarf had piled up in the first few months of being open for business. Or in saying she hated the taste of alcohol and the feeling of even a light buzz and preferred a strong-ass cup of coffee, now that she'd grown more used to *that*.

"Let's check out the other things down here," she said instead. "They obviously still follow drinking-age laws down here, and we'll find something *way* better."

"There's a way." Summer tossed the long half of her hair over her shoulder and kept walking. "George Harland came back with a whole jug of wine last semester. No idea how he smuggled it past the teachers, but he did it. *I'm* gonna do it too."

"Not without any money, you're not." Amanda patted the back pocket of her jean capris. Sure, Johnny had given her a credit card for *emergencies*, but using it now as leverage to keep Summer from getting them in even more trouble felt a lot like an emergency.

The black-haired witch chuckled. "Just because I didn't live underground with the rest of those LA weirdos for however long doesn't mean I don't know my way around a little sleight of hand, shifter girl."

She turned and wiggled her fingers at Amanda before shoving them into her hoodie pockets.

"No. No sleight of anything. I'm serious. We were only supposed to come down here to check it out."

"Ugh. Stop being such a *nag*."

Amanda stopped on the walkway in front of the storefronts and glared at her friend. "I'm not gonna help you steal stuff."

"Oh, yeah? The way you didn't steal that little radar-what-ever-thingy in your pocket?"

"Yeah, because I didn't steal it!" Amanda hunched her shoulder when the shout she hadn't intended echoed across the buzz of the kemana's late-night activity.

A group of dwarves dressed in camo from head to toe looked her over as they passed. One of them raised a cigar to his lips, inhaled, and exhaled a cloud of glittering blue smoke, frowning at the shifter girl.

She hurried toward summer again and lowered her voice. "I *borrowed* it. There's a difference."

"How about you quit trying to shit all over a good time, huh?" Summer wouldn't look at her but instead studied the storefronts on the adjacent kemana wall and across the wide thoroughfare on the other side of the giant hovering crystal. "I didn't come here to be a—"

"Hey. Look." Amanda tugged on the other girl's sleeve and pointed two shops down in front of them. "The Alchemist's Throne. That's gotta have something good, right?"

Summer turned slowly around, and her eyes widened with excitement. "Alchemy supplies. You're okay, shifter girl. Come on."

She took off toward the shop, which was still open for business even in the middle of the night, and Amanda puffed out a sigh before hurrying after the witch once again.

*This was already a long night, and now it's gonna be even longer.*

A quick glanced at the shops around them made her briefly stop when she saw the sign hanging over another storefront with the words High Tide Ammo painted in thick black letters. Behind the store's name was an image of a crossbow. Amanda fought back an eager grin.

*Yeah, okay. I'll humor her with alchemy. Then we'll hit up the weapons shop.*

Two wizened magicals so old they were barely more than lumps of wrinkled flesh within oversized jackets and slacks sat in identical wooden rocking chairs on either side of The Alchemist's Throne's front door. They smelled like mothballs and lemons—mostly—but there was a hint of wizard scent from one and some kind of Elf from the other. Amanda rolled with it.

"Evenin'," the wrinkled old wizard muttered, rocking slowly back and forth. Even his eyes were mostly obscured beneath folds of sagging skin.

"Hey." Summer didn't look at him as she pulled open the front door and stepped inside. A little bell hanging over the class pane jingled when she entered.

Amanda nodded at the old-timers rocking away on this kemana's version of a southern front porch. The maybe-Elf hissed out a laugh and grinned at her, revealing a gaping hole of a mouth where teeth should've been. "Y'all ain't gettin' yerselves into too much trouble, naw, eh?"

She barely had time to register what he'd said as she caught the door before it closed. "Having a look around."

"Aw, sure. Youngin's be rollin' roun' down these parts lookin' fer net but wizbang dun-up, what ah reckon," the old wizard muttered.

*Okay, I have absolutely no idea what* he *said.*

Amanda chuckled politely, then scurried through the door and let it shut behind her with another jingle from the bell. She scanned the shop's front intently for Summer and found the young witch already standing in front of two glass cases along the far wall beneath a sign that read: Potent Reagents. Please Ask for Assistance.

The gray-haired witch behind the counter with her hair pulled back in a severe bun and her gray sweater buttoned up to her neck looked even sterner than their Alchemy teacher Mrs. Zimmer. Also a lot less happy to see two teenage girls walking into her shop way past midnight.

"Summer." Amanda tried not to run through the store.

"You have some seriously good ideas, shifter girl," Summer muttered, grinning at the collection of alchemy supplies protected by the glass cases in front of her. Her eyes shimmered with excitement. "I'll give you that. This is *way* better than sneaking into a bar."

A glance at the counter showed the store owner scowling at them.

*Summer's not exactly whispering, either.*

"There's gotta be something else in here that isn't as—"

"Explosive? Deadly? Glorious?" Summer drew a deep breath and leaned toward the glass cases.

"No. That isn't as likely to get us kicked out of *here* too," she replied through gritted teeth. "Like maybe something to help with spells? Or *tiny* experiments, if you have to—"

"Nah. This is perfect." Summer tapped a finger against the glass and turned toward the store owner. "Hey, lady. How much for this jar of volatile fairy seeds? I've been looking for these all my life."

Amanda rolled her eyes and backed away from her friend as the gray-haired witch's scowl darkened even more.

---

They were, in fact, kicked out of The Alchemist's Throne. And the cigar store filled with all manner of magical brands—including the one she'd seen a dwarf in full camo lighting up with the glittering blue smoke. They needed IDs for that too. The nightclub turned them away next, which was just as well. Amanda had no idea how many magicals Summer would end up pissing off when the whole place was decorated like a hunting trip—camo and neon orange everywhere—and played some weird half-banjo, half-EDM mashup music.

Summer made a final attempt to sneak into what served as an alley between two rows of shops—namely the one filled with magitech gadgets on one side that looked more like Renaissance torture implements and a small store on the other side with signs for "The Best Beauty-Illusion Techniques in the South." The alley itself was nondescript, but the farther they walked, the more the stringent scent of alcohol permeated the air. It got so bad, Amanda could almost taste it, and her eyes continuously watered before they stumbled upon a group of old-timers huddled around a massive steel contraption against the kemana wall. Thick steam billowed up from the machine and into the thick pipe running up to the ceiling and funneling out into the air aboveground.

*Swamp creatures up there are getting a serious buzz right now.*

Amanda wiped the tears from her eyes, then snatched the back of Summer's hoodie and tried to pull her away from the old-timers huddled around the machine and drinking from flasks as they worked. "Time to turn around."

"What? Are you crazy? This is exactly what I was looking for—"

"They're making moonshine, Summer."

"*Perfect!*" The girl rubbed her hands together. "Look at the size of that thing. I bet I can get these old farts to hand over a bottle or two."

Those "old farts" squinted at the girls from beneath wide-brimmed hats and furrowed brows. One of them summoned a warning flicker of sparking yellow magic in his hand and stepped forward. Summer didn't even notice.

"We need to leave," Amanda muttered.

"Aw, come on. You think they take credit cards—"

With a growl, Amanda leapt after her friend, grabbed Summer's arm, and spun, all but tossing the young witch back down the alley.

"Hey, what are you—"

"I said we need to leave!" Amanda snarled. The tingle of an imminent shift blazed beneath her skin, and she knew her eyes had taken on their silvery shifter glow when Summer froze and her eyes widened.

"Okay. Jesus."

Breathing heavily, Amanda looked over her shoulders at the magicals making their giant batch of 'shine in the kemana itself. The one who'd stepped forward snuffed out the yellow burst of spell energy in his hand and nodded once. "These aren't the kinda locals who part with a bottle or two. *Or* take credit cards."

"Yeah, I get it," Summer hissed. "Amanda."

"*What?*"

The witch glared at her, their faces inches apart. "I like you and everything, but if you don't get your death grip off my arm, I have no problem socking you in the face."

Only then did she realize how tightly she'd been clenching her friend's arm. She looked down at her fingers buried in Summer's hoodie sleeve and immediately let her go. "Sorry."

"Yeah, I bet." Summer rubbed her arm and turned back toward the mouth of the alley. "Christ. Do you always have asshole strength, or is that only when you lose your shit?"

"Pretty much always," Amanda muttered as they headed quickly down the alley. The sting of alcohol fumes faded from her nostrils, but her eyes still watered, and she wiped them absently. "I only use it when my friend's acting stupid, and I have to save her from getting her ass kicked."

Summer snorted. "Pretty sure that's not the only time. Fine. Good enough reason."

The shifter girl couldn't help a small smirk as they emerged from the alley and continued into the main thoroughfare of the kemana's open, cavernous expanse.

There had been other times when she'd lost control and used that strength, some of them on purpose. Like shifting out of a pair of handcuffs and a black bag over her head in the back of a van before tearing out a few throats. And a few times that weren't so much on purpose as they were pure instinct. Like squaring off with a bunch of thugs sent to take care of Johnny Walker's ward while he was off on a case.

She shook her head and wiped the last of the stinging tears from the corner of her eyes.

Summer chuckled. "You know, I think I'm good with hunting for booze." She turned a lazy smile onto Amanda and sighed.

"Why?" *What's she cooking up now?*

"Come on, shifter girl. Don't tell me you don't feel it too." Summer slapped her hand weakly against her friend's shoulder. "Shit. I think the fumes gave me a buzz."

"Huh." Amanda nodded and pretended to go along with it, fighting back a laugh.

*Lightweight. I feel fine.*

CHAPTER SEVEN

They wandered around the kemana, peeking into storefronts and being turned away by surly shop owners who didn't want anything to do with a couple of kids perusing their wares in the middle of the night. Amanda ended up using her emergency credit card only once to buy them each a bottle of orange soda called Juicy Tune—the intensely carbonated drink sang obnoxiously off-key every time they twisted off the lid to take a sip. It went well with the paper plates of pickle chips and heavily peppered fried shrimp they bought from one of the food trucks.

They took their food to one of the benches scattered around the kemana without any real rhyme or reason and sat to eat. The place was still as busy as it had been when they'd arrived, though the magicals down here at this time of night seemed a lot more likely to toss them aside with a snarl than offer friendly directions around the underground city. So the girls decided to keep to themselves while they ate, and from their perch on the bench, Amanda had a perfect view of the weapons shop High Tide Ammo and the Atlantean who owned the place. Or at least had the night shift during their twenty-four-seven business hours.

"We should head back soon," she said through the crunch of perfectly fried pickles.

"Why? This place is amazing—" A squeal of a high-pitched song erupted from the top of Summer's soda bottle, and she immediately smothered it by chugging down the rest of it in one breath. When she belched, the same high note emerged from her lips, and both girls cracked up. "I could stay here forever."

"And do what?"

"I don't know. This." Summer shrugged and dusted the breading crumbs off her hands. "We haven't even scratched the surface of this place. I know that much."

"Yeah, but we can't stay here all night…" Amanda's gaze returned to the front of the weapons store.

"You got a crush or something?"

"What?"

Summer wadded her plastic plate into an amorphous blob of trash, spilling pickle-chip crumbs all over the place, and laughed. "You've been eyeing that door since we got here. I know it doesn't *seem* like I pay attention to anything, but I do."

"Yeah. I wanna go in there." Amanda studied what she could through the store's front windows. "As soon as I finish eating. We'll take a quick trip, and I'll look around, and—"

"Then you can buy something awesome, and we'll take it back to campus." Summer gestured toward her friend's remaining pile of pickle chips. "So hurry up, already."

"I'm not gonna buy a weapon and take it back to *school*."

"Why the hell not?"

Amanda barked out a laugh. "Where am I gonna hide it, huh? Stuff a giant crossbow under my shirt like there's nothing weird about that?"

"A *crossbow*. I like that it's your first choice, shifter girl."

She shook her head. "No, I only wanna look."

"Oh, come on. If George Harland could sneak a whole jug of wine back to the Academy, you can smuggle in a crossbow."

Amanda pressed her lips together and forced herself not to say anything.

*Like how I smuggled a few other things into the dorm already.*

"Let me finish my pickles."

"Right. They're good but not *that* good."

Ignoring her friend's habit of dissing practically everything, Amanda stared at the front door of High Tide Ammo and took her time with her pickle chips. It was easy enough to daydream about all the different kinds of weapons she'd find in that shop—most of them less exciting versions of what Johnny kept in his workshop, the toolshed in the back yard, and hidden away in the back of his red Jeep. Still, there might be something in there Johnny hadn't thought of, something that would be more suited for a shifter girl who'd discovered only seven months ago that she was born to be a bounty hunter.

A woman in bright red, two-inch heels headed for High Tide Ammo's front door, the *click* of her shoes lost amidst the low buzz of conversation and music and late-night transactions inside the kemana. The bright red handbag slung over her shoulder matched her shoes perfectly, and everything else she wore was gray—from the top of her tailored suit jacket to the matching pencil skirt and the light jacket draped over her arm.

*Who needs a jacket over a jacket in Florida?*

The woman opened the door and stepped inside. Amanda thought she saw a flicker of white light along the doorframe—or maybe she only thought she did, since the door didn't quite close behind the woman in red heels.

*Huh. She doesn't* look *like someone who'd walk right into a weapons store. I guess I don't really, either.*

"Look at this bitch. Walking in like she thinks she owns the place."

The snarled voice was muttering to whoever else was listening, but Amanda was already paying attention to the store and its newest occupant. Her shifter hearing caught it immediately, and she leaned forward a little, staring at the ground as she strained to listen.

"It's the ones like this who keep us *out* of business. You know what I'm saying?" The second voice was equally low and hateful. "Want me to get rid of her?"

"Only if she starts asking a million questions and wants to try on every single holster to see if it goes with her purse."

Hissing, unamused laughter followed. The woman passed in front of the glass door, perusing the items on the racks without hearing the conversation Amanda had so easily picked up on.

"Can I *help* you?" the pissed-off owner asked.

"Oh, no. Thank you." The woman's voice was soft and innocent. "I'll be out of your hair in a moment. Is this your entire selection of gun cases, or do you have a wider selection somewhere else?"

"What you're looking at is what we got."

"Wonderful."

Summer heaved a massive sigh. "Dude. I thought you wanted to finish your stupid pickles first. You're taking fore—"

"Shh." Amanda held up a hand, her eyes narrowing as she strained to focus on the voices. "Something's happening."

"Huh?"

"Shut up." She must have snapped it convincingly enough because Summer did exactly that, and Amanda returned her attention to the voices inside the store.

"Goddamnit, Marley. She's taking forever."

"Naw, she won't take more'n two minutes. Get the heavy hitters ready, huh? Soon as this stuck-up broad's outta here, we're moving on Rooney and his guys. Tonight."

The second voice sniggered. "Bastards won't know what hit 'em."

"That's the plan."

Amanda's hand automatically clenched in her lap, which

crumpled up the paper plate and sent the rest of her fried pickles toppling all over the bench.

"Earth to shifter girl..." Summer pointed at the ground. "Hey. You having some kind of shifter problem? 'Cause I have no idea how to deal with that. I wanna make that clear."

Amanda slowly lifted her gaze to the front of the shop, where the woman had now approached the counter to purchase the gun case she'd selected.

"I'm good," she whispered.

The half-Kilomea behind the counter sniggered. "You even know how to shoot a gun?"

"Oh, it's not for me. My dad's finally out of the hospital and can't wait to take up his target practice again. It's a little present for—"

"Yeah, yeah. You payin' in cash?"

"I *can.*"

"Great. Throw down thirty, and we'll call it good."

"The price on the display said forty-three—"

"I know what the hell it said, lady. I'm givin' you a deal. Look, we gotta close up early tonight. So you want the damn case or not?"

The woman pulled a matching wallet from her red purse and rifled through it for the bills.

Just like that, all the excitement that had built up in Amanda at the prospect of catching some jerkface in the act of hurting someone—the way she planned to do all the time when she became a real bounty hunter—fizzled away.

*I thought for sure they were gonna hurt her.*

"Hey!" Summer shouted. "What the hell is going on with you?"

"What? Nothing." Amanda looked away from the store and reached for the pickles on her plate, but they were all over the ground. "Crap."

"I know you like to zone out sometimes, but that was one of the worst." Summer ran her hand through the half of her long hair that still existed and snorted. "You said something was happening."

"Yeah, I was wrong." The Juicy Tune soda let out a bellowing opera note from a male voice when she twisted off the lid, cutting off when she drank. "I'd rather go back to campus now."

"Wait, what? What about your crossbow?"

"Hey, we know the way here." Amanda glanced at the bulge of the radar device in her hoodie pocket. "This isn't the last time. Obviously."

They both stood, and Summer sighed. "You know, this kinda feels like you were wasting my time on purpose."

"Relax. I changed my mind." Amanda scanned the kemana walls, searching for the high platform and the rebar ladder they'd climbed down to get here. "There it is. Let's go."

"Uh-huh." The young witch shot her a skeptical sidelong glance. "You're hiding something."

"No. I'm tired. What is it, like, three o'clock in the morning?"

"Like you've never stayed up this late before. Please."

As they headed toward the opposite side of the underground city toward the staircase to the platform, Amanda turned for a final glance at High Tide Ammo. The woman stood right outside the door, which was now shut behind her as the two magicals running the place scowled and walked around inside, shutting down for the night. She bent to scratch her ankle with her cell phone pressed to her ear and set her purse down in the process.

The next second, she straightened, nodded as she said something else into her phone Amanda didn't catch and walked away.

Amanda stopped and turned all the way around.

*She forgot her purse.*

"Hold on a sec."

Summer groaned and slowly turned as she rolled her eyes up toward the ceiling. "What *now*?"

"That lady left her bag right there in front of the store."

"So?"

"She was talking on the phone. I don't think she even realized it."

"You think it's your job to—ugh." Summer rolled her eyes again as Amanda took off toward the front of High Tide Ammo one more time. "Of course you do. Of course, you think it's your job to help a rando lady with her purse. Hurry up!"

Amanda didn't have enough of an attention span to keep one eye on the lady in heels, one on her red bag, and think about replying to her friend all at the same time. She darted through a group of Atlanteans chuckling over something one of them pushed around in a metal crate on wheels that thumped around and hissed like all their hair snakes.

The woman had made it halfway across the kemana at this point, but at least Amanda could still see her. She didn't even slow down before she snatched up the red leather purse and hurried after the woman. "Hey! Excuse me! Ma'am, you left your—"

A surge of magicals wearing costumes made of neon orange and yellow reflective vests cut her off when they streamed out of the camo-themed nightclub, shouting and laughing and stumbling drunkenly all over themselves. Half of them had painted their faces in glow-in-the-dark stripes, and they whooped and hollered, staggering around before the weird club music muted again behind the closed door.

Growling, Amanda tried to dodge through them and eventually shoved two cackling Light Elves out of the way so she could follow after the owner of this purse in her hand.

"Hey! Your bag!"

But the woman was gone.

*What?*

She spun, looking for the red heels and the gray suit and the woman's auburn hair cut short against her head. Nothing.

Frowning in confusion, Amanda stared at the purse in her hands and slowly headed back toward Summer, who hadn't moved an inch since she'd been left halfway to the kemana's exit.

"Now what?" The black-haired witch spread her arms. "You tried to be a hero and...bam. Now you might as well have stolen the lady's purse yourself."

"Shut up." Amanda spun again, still searching. "I was trying to help. She just...disappeared."

"Can't you, like, sniff her out or something? Track her down that way?"

"Yeah, but..." Wrinkling her nose, Amanda slowly looked down at the red leather purse zipped completely closed and realized the other thing that had been bothering her. The bag didn't have a scent.

She lifted the purse to her face and sniffed. Nothing.

"Hey, come on. A little discretion maybe, huh?" Summer glanced at the other magicals in the kemana, but no one paid any more attention to them than they had all night. "So?"

"Nothing." Amanda sniffed again, but that only confirmed the weirdness of it. She wrinkled her nose. "How does somebody *not* have a scent?"

"Clean freaks? Robots? I don't know. I *do* know she's gone. So if you wanna get back to campus, let's go. We can go through her stuff later, okay?"

"No, that's not why I took her..." The shifter girl's attention trailed off again when she saw two wizards approaching the front door of High Tide Ammo. She normally wouldn't have thought anything of it, but they were scowling, and one of them carried what looked like a baton in his fist. The thing left a trail of crackling red light behind it through the air as he walked.

*That's cool.*

"Amanda. You're blanking out on me way too much. Let's go."

She ignored Summer and stared at the wizards, who leaned around the corner of the weapon store to search the side wall, spun in a slow circle, and stepped closer to each other for a low conversation.

"Where the fuck is it? She said it would be right here."

"It *was* right here. I just talked to her. Somebody must've snatched it up."

"Bullshit. Those assholes got to it first and tried to give us the slip. I say we go in now and remind 'em who they're fucking with."

The guy with the buzzing magical baton nodded, scanning the magicals milling around the kemana, and whipped the baton out at his side. "Go. It's unlocked."

"Oh, man..." Amanda took two steps forward as the wizards jerked open High Tide Ammo's front door that was supposed to be locked and disappeared into the dark shop.

"Yo. Shifter girl. Whatever you're staring at needs to—"

A curdling shriek rose from inside the weapons shop, followed by quick, sputtering bursts of red light and crackling sparks flying up against the windows.

"Whoa, shit." Summer's attention was wholly focused on the store now too, and she let out a disbelieving chuckle. "Are we watching some kinda robbery right now?"

"I don't think so." Amanda's eyes were glued to the windows and the flashing lights beyond, illuminating the struggle between the two wizards and the two other magicals in the shop in intermittent bursts. "I think they—"

Something like machine-gun fire cracked through the shop, and the windows spiderwebbed and shattered.

# CHAPTER EIGHT

The magicals in the kemana shouted and scurried away from the chaos, some of them watching the destruction in delight while others hurried to avoid it. Two giant Crystals two doors down poked their heads out of the Big 'N Magical tailor's store, shouted something behind them, and stormed toward High Tide Ammo to either break up the fight or get involved.

A group of gnomes wearing all white raced past the giant crystal from the other side of the kemana, shouting and tossing flickering, humming orbs that looked like glass.

The lights inside the weapons store flicked on, and the girls had a front-row seat at the four-magical battle raging inside. Shelves of arrows and crossbow-bolt boxes toppled to the floor. The wizard with the baton cracked it like a whip at the half-Kilomea storming toward him and sent the guy slamming back into a glass case filled with firearms.

"I...think we should get out of here," Amanda muttered. "Like, right now."

"No way. Not now that it's getting good!" Summer grinned as she stepped slowly across the kemana to get a better view.

Magicals were running all over the place, either trying to get help for the guys battling the wizards, or wanting to join the wizards, or trying to break up the fight itself. Magical projectiles popped off inside High Tide Ammo without rhyme or reason, creating a deadly light show for the spectators, whoever they happened to be.

"Seriously, Summer." Amanda took off after her, still stupidly holding the straps of the woman's red purse. "I don't think things are gonna get any better for us down here right now."

"This is *awesome*." The witch couldn't take her eyes off the fight. "Hey, you ever see one of those weird flashy electric sticks before? That wizard's using it like a pro."

"Summer." The bag felt heavy in Amanda's hand, and she was pretty sure she was partially to blame for the magicals running High Tide Ammo getting their asses kicked right now. "We should—"

"I gotta get a better view." The witch darted away and scrambled up the side of a huge, pyramid-shaped stack of crates resting beside a dolly in front of some shop she didn't bother to catch the name of. The crates wobbled beneath her, and halfway to the top, the precariously stacked boxes shifted. "Shit."

Summer leapt off and tried to stabilize the pile, but the crates were already toppling all around her. The deafening crash was almost as loud as the battle raging inside the weapon store.

"Maurice!" A giant Crystal stormed out of the closest storefront, hissing in frustration. "How many times do I have to tell you to—"

He stopped when he saw Summer standing in the pile of his stuff, his ice-encrusted beard swinging side to side.

The witch spread her arms. "Sorry. Just an accident—"

The top of one crate burst from its setting, and a high-pitched whine filled the air as multi-colored sparks blazed from something spinning madly like a mechanized top. Summer bolted from the pile of toppled supplies—whatever they were—and ducked a blast of blisteringly cold Crystal magic spewing right over her head. "Time to go!"

"Oh, *now* that you got us in trouble, you're ready to leave?" Amanda shouted.

The Crystal snarled at her, and her eyes widened before she darted around the fallen crates after her friend.

"Get back here, you no-good little—" The Crystal roared and stomped after them, leaving frozen patches of ground in his wake and tossing icy blasts at the girls whenever he had a clear shot through the frazzled crowds in the kemana.

"Back here," Summer shouted before ducking behind two more buildings and narrowly avoiding running face-first into a gnome taking out a bag of trash nearly as big as he was.

"Hey! You know what happens if this bag breaks—whoa, whoa, whoa, watch it!"

Amanda skidded around the corner and spun out of the way before she would have stepped right through the trash bag and maybe the gnome as well. "Sorry. Sorry."

The Crystal lumbered after them and stopped at the back of the building before snarling at the gnome. "They come back this way?"

"Yeah, but—" The gnome released the bag and leapt backward when the Crystal's racing footsteps brushed against the trash and froze it all the way through. "Goddamnit! You know how heavy this shit is now?"

An explosion and more sounds of gunfire and crackling magical attacks came from High Tide Ammo, joined by the shouts of onlooking kemana visitors—both encouraging and discouraging. The Crystal roared behind them and blasted shards of ice above the girls' heads.

Summer snapped her fingers, and a tiny spark of fire ignited between them. As they raced past a wizard stumbling around with an open flask waving in his hand, the witch snatched it from his grasp before he knew what had happened and dumped the whole thing in a trail of splashing booze that smelled as strong as the moonshiners' machine.

Amanda leapt out of the way to avoid getting splattered with what might as well have been rubbing alcohol. "What are you—"

This time when Summer snapped her fingers, a tiny fireball ignited in her hand. She tossed it at the trail of spilled liquor and pointed at the flying fireball. It hit the wet trail, catching it on fire, and whatever spell she cast next was at least partially successful. The blazing alcohol exploded into a fiery wall racing up between the buildings as the Crystal skidded to a halt on the other side.

"Yes. Finally." Laughing, Summer flipped him the middle finger, then tossed back what was left in the flask before chucking it aside. "Oh, gross. No wonder that wizard couldn't keep his eyes open."

"Okay, how about we focus on getting out of here before you burn the whole place down, huh?" Amanda snatched her friend's arm and tugged her fiercely toward the base of the zigzagging staircase up to the platform. "Fast."

"Yeah, yeah. Don't get your little shifter panties in a—" A spear of ice sliced through the air six inches from Summer's shoulder. "Shit. Run."

Apparently, the Crystal didn't care that the wall of flames cutting him off partially blinded him. He tossed spell after spell at the girls racing up the staircase toward the highest platform below the ladder. Amanda slung the straps of the lady's purse over her shoulder and booked it up the rebar rungs, ducking her head when the occasional icy blast raced toward her only to crash against the kemana wall.

"Jesus Christ, you're fast." Summer scrambled up after her, leaving the chaotic explosions and tossed spells and battling magicals in the kemana far below them.

Then Amanda shoved her forearm up against the underside of the toilet seat she hadn't remembered closing after herself on the way down and scurried up through the wooden john. She grabbed Summer's hands when the witch reached the top and helped to haul her friend out before they raced out of the outhouse in the center of the island and back toward the airboat.

"Untie the rope." Amanda leapt onto the boat and got ready to turn the thing on the second Summer had the rope off. It *thunked* down onto the deck as the large propeller blades whirred to life in the giant fan, then Summer leapt onto the airboat, and they were off.

The river's tide sloshed all around them, rocking the other crafts moored at the island.

*I know it's bad form on the water. Even worse form to get turned into a shifter popsicle because this witch can't use her brain.*

Doubled over with her hands propped against her thighs, Summer panted to catch her breath and looked up at the slowly receding island. "Okay. I think we lost him." She barked out a laugh and straightened. "Man. I'd like to see him try to crawl through *that* toilet seat."

As she navigated the airboat around the bend in the river, Amanda spared a glance back at the island and saw a huge, hulking figure standing there in the darkness beside the outhouse. A shimmer of blue-white Crystal light flared around his body before winking out again. With wide eyes, she slowly turned back to face the bow.

*Focus on getting us back to campus. If he wanted to follow us, he'd still be following us.*

"Ha! That was the craziest—" Summer cackled wildly and swung a fist through the air, making the airboat rock a little. "Man, I haven't had that much fun since I snuck into the—no. This was *way* better. Turns out you *do* know how to have a good time!" She smacked Amanda's shoulder, then paused when she saw the red purse dangling by its leather straps. "For real? You kept the freakin' bag?"

"Yeah." Amanda shrugged.

"You should've dropped that thing when we split, shifter girl. You wanna get popped for trying to help a lady out? This is the way you do it. That thing on your shoulder makes you look *really* guilty."

"There's no way she would've been able to find it again, even if she noticed it missing right after we left." With a sniff, the shifter girl shot her friend a sidelong glance and tried to look noble about it. "Like you said. I bet her wallet's in here. If we find some ID, we can get hold of her and give it all back."

"*Or* we could *use* that ID to get into The Front Porch. *Then* give it back." Summer wiggled her fingers at the purse. "Hand it over, then. I'll check it out."

The purse straps slipped off Amanda's shoulder, and she handed over the purse, trying to keep her focus on navigating them upriver at what had to be almost 4:00 a.m. now. The moon was already on its way down toward the horizon, so it had to be ridiculously late. "We're not going through her stuff so we can use it. She was buying a present for her dad and got distracted. That's it."

The zipper ripped harshly under Summer's eagerness to get into the purse.

*Do I believe that?* Amanda tried hard not to look down at the purse. *Like I can convince myself there's no way that purse and the wizards weren't connected.*

Summer sat back on the deck of the airboat and cocked her head. "You *sure* that's what happened?"

"What?"

With a smirk, the witch popped open both sides of the bright leather bag and raised an eyebrow as she met Amanda's gaze. "Because this doesn't look anything like the belongings of a busy businesswoman whatever-she-was out buying presents."

"Show me." Amanda's mouth ran a little dry, and she tried to lick her lips enough to at least feel like she was in control again.

"Okay, shifter girl. Spill it."

"I don't know what you're talking about. What's in the purse?"

Summer sat back and propped herself up with both hands on the deck behind her. "You were in La-La Land before that super awesome fight broke out in the store *you* wanted to see before you suddenly didn't. You said something was happening. You told me to shut up."

"I was trying to pay attention to—" *Crap. I was trying* not *to bring that up.*

"Yeah. That's what I thought. What'd you hear with your superpowered little shifter ears, huh?"

"Okay, fine." Amanda swiped the hair out of her face, but it kept blowing back as the airboat took them upriver because they were traveling downwind back to the school. "I heard the guys in the shop talking about maybe getting rid of the lady, maybe not. I heard them talking about taking somebody out. Ronnie or something. No, wait. Rooney."

"And that meant something to you?"

"No, but they were planning some kind of attack. Or…I don't know. That's what it sounded it like." *Now I sound like I've completely lost my mind because I have no idea what happened.*

Summer cleared her throat. "Then…"

"Then what?"

"Quit screwing with me, Amanda. I'm sitting here looking inside this purse that is most definitely *not* only a purse, and I'm pretty sure you know exactly why."

"No…" She swallowed thickly, glanced at her friend, then quickly looked back upriver at the tunnel of overhanging branches coming up ahead of them as the river narrowed. "Crap. Okay. She set down her purse, and I thought she'd forgotten it, 'cause she was on her phone. So—"

"Yeah, forget the part where you tried to be a magical Good Samaritan." Summer frowned. "What else?"

Amanda wrinkled her nose and stared straight ahead. "Then the wizards showed up, got pissed about something not being there anymore where it was supposed to be, and they decided to go break into the weapons store anyway. Then, you know... magic fight."

Summer's mouth popped open.

"And... I might've seen the woman cast some kind of spell on the door to keep it open. Pretty sure the guys inside thought their locks still worked."

"Holy shit!" Summer burst out laughing, clutching her sides and rocking back so far she almost fell to the deck of the airboat.

"It's not that funny."

"You got into the middle of somebody else's serious business and screwed the whole thing up."

Amanda rolled her eyes. "Yeah..."

"You didn't try to do a good deed and fail." Another shrieking laugh escaped the witch and echoed out over the mostly silent water of the swamp. "You stepped right into the middle of a *drop*! You took the one—ha! The one thing those wizards were supposed to have before they blasted up that store!"

Gritting her teeth, Amanda glanced down at the open purse sitting in front of her friend and quickly snatched it up. "I figured that out without you laughing in my face and screaming it to the whole stupid Everglades."

"You...you're trying so *hard*!" Summer finally did fall back onto the deck of the airboat and rolled back and forth, caught up in a seemingly unending fit of laughter.

Resting her shoulder against the throttle control stick to keep them steady upriver, the shifter girl plunged her hand into the purse and only felt...one thing. Not a wallet, not a sunglasses case, not even a cell phone or anything that would normally go inside a purse.

It felt like stone.

"What is this?" She pulled the item the size of her fist from the bag and studied it in the fading moonlight.

"Oh, *wow*." Summer flung the long half of her hair out of her face and pushed herself up, fighting to catch her breath. "You really crack me up. You know that?"

"You know me. Just trying to entertain…" Amanda turned the figurine back and forth in her hand as she lowered it and tried to catch some of the moonlight on it. "It's a statue."

"Well, good thing it's not another freakin' soul stone, huh?" Summer leapt to her feet and reached for the fist-sized hunk of stone carved in the shape of a round humanoid figure sitting cross-legged on a stone cushion. Its features were soft and not very detailed—except for the eyes. Those looked like they could've been real, miniature eyes staring out of the stone face and watching everything they did. "What is this supposed to be? A Buddha statue?"

"Yeah, Summer. Two wizards armed with a sparking baton and blasting up the weapons store wanted to make sure they had the Buddha's blessing before getting down to the violence."

The witch snorted. "That doesn't sound very Zen."

"Because it's not a Buddha statue." Amanda reached out for the figurine, but her friend jerked it out of her reach. "Hey, come on. It's not *ours*, either. You don't know what it's for."

"No, but I can figure it out pretty damn quick. Like I did with the soul stone."

"That worked out *so* well for us last time. Come on. Give it."

"Give me a few seconds, shifter girl. Jeeze. It's not a stick of dynamite or anything—"

The figurine's eyes blazed with a dark, burnt-orange light growing steadily brighter by the second.

"Huh. Or maybe it is…"

"Summer, put it back in the purse."

"I wonder what else this thing can do…" The witch turned the glowing figurine over in her hand, and a spray of multi-colored sparks flew from those burning orange eyes. "Ow! Shit." The figurine toppled to the deck as Summer shook out her hand and sucked the tip of her finger. "Damn thing burned me."

"Because we're not supposed to be screwing around with it!" Amanda abandoned her post at the throttle control and leapt toward the figurine. The thing had already started spinning on the deck, throwing a spiral of multi-colored sparks around itself as the rest of the stone glowed with the same orange light. A high-pitched whine rose from the artifact, and right before Amanda's fingers closed around it, a thin beam of orange light shot straight up into the sky.

"Ow! Come on." She shook out her hand—the figurine was too hot to snatch up the way she wanted—and tried again, this time playing hot potato with a magical carving that was acting a lot like a bomb.

"What are you *doing?*" Summer shouted.

"We need to put it back in the bag!" Amanda tossed the thing from one hand to the other, snarling at the minor burns across her palm.

A thick tree branch snapped and cracked overhead when the thin sliver of orange light blasted through the overhanging trees. Sawdust and splintered wood and a few stray leaves toppled down around the boat, and the severed branch dropped. It caught on a lower bough and bounced, making the other branches snap.

At the same time, Summer snatched up the purse and raced toward the shifter. "Shit, it's a freakin' *laser!*"

Amanda tossed the figurine into the wide, gaping darkness of the large red purse a second before the heavy branch she'd inadvertently sawed in half broke the other branches catching its fall and crashed down toward the airboat's stern.

"No, no, no!" She leapt toward the throttle control stick and shoved it away from her with all her strength.

The fan turned as she cranked the throttle and propelled them to the starboard side. A *clank* of small branches and leaves scraping against the metal cage of the large fan split through the air, a few leaves got shredded in the process, and the branch crashed into the river, sending up a spray of salty water over the back of the airboat.

Amanda jerked the throttle control back toward her to level them out before they would've crashed bow-first into the river-bank and tossed her hand out toward where she thought Summer was. "Get that thing—"

Instead, her hand smacked against the leather purse in Summer's arms as the witch finished zipping the thing shut.

"Hey, what the—" Summer tried to catch it and stopped at the portside edge of the airboat, her arms flailing to keep her from toppling over in the water. The purse landed in the swamp with a *plop* and a small splash.

Amanda immediately cut off the airboat's fan and raced to the edge of the deck. Both girls stared at the dark, muddy, churning water where the random woman's purse and some secret carv-ing-slash-laser-weapon had disappeared.

The river settled back into its natural rhythm, lapping a little more heavily than usual at both banks now that the tide was partially obstructed by a giant sawed-off branch halfway submerged in the water. The swamp fell back into its nighttime silence a few hours before dawn.

Amanda huffed out a sigh.

"Well, now *no one* gets it," Summer muttered.

The shifter girl clenched her teeth and stomped back to the stern before starting the boat's fan again. The airboat lurched forward, and they zipped across the river toward the Academy.

"Hey, don't be pissed at *me*."

"I'm not," Amanda said through clenched teeth.

"*You're* the one who slapped it out of my hand."

"I know!" She drew another deep breath to calm herself and shook her head. "That's probably not a good thing."

"Hey, but look on the bright side." Summer returned to the stern and stopped beside her friend, folding her arms. "Now we don't have to worry about getting rid of the evidence."

"I guess."

"A little more time to figure out how that thing works would've been cool, though. Did you *see* the way it sliced through that branch?"

"And almost crushed off the fan so we'd have to swim with the gators back to campus? Yeah. I saw." Amanda scowled at the grouping of narrower tributaries leading to this part of the river, which she recognized now after at least a dozen trips spent trying to find the kemana before tonight.

*We were only supposed to go out and have a little fun. And we almost seriously screwed up.*

"Hey." Summer bumped her shoulder lightly against the shifter girl's. "Amanda."

"What?"

"There's something really important I want you to remember about tonight."

Amanda turned her head to meet her friend's gaze in the semi-darkness and raised her eyebrows.

Summer's lips twitched as she fought to hold back a laugh. "We climbed into a porta-potty." She choked on her next words and had to try again. "And climbed back out again with a laser-Buddha."

The only way Amanda managed to choke back a laugh was by forcing a cough instead. "Don't."

"Pretty heavy-doody stuff."

Both girls stood rigidly in front of the fan mount, and when they looked at each other again, they burst out laughing.

"Okay, cut it out so I can focus on getting us back to the dock."

"Sure. I'll cut the shit."

"I'm serious."

"Laser-Buddha could've done a pretty good job of that too, you know. Now he's swimming with the fishies—"

Amanda bumped her shoulder against the witch's harder than

she'd intended and sent Summer stumbling forward across the deck. "Next time, we're not touching *anything* but food. Got it?"

"Oh, so there's still gonna be a next time, huh?" Summer righted herself and turned her face into the wind as the airboat slowed and Amanda steered them around the bend.

With the dock in view behind the thick overbrush and a giant stand of cattails she had to maneuver around, she finally let herself relax about the whole thing. "Oh, yeah. Definitely a next time."

# CHAPTER NINE

Amanda had a hard time getting to sleep that night with the memory of the woman with the red shoes and the guys running High Tide Ammo racing over and over in her mind. The craziest thing was that she didn't feel bad at all about the latter. Those magicals in the store—Marley and whoever else he worked for, or at least the other guy calling the shots—had been planning to storm into someone else's shop or home or wherever and *take them out.*

*"Bastards won't know what hit 'em."* That's what the Marley guy had said.

She stared at the tiny holes in the panels of her dorm room ceiling and sighed.

*I don't feel bad that they got their asses kicked by those wizards. They deserved it. I feel bad for screwing it up.*

Maybe the fight would have been faster, more precise, and less of a spectacle in the Everglades kemana if Amanda hadn't tried to be a teenage hero and return a forgotten purse.

She snorted and rolled over in her bed, trying to ignore everything racing through her mind. Summer hadn't seemed to care one way or the other. The witch had thought the whole thing hilarious.

*Not hilarious when I did the exact opposite of what I even came here to this school to do. Johnny would've waited and watched. That's what I need to do more of.*

The alarm clock beside her bed flashed its blue-green numbers in the darkness—4:23 a.m.

*I'm so glad we don't have a wake-up alarm tomorrow. Maybe we should leave the kemana trips for the weekend.*

She woke with a start, feeling as if she'd missed something incredibly important. Her stomach let out a furious growl in response, and Amanda pushed herself up in bed before rubbing her belly.

*Only breakfast. Better go smile and tell the pixies pretty please.*

Hopefully, there was still something left at breakfast, which the kitchens served later on the weekends. Even high-school kids slept in on Saturday and Sunday mornings, including students at the Academy of Necessary Magic.

Amanda was up and dressed and ready to feed the growling beast in her belly in under five minutes. She slipped into her sneakers and reached for the doorknob.

It wouldn't budge.

"What?" She tugged on it, jiggled it back and forth, and bent to peer at the brass knob that didn't have a keyhole on *this* side of the door. She closed her eyes and drew a deep breath. *Shifters have magic. Right? All I have to do is focus more than ever, and...*

Her hand trembled in front of the doorknob as she tried to work a spell she'd seen Summer use countless times to open locked doors but only half understood. It wasn't exactly the kind any of the teachers here would include on their lesson plan. Nothing happened.

*Who am I kidding? The only reason I could change the color of a stupid piece of paper last semester was because of that soul stone. Why the heck is my door locked?*

She jiggled the doorknob again, but it wouldn't budge.

"Hey!" Her palm slammed against the door, then she pressed her ear to the wood and listened.

No movement in the hall outside. No sound of footsteps or morning conversation from the other girls shuffling sleepily down to what amounted to weekend brunch. She did hear the very faint sound of someone's slow, steady breathing, almost as if someone were trying to stay so quiet, even a shifter couldn't hear.

She recognized the scent wafting through the crack in the door when she leaned toward the doorframe and sniffed.

She pounded the side of her fist against the door once. "Summer, what gives?"

"Damn, shifter girl." The witch chuckled on the other side. "I thought for *sure* I was quiet."

"No, you're annoying. Why's my door locked from the outside?"

"It's a little something I whipped up to—"

"Open it. I'm starving!"

"Okay, okay. Keep it together. Jeeze." The flash of a faded yellow light flickered around the edge of the door. "There. You're all good—"

Amanda jerked open the door and found her friend standing right there in the doorway, grinning. "What are you doing?"

The black-haired witch slammed both her hands against the doorframe and wiggled her eyebrows. "We need to talk."

"Great. Let's talk on the way to breakfast." Amanda tried to step out of the room, but her friend blocked her.

"Here's the thing. I've been thinking a lot about what it means to care about anything at all, you know? Like, whether it's a nice sunny day out and the birds are singing or if I'm gonna step in a pile of dogshit with my bare feet. You ever have that feeling?"

Amanda clenched her fists, glared at her friend, and ignored the painful imploding of her empty stomach. "The only feeling I have right now is hunger. Quit screwing around and let's go get breakfast."

"Wait, wait, wait. Amanda." Summer dipped her chin and shot the other girl a trying-to-be-serious stare. "I found out over break that they built this entire school in a *month*. Did you know that?"

"Yeah. Who cares?" She tried to muscle her way past Summer again, but the witch stepped into the room and slammed the door shut behind her before leaning back against it and folding her arms.

"*And* I heard a rumor you built yourself a copy of Petrov's obstacle course. Doesn't that feel a little like cheating to you? Not that I care or anything. I'm only saying it's a little—"

"What are you *doing*?" Amanda shouted and gestured at the door. "You're not making any sense."

"That's kinda the point, right?"

"No!" The tingle of an imminent shift raced across her body, and Amanda growled. "Maybe you don't understand what's happening right now. I'm hungry. You ever seen a shifter get really, *really* hungry?"

The witch's eyes widened, and she chuckled, shaking herself in a mock shudder. "Ooh…tell me more."

*I know what this is. She inhaled too many moonshine fumes and left her brains in the kemana.*

"Summer!" The shout came out as a snarl, and Amanda leapt toward the door, grabbing two fistfuls of her friend's hoodie at the shoulders without even thinking about it. "Get out of my way!"

A brief flash of surprise and a little fear flickered across the witch's face, but she quickly covered it up with a smirk. "You need to relax."

"I need breakfast."

Summer spread her arms and stepped away so Amanda could finally jerk open her bedroom door. The shifter girl stalked into the hall and headed for the staircase at the front of the building. She heard her door closing and Summer's hurried footsteps coming after her.

"Seriously, shifter girl. I was only playing around."

"Yeah, well, maybe you should pick your timing a little better. Like, *after* I've had something to eat."

"What, you're gonna rip my head off because I stood between you and a stack of pancakes?"

After whipping open the door to the staircase, Amanda stopped and glared at her friend. "What do *you* think?"

Summer laughed and ran a hand through her botched haircut. "I think you're all bark and no—Hey. Hey, slow down. Come on. I'm screwing with you."

The door creaked shut behind them, and Amanda jogged down the staircase, hungry and agitated and pissed off. *Not a good combo in a shifter. How does she* not *know that?*

"I don't know what you were trying to pull, but don't do it again."

"Oh, come on. You can take a little practical joke here and there."

"Not first thing in the morning. Not when I feel like I could eat the whole spread laid out. There's still food, right?"

Summer shrugged as they entered the common room on the first floor, which was completely empty and deathly silent.

Frowning, Amanda turned and scanned the tables and chairs, all of which had been put back in their usual places after the girls' movie night and chaotic sleepover down here the night before. No one was here.

"Where is everybody?"

"Probably out eating the whole spread. Shall we?" Summer gestured toward the front door of the dorms, and Amanda stormed away with a scowl.

"You're freaking me out."

"You're over-reacting."

The sunshine practically blinded her for the first few seconds when they stepped outside, and Amanda squinted against the glare before her vision adjusted. The air was warm with a light January chill, birds were singing, insects droned in low, sleepy voices, and…

"What's going on?"

"What do you mean?" Summer shoved her hands into her hoodie pockets and waltzed across the grass, staring up at the puffy clouds moving lazily across the sky.

"It's too quiet."

"If you ask me, everyone here could *seriously* use a little more quiet time, know what I mean?"

Amanda turned to scan the central field, the grouping of main buildings, and then the boy's dorm on the other side of the girls'. "There's no one here."

"So what? It's a Sunday."

"Summer, it's not like they have somewhere else to go over the weekend. Where *is* everybody?"

"Look. You need to quit thinking about everyone else's problems, huh?" Summer spread her arms. "Five minutes ago, you were about to go full wolf on me because I stood between you and your breakfast. Now there's *literally* no one here to stand in your way. Are you hungry or not?"

The shifter girl scowled, scanning the swamp surrounding the Academy campus and straining to hear a single noise from anyone else on the property. "What did you do?"

The other girl barked out a laugh and headed around the buildings toward the outdoor cafeteria. "Just so we're clear, not everything's *my* fault."

*Something's really, really, really not right.*

With a final glance toward the teacher housing on the other side of the main building, Amanda headed after her friend, trying to fit all the pieces together. None of them made any sense.

"Hurry up, shifter girl. If there's any food left, you're gonna want it pretty much right now." Summer strode along as if she didn't have a care in the world—which wasn't all that different than usual, except for the fact that the Academy had become a ghost town in the five hours Amanda had spent passed out in her bed.

The witch reached the edge of the field holding the outdoor cafeteria and stopped halfway to the banquet table. She turned and spread her arms. "What are you waiting for?"

Amanda froze. The pavilion was empty. All the picnic tables were empty. The banquet table didn't have a single plate or serving dish on it, let alone a speck of food. She swallowed thickly. "You gotta be kidding me."

"Come *on.*"

"No. We should go find Glasket or one of the other teachers to—"

Rolling her eyes, Summer stormed back toward the shifter girl and set both hands firmly on her friend's shoulders to guide her toward the eerily empty cafeteria. "You seriously need to learn how to go with the flow," she muttered, leaning toward Amanda's ear. "Everything'll be a lot easier for you that way."

"What are you talking ab—"

A ripple of prickling energy washed over her face first, then across her chest and shoulders, and into her back. She sucked in a sharp breath, and over a hundred voices shouted all at once, "Surprise!"

She jumped and shoved Summer's hands off her as the black-haired witch burst out in a fit of laughter. Because the outdoor cafeteria suddenly wasn't empty anymore. The Academy's entire student body stood there, filling the space between the pavilion and the kitchens and surrounding the salad bar turned drink station.

Someone shot off a spell of glittering black and green sparks —a poor attempt at fireworks—and what sounded like a million conversations kicked up all at once.

Amanda's mouth dropped open, and she couldn't help a surprised laugh. "What?"

"Happy Birthday!" Summer shouted through her laughter, sweeping her hand across the cafeteria. "Late, obviously. Or so I heard."

"Wait, did you do this?"

"Me? Hell no. I'm only the messenger." Summer headed straight for the banquet table now piled high with their regular brunch spread—eggs, bacon, sausage, pancakes soaked in butter, real maple syrup, biscuits and gravy, and a massive three-tiered cake at the far end decorated with fake teeth and huge, dark-stained slashes across the side that were probably supposed to be claw marks.

*Now* Amanda smelled the food.

# CHAPTER TEN

The other students poured toward the banquet table after Summer, talking and laughing and occasionally shooting broad smiles Amanda's way.

"What do you think, Coulier?" Jackson jogged toward her, grinning from ear to ear and spreading his arms as he looked up at the decorations hanging from the side of the kitchen and the pavilion's roof over the picnic tables.

"Um...I don't—"

"I *told* you she wouldn't know what to say," Grace added as she joined them, wrapping her fuzzy sweater tighter around her shoulders.

"Speechless! That was the point." Jackson bit his bottom lip and waited for Amanda to say something.

"I'm..." She couldn't think of anything else but, "You know my birthday was a week ago, right?"

"Yeah. December thirtieth. Lemme tell ya, Coulier, *that* was the hardest thing to drag out of Principal Clam-Up over there." Jackson nodded toward the teachers who stood at the far end of the banquet table beside Fred, the head kitchen pixie, and Gloria. The rest of the pixies had opted to stay in the kitchens for the celebration, but the adults who *were* here smiled and looked at least halfway entertained.

"Okay…" Amanda chuckled uncertainly. "I hope Glasket didn't think it was a good idea to call the shifter out with a school-wide birthday party."

"What's wrong with that?" Jackson folded his arms.

"I mean, no one else has had a party like this."

"That's because the teachers had nothing to do with it." Alex approached them calmly, licking frosting off his fingers.

"Dude, you got into the cake already?"

Alex stared at the wizard and didn't reply.

"Wait, what do you mean the teachers had nothing to do with it?"

"It was all Jackson." Grace clapped a hand on his shoulder and gave him a little shake. "He took the reins. I mean, yeah, he had to get it *approved—*"

"That was the hardest part. Everything else was easy." Jackson gestured at the streamers fluttering in the breeze and the large sign that said, "Happy Birthday Amanda!" hanging from the pavilion roof. Random drawings of wolves chasing down pigs were tacked up to the pillars of the pavilion and on the kitchen wall over the banquet table.

Amanda bit her lip. "Nice new take on the Three Little Pigs story."

Jackson rolled his eyes. "Why does everyone keep *saying* that? It's supposed to be you chasing off the deadly hogs that came through here last—hey! Hey! You jerks better save some cake for Coulier, got it? It's not *your* party."

He took off toward the banquet table, and Alex snorted. "Cake police over here."

"This is awesome, guys." Amanda's cheeks grew warm, and she stuffed her hands into her hoodie pockets. "Really. Thanks."

"Thank the guy who put it all together." Grace laughed when Jackson shoved his finger in Corey Baker's face and told him not to eat half the cake just because he could. "He wouldn't shut up about it all break."

"What he *really* wanted to do was take the party to your house on your actual birthday," Alex muttered. "Glasket almost threw him out the window when he wouldn't stop asking."

"Just like everyone else." Amanda's friends both sniggered.

"Because he wanted to throw a party?"

"Because he wouldn't quit bugging *everyone* about helping him out with it. Obviously, the pixies were on board from the very beginning." Grace nodded at Fred, who grinned through his beard and wiggled huge fingers at them in a joking wave. "I'm pretty sure everyone else who had something to do with it gave in so he'd stop hounding them about it."

"Oh, boy." Amanda wrinkled her nose. "*That's* what you guys were talking about last night."

The blonde witch shrugged and shot her a coy smile. "Maybe. Or at least part of it."

*Nope. He did it as a friend. That's all it is.*

Amanda's stomach growled again, and she inched her way toward the banquet table. "I'm gonna grab some breakfast."

"It's *your* party, shifter girl!" Emma Teal shouted from the other end of the table as she flopped a huge slice of cake onto her plate. "We're only here for the cake. For breakfast. Good job lasting another year."

The other upperclassmen around her burst out laughing and took their plates of cake and no actual breakfast to the picnic tables.

Amanda grabbed herself a plate and piled it high with some of everything laid out this morning. Two slices of bacon disappeared in her mouth instantly, and she felt like she could hold off on the rest until she sat with a fork.

*They did all this for me. I had no idea...*

The teachers still stood at the far end of the table, overseeing the "party" with their plated cake slices in hand. When Amanda reached for the cake that now looked like a wolf *and* a school full of hungry teenagers had demolished it, Fred waved her away.

"I got ya, kid. Big-ass slice for the belated-birthday girl, right?"

"I mean, why not?" She grinned at the pixie as he handed over a plate.

With a wink, he leaned toward her and muttered, "If that scrawny wizard's energy had to be directed *somewhere*, I'd say he picked the right target to aim it. You got good friends here, kid."

"And good cake." She lifted her plate toward him and turned away to head for the picnic tables. "Thanks. Tell everyone else in the kitchen I said thanks too. I know a giant cake probably wasn't in the plans."

Fred chuckled. "Neither were baskets of midnight snacks, but I'd be lying if I said we don't enjoy it. Happy birthday, kid."

Amanda avoided the teachers' gazes altogether, feeling more than a little self-conscious, and focused on finding an empty table to eat her giant, sugar-filled breakfast.

"I can't believe these guys." Carrying a tiny slice of cake and huffing in frustration, Jackson joined her at the table. "Half of them didn't do crap to help, and they're sitting here smashing cake in their faces as though they deserve it."

Amanda crammed scrambled eggs in her mouth and tried not to laugh. "This is awesome."

"It *better* be." He stared at her plate, then flicked his gaze up toward her, shifting nervously on the bench across the table. "You looked really pissed before you stepped through that illusion. I thought I'd screwed the whole thing up."

She choked down her eggs and washed it down with an entire sausage link. "That's because Summer played the whole 'distract the shifter card' a little too hard. I was…hungry."

"Yeah, obviously." Jackson chuckled and finally got down to eating his cake. "You're okay that we threw you a party? I mean, I know it's kinda cheesy, and it's not like I could get anything fancy out here in the middle of—"

"No, it's great." He lit up at the words and grinned, making her even more aware of everything the other girls had shouted at her during the movie last night. *Don't even think about it.* "Seriously. I haven't had a birthday like this in…, probably ever."

"What? You mean you haven't spent your entire life at a bounty-hunter school surrounded by a bunch of crazy magical kids?"

They both laughed.

"No. But all my other birthdays were small. You know, only family. They were—" Amanda swallowed thickly and stabbed up a forkful of pancakes. "I mean, I have a—*had* a twin, so…"

"Oh. Right." Jackson stared at his plate. "I didn't mean to bring that up."

"No, you didn't."

"Bring what up?" Alex sat beside the wizard with a stack of five pancakes overflowing with syrup on his plate and nothing else.

She snorted as he dug in. "That this is the best birthday party anyone's thrown me."

"Really?" Alex studied her with his bright green eyes and squinted. "I can't tell if you're saying that to be nice. 'Cause that might mean you've had a seriously screwed-up childhood before coming here—" The pancakes dropped from his fork when Jackson elbowed him in the ribs. "What's *your* problem?"

"You're ruining it," Jackson muttered through clenched teeth.

"Uh…looks to me like she's pretty happy. So maybe chill out." The half-Wood Elf went back to eating his syrup with a side of pancakes and didn't look up at either of them again.

"Okay." Grace joined them with her plate and sat beside Amanda. "I wasn't sure how this was gonna play out, but this might be the best cake I've ever had. Good job having a birthday. And officially being old enough for high school now, right?"

Amanda playfully rolled her eyes. "Yeah, thanks. Good

surprise. Hey, whose idea was it anyway to make Summer lock me in my room?"

Jackson choked on his cake. "Wait, what?"

"She *locked* you in your room?" Grace snickered and wiped bacon grease from the corner of her mouth with the back of a hand.

"Yeah. And started talking gibberish."

"She was supposed to make sure everyone was out of the dorms and behind the illusion before you woke up. No one told her to lock you in your room."

"Of course not." Amanda shoveled more food in her mouth and couldn't help a wry laugh. *That was Summer's special version of throwing a party. Awesome.* "The illusion was a good touch. I thought everybody was…I don't know." She laughed. "Dead or something."

All three of her friends paused mid-bite and stared at her.

Then Grace wrinkled her nose. "You have a morbid sense of humor sometimes. You know that?"

"No, I don't."

Alex pointed his fork at her. "You laughed before you said you thought we were all dead. That's pretty morbid."

"I didn't know *what* to think, okay? I couldn't hear anybody or even smell the food."

"Yeah." The half-Wood Elf turned slowly to cast a longing glance at the teachers in casual conversation with Fred and Gloria. "That was all Mrs. Zimmer."

Jackson elbowed him in the side again and wiggled his eyebrows. "You still got it hot for teacher, huh?"

"I can appreciate someone's skills with illusions." Alex scooted down the bench away from his friend. "That's all."

"Oh, that's right." Grace laughed. "There really is a fine line between appreciation and obsession."

Jackson barked out a laugh. "Yeah, they both make him drool in Illusions class."

Alex shook his head and focused on his pancake stack.

Amanda couldn't help a constant smile as she finished the rest of her hearty breakfast and got to work on the cake, which was admittedly better than any of her other previous birthday cakes. *It'd still taste better if Claire were still here with me. She'd be happy I finally have friends, at least.*

After breakfast, Jackson fell all over himself trying to apologize for the fact that there weren't any presents for her. "Not like we have a bunch of dough to spend on anything. Doesn't mean we didn't want to. So don't—"

Alex clapped a hand on the wizard's shoulder and stared at Amanda. "Stop rambling and give it to her already."

Jackson's cheeks flushed, and he shrugged out from under the other boy's hand to race around the back of the kitchen.

"Give me what?" Amanda tossed her paper plate in the trashcan and shook her head. "I don't need presents."

"Yeah, but what kinda friends would we be if we didn't get you *anything*?" Grace tucked her blonde bob behind her ear. "Or *make* you anything, at least."

"You guys threw me a party. That's enough."

Alex rolled his eyes. "Just shut up and take your presents, Amanda. Otherwise, I'm pretty sure Jackson's gonna spend the rest of the semester in a seriously deep depression."

"Jeeze. Okay."

The wizard scurried back toward them holding what looked like a cake box. He shrugged and handed it to her. "The pixies had extra boxes, so…"

"Thanks." Amanda cradled the box under one arm and tore off the lid. "Oh. Whoa. This is…"

"You don't like it." Jackson rubbed the back of his neck and scowled at Grace. "I *told* you she wouldn't—"

"You need to chill out," the witch replied. "She loves it."

Amanda glanced around the outdoor cafeteria and made sure the teachers weren't paying attention too closely. "You *made* this?"

"Yeah. Had to ask Tenney Rorke to sneak us some extra wi-fi to look up the parts and everything." Jackson shrugged. "Then, well…there was the issue of finding the parts."

"To be clear, that was all Summer." Grace folded her arms. "Apparently, she figured out how to break into LeFor's supply room, but at least she can read a list of parts and didn't have to blow anything up to get them."

Amanda grinned at the collapsible and therefore highly portable crossbow sitting at the bottom of the box. "This is awesome. I can't even… Thanks."

Alex took the lid from her and placed it back over the box. "Don't take it out where everyone can see. We wanted to put some bolts in there, but Petrov's a lot better at putting wards around the training building."

She laughed and stared at her friends. "Thanks. I love it."

"*Told* you." Grace shoved Jackson in the shoulder, and he shuffled his feet with a crooked smile. "I'm going back for more cake. Anybody want some?"

"Definitely." Jackson leapt after her as they headed back to the banquet table, and Alex stood there, staring at Amanda with a deadpan expression.

"So you're what, now? Ten?"

"Very funny."

A tiny smile flickered at the corner of his mouth, and he pointed at the box. "Seriously. Don't let anyone else see that thing. If they do, don't tell them where you got it. Unless you, like, use it to save the day or something. I'm gonna go now."

"Okay…" She laughed as he brushed past her and headed back to the boys' dorm.

*Thirteen's definitely the best birthday so far.*

With all the other students either cleared off after the surprise party or still making serious dents in the giant cake, Amanda turned and headed back toward the girls' dorm to find a good hiding spot for the homemade crossbow that counted as contraband on campus.

*I can't wait to use this thing—*

"Amanda?"

She spun to find the History of Oriceran teacher jogging to catch up with her, and her smile faded. "Ms. Ralthorn. Hi…"

The witch stopped and readjusted her glasses on her face. "Don't look so terrified. Nothing's wrong. I was going to give this to you after class this week, but I guess now might be a better time. Think of it as a birthday present."

Amanda couldn't help a confused frown as the teacher reached into her pocket and pulled out a piece of paper folded into a small, neat square. *A present from the teacher who doesn't like shifters?*

"I told you last semester I'd brush up on my… Well. That I'd do better as a teacher when it comes to opening my mind to different perspectives. When I found this, I thought it might be of some use to you."

"Um…thanks." Awkwardly tucking the cake box full of illegal weaponry under her arm, Amanda took the folded paper from Ms. Ralthorn and forced a smile.

"I'm afraid I won't be very useful if you have specific questions, but I'm sure *they* will be. Happy birthday." The history teacher walked away, paused, and turned with her mouth open, weighing the pros and cons of whatever else she wanted to say. Then she shook her head and headed back toward the other teachers gathered beside the banquet table.

Amanda frowned at the paper and didn't bother to read the weird note from her teacher until after she'd slipped back through the front door of the girls' dorm. The box went down on the closest table, and she unfolded the neat square of paper to reveal a very short message in Ms. Ralthorn's incredibly neat handwriting.

**The Coalition. Current chair: Connor Slate. I will vouch for you with Dean Glasket if you're interested in more.**

That was it.

She flipped the paper over, but the other side was blank. So she shoved it into her pocket instead and headed toward the closest staircase.

*I get it. She was trying to make up for last semester. I'll take the present I understand.*

Another glance at the box in her arms made her smile.

*Like homemade weapons from my friends.*

# CHAPTER ELEVEN

The next day, the spring semester officially started at the Academy. Amanda was more than ready to put her two weeks of practice over the winter break to good use with Mr. Petrov's obstacle course, but she never got the chance. Havalah had to start the day with a complaint about how they weren't *learning* anything in their first—and incredibly physically demanding—class of the day.

Mr. Petrov had seemed uncharacteristically amused by that and made his point by ordering the whole class to run laps for the first third of the class while Havalah stood in the center of the training field and watched. For the second third, he made her run on her own.

"Break's over, kiddies," the bald teacher shouted from the comfort of his folding lawn chair in front of the training building's open door. "Time to look alive and act like you've earned your place at this school. You haven't. Not yet. So you know, I wanted to call this class Fake It 'Til You Make It One-oh-One."

The final fifty minutes of class, Mr. Petrov had them pulling weeds from the training field and sanding down the poles and platforms of the obstacle course.

None of the freshmen were in much of a laughing mood after that, all of them drenched with sweat at the end of the class and ready to get the hell away from the teacher they called "the sergeant" behind his back.

Jackson wiped sweat from his forehead beneath his shaggy blond hair and puffed out a sigh as they filtered away from the training field. "Good thing it's not the middle of summer still, right?"

"He likes to torture us," Grace grumbled and nodded at Amanda. "Did you get to practice on your obstacle course over break?"

Amanda stretched out her shoulder after having spent way too long sanding the underside of a wooden platform. "Yeah. Got all the way through a few times too."

"Good. Next time we get up there, finish the stupid thing." Grace upended her water bottle with the Academy's logo on it into her open mouth, then sighed. "Maybe that'll torture the sergeant."

"Oh, man." Jackson snickered. "I can't *wait* to see his face when that happens."

"We won't have to go through all this again next year, will we?" Amanda asked.

"Who knows? Every time I try to ask an upperclassman what *they* do in his class, I get the same answer."

Alex retied his hair in its long ponytail. "If they told us, they'd have to kill us."

"Yeah, what he said."

"Awesome."

---

Illusions class wasn't nearly as bad, fortunately. Ms. Calsgrave welcomed them back and dove right into what they'd be working on for the first part of the semester, at least—casting illusions to change not only the color of flat objects but now the shape and size as well. Only after she finished instructing the freshman class on how to do so did Calsgrave call Amanda to join her in the back of the room.

The shifter girl glanced at Grace, who shrugged and turned immediately back to scrutinizing the rock on her desk. Ms. Calsgrave had instructed everyone to make their stone look like a pencil.

*Great. This is the part where I get reminded of how useless I am in a class that's all magic and nothing else.*

Amanda slowly moved toward the teacher at the classroom door, and Calsgrave gestured into the hall. "I'll be twenty minutes," she said to the class. "If I come back and see a single one of you not focusing on the assignment, I'll pull those students out individually. I promise you that I'll find the one thing you hate the most and make you sit alone in a room with it for the rest of the class."

With a pert smile, the witch with a short brown bob turned smartly on her heels, closed the door behind her, and followed Amanda into the hall.

"Is…something wrong?"

"Not at all, Miss Coulier. I can't in good conscience let you sit through the entire class without fulfilling your potential. Which, as we both know, doesn't necessarily coincide with illusion spells. Come with me." Calsgrave's flats whispered across the linoleum floors as she hurried down the hall and led Amanda toward the east wing.

"Isn't this where the seniors have their classes?" the girl muttered as she tried not to look through the windows into the other classrooms. It was impossible not to; a bright flash of green light followed by explosive laughter strobed through the windows of a classroom coming up on their right. She caught a brief glimpse inside of a senior boy standing at the front of the room with a large seagull standing on his head, wings fluttering madly, and a spray of what had been the seagull's last meal—now fully digested and expelled—dripping down the front of the kid's shirt.

Mrs. Zimmer glanced up and pointed at the door before the blinds automatically spilled down to cover the window.

"It is," Calsgrave replied. "You'll get to your advanced classes in the east wing soon enough. I have no doubt."

"In two and a half years..."

The teacher turned halfway around to smile at Amanda. "I know it feels like a long time, Miss Coulier, but trust me. Your time here at the Academy will fly by faster than you know. For now, let's focus on the present. It includes a few changes to the freshman curriculum." Calsgrave's smile faded a little, and she blinked quickly as if her thoughts had confused her. "Specifically yours."

They stopped at a nondescript door on the right, almost at the end of the east wing's final hallway, and the witch jerked down on the shiny new handle. "Fortunately for us, the Academy's budget for additions and improvements is more than adequate, especially as we move through this first year and work out some of the...kinks. Our top priority is the well-rounded and preparatory education for *all* our students. Including those who may not possess certain qualities and skillsets that apply to all classes."

Amanda stopped in the hallway without bothering to look inside this next room and sighed. "Say it. Because I'm a shifter and I can't do magic, and I'm useless in your class."

Calsgrave drew in a deep breath and held it. "You're absolutely *not* useless, Miss Coulier. You made that clear last semester. Several times. It was an oversight on all our parts not to have fully thought through which classes would be beyond your inherent capabilities, through no fault of your own. We took the chance to implement some changes over the break."

"Great." The shifter girl grimaced. "I'm gonna be organizing files or cleaning out supply closets, right? Something boring but still useful enough to say you put me to work so I get credit for your—"

"Okay, let me stop you right there." The smirk on Ms. Calsgrave's face flickered in and out, and she released the handle of the open door. "I should've known something was up when you excelled through that handful of assignments in my class last semester after weeks of staring at a piece of paper with no results. No, you don't have a very ancient, very *dead* magical's soul stone anymore to help you cast spells. On the bright side, you may be the only shifter in history to have cast any spells at all. Or at least the only one I know of. Still, you *do* have a special brand of magic, and this is a school. It's our job to help you find your strengths and hone them to the best of your ability. Which I think you exhibited perfectly during our Samhain celebration when you did what you realized had to be done. When no one else did."

Amanda wrinkled her nose. "So my Illusions class is now being replaced by How to Avoid Angry Spirits As A Wolf class? No offense, Ms. Calsgrave, but I'm pretty sure *I* should be teaching that one instead of the other way around. You know, if there were any other shifters here."

"That's an excellent idea to keep on the back burner." The witch chuckled. "Who knows what kind of freshman class we'll have on our hands next year? For now, why don't you at least *try* to put aside your doubt and frustration and join me?"

"Yeah. Sure." *As long as it's not scrubbing walls or picking up ward-eating grubs, I guess it's fine.*

She followed the teacher into the room beyond, which was dark and smelled like dirt. Once inside the door, Calsgrave snapped her fingers, and the air along the ceiling and walls shimmered before the blackness fell away like a fluttering curtain dropped from somewhere very high.

Bright light spilled through the panes of clear glass that made up the walls and ceiling of the massive greenhouse twice the size of any other classroom Amanda had seen so far. Five large troughs slightly taller than waist height lined the greenhouse from one side to the other, with three-foot rows of space between them and a workbench at both ends of every trough.

*No wonder I smelled dirt.*

Amanda looked up at her Illusions teacher, who smiled expectantly and raised her eyebrows. "What do you think?"

"Um…I guess I'm wondering where all the plants are."

"Yes. Well, that's why you're here." The witch took off across the room, gesturing toward the troughs and the large, bright green metal cabinet rising to the ceiling on the far-left side. "We don't have an herbalist on staff currently. Dean Glasket insisted on offering Ralston Herod a position here at the school, but of course, he refused. She refused to consider anyone else."

"Who?"

"Ralston Herod. You've never heard of—you know what? It doesn't matter. The Academy doesn't need the topmost expert of the last century in magical cultivation and enhanced herbal applications to… I'm sorry. I'm rambling."

Amanda pressed her lips together and kept her mouth shut.

Calsgrave cleared her throat and clapped her hands together. "Last semester was a learning experience for all of us, as I'm sure you recognized. A month of construction and organization before opening the Academy wasn't nearly long enough to prepare for a greenhouse of our own, so that endeavor fell to the wayside. Until it was repeatedly brought to our attention that we needed an alternative for students like yourself, Miss Coulier, who would benefit more from hands-on experience with more…physical-based magic than what was offered before—"

"This was Johnny's idea, wasn't it?"

The teacher started, blinked furiously, and tucked her hair behind one ear. "I'm sorry?"

"Look, I know he talked to someone here about having a

shifter as a student and not forcing me to do impossible magic I can't do, so you don't have to pretend it was anything else."

"I see." Calsgrave cleared her throat again. "Yes, he was very...passionate."

Amanda snorted. "That's one way to think of it. But *gardening?*"

"Your guardian didn't have quite as much to say about the specifics of alternate courses for you, but Ms. Breyer was very helpful. In a separate conversation."

*Great. Both of them had big ol' meetings with my teachers just like every other helicopter parent.* Amanda laughed and tried to cover it up with a forced cough. *One who happens to own at least a third of the school and all of the land it's built on.*

"Okay. So instead of learning illusion spells I can't cast, I get to...what? Grow tomato plants?"

The teacher folded her arms and cocked her head. "I know it's hard to believe that adults who would choose to dedicate their lives to the instruction of teenage magicals heading down a path toward bounty-hunting—or at least something like it—would have much imagination at all. I'm asking for a little more credit. You will *not* be growing tomatoes."

With a smirk, the witch turned toward the cabinet and produced a key from her pocket before unlocking both doors. Different-colored bags of soil, labeled binders, gardening spades, gloves, various sizes and shapes of watering cans, short-handled rakes, and whatever else the Academy thought was necessary to run a successful school greenhouse filled the cabinet.

Amanda forced back another laugh. "Is that a fire extinguisher?"

"Yes. And a first-aid kit. Because the specific strains you'll be planting, growing, harvesting from, and caring for in this green-house are the kind that should probably come with a signed liability waiver." Calsgrave grinned.

*Okay, now this is finally starting to sound like a good idea.*

"Seriously?" Amanda headed toward the open cabinet, viewing the contents without knowing what half of them were. "Like what? Flesh-eating plants?"

"At some point, yes."

"What about *explosive* plants? Obviously, there's already a kind that has to…what? Spit fire or something, right? When do I get to grow *that*?"

"First things first. You'll work your way up, Miss Coulier. I have no doubt. Because we're starting from scratch here, we have to build our way up."

"Yeah, by planting badass seeds."

"Eventually." Calsgrave grabbed the thinnest binder from the cabinet's top shelf, then hauled a massive hardback book twice the size of a regular textbook and at least a foot thick. She brought them both to the workbench built against the end of the closest gardening trough and *thunked* them both down on the sturdy wooden surface. "We're working with what we have right now. The plants you're talking about only thrive under certain conditions. We'll create them in the soil and the atmosphere of this greenhouse, which already has a climate-control enchantment. Meaning nothing you do here will affect the rest of the school if you were to, say, prematurely trim the leaves of a disconsideous."

"Why?" Amanda gave her teacher a sly smile. "What would that do?"

"We'd all be hallucinating for a week. This way, if you make a mistake, *you're* the only one who suffers the consequences." The witch obviously saw the confusion on her student's face and nodded. "Yes, you'll be the only student with access to the greenhouse. At least for this semester. At the end of the year, we'll reevaluate and see what else, if anything, needs to be tweaked."

"Okay, so where do I—"

"As I said, we're working with what we have *right now*. We'll keep building from there." Calsgrave opened the thin binder on the workbench and pointed at the first page of printed instructions. "This is what you'll be working on today for the remainder of the class." She tapped the giant paperback book—*Magical's Guide to Magical Greenery.* "If you have any questions or feel like drumming up a little inspiration, feel free to browse through this. Several different species will be especially useful for work in your other classes and the other students. Such as these."

Before Amanda could open the large encyclopedia, Calsgrave reached under the closest trough and hauled up a large, bright orange five-gallon bucket. A very familiar five-gallon bucket.

"Wait..."

"Yes. We like to find a use for everything." The bucket plopped into the packed dirt in the trough with a light *thump.* "As it turns out, these are particularly useful for fertilizing fresh soil with everything it needs to become the perfect breeding ground for *magical* plants. You'll find detailed instructions in that starter binder. Mrs. Zimmer is expecting the first pound of dried husks before spring break."

"The first *pound*?"

"Oh, don't look so dubious, Miss Coulier. You and Miss Flannerty collected more than enough of these, and now we have a use for them." The teacher tossed Amanda the keys to the cabinet and grinned. "Lock up when you're finished. Don't worry about the lights or the state of the windows. I've taken care of that already. However, I do expect everything to be put back neatly in place until your next class on Wednesday. I'll be checking too."

"Okay, but..."

"Yes, this will be your second class every other day instead of Illusions. Better get started. Those things are already losing a little of their color." With that, Ms. Calsgrave practically skipped out of the greenhouse and pulled the door shut behind her.

"Wow." Amanda gave herself a second to look over the sizeable room one more time. *The only student with access to this place. I could get some really cool stuff done in here. Eventually.*

She walked down the side of the closest trough and stopped in front of the orange bucket. She tipped it toward her on the dirt to peer over the rim and saw exactly what she expected to find in there. She'd been the one who'd tossed these grubs into the bucket in the first place.

Hundreds of purple and orange little worm things the size of her thumb writhed against each other, filling the bucket almost halfway. They weren't as bright or as plump-looking as when she and Summer had tossed them in here as part of their final round of detention last semester, but at least she didn't have to go looking for more to get started.

"Okay. What the heck am I supposed to do with these?"

She went back to the thin binder and read all of two pages written out about the energy grubs, their magical properties, and their documented uses, most of which were specifically for the process of growing magical plants.

Her finger stopped at the second-to-last entry of such uses, and she rolled her eyes. "Of course, Zimmer wants them *now*."

At least she didn't have to spend two-and-a-half hours every other day staring at whatever object Calsgrave had placed on her students' desks and willing it to look like something else. She could follow directions and get started fertilizing all these troughs with the gross, writhing grubs that tossed shimmering goo when they were popped and smelled like rotting fruit.

CHAPTER TWELVE

"I don't get it." Jackson scratched the back of his head as they filtered out of Mrs. Zimmer's Alchemy class, now in the middle of the spring semester's third week. "You get an *entire* room to yourself, and we have to sit around staring at a bunch of rocks until they look like something else. How is that fair?"

"Because *we* have magic," Grace said as she elbowed the wizard in the ribs. "And because Amanda's not here to waste her time. Right?"

"I guess. Not like those weird worms are good for much of anything." Amanda shrugged and readjusted the straps of her backpack over her shoulders. "I bet they'll end up making money off whatever I grow in there. If I can ever get anything to grow."

Grace shot her a sly smile. "How *much* money?"

"I don't know. I guess there aren't any herbalists or whatever around here, so they'll probably end up selling things to the locals."

"They want the ingredients for classes," Alex muttered, staring at Zimmer's chicken-scratch handwriting all over his first paper of the semester. He looked like he was about to either break down crying or spin right back around to try arguing his low grade with their teacher. "You know, potions and stuff."

"We don't have a potions class," Grace said. "Or a potions teacher."

The Wood Elf looked up at her with wide, disbelieving eyes. "Because we didn't *have* any ingredients. Until Amanda got her special garden."

"Hey, there *still* aren't any ingredients," Amanda cut in. "I've been babysitting giant worms for two weeks. I'm starting to think it's even more boring than sitting through Illusions without being able to, you know, do illusions."

"You said you'll be able to grow some of that other stuff, right? Like those little white flowers you can eat that taste like a five-course dinner?" Jackson shrugged. "*That* sounded cool."

"Hermit's Feast. Yeah."

"Listen to *you*." Grace laughed. "The shifter gardener already."

"I read the book. Those things have to have, like, all kinds of stuff in the soil to grow. I only have grubs."

"Why does Zimmer want their skin?"

"Because it's like...some kind of ward-repellant. Which doesn't make sense when they were popping up out of nowhere with the new wards around the school, but she's probably gonna use them to show us how to—"

"Break through wards!" Jackson's eyes widened, and his mouth popped open in realization. "Break through *anything*. Coulier, you're a genius!"

"I didn't—"

"Told you the whole greenhouse thing is for class supplies." Alex rolled up his red-marked paper and shoved it into the back pocket of his cargo pants.

"Yeah, right. Zimmer's not gonna teach *freshmen* how to repel wards. We won't get to see that stuff until next year at the earliest."

Jackson frowned. "You don't know that."

"They don't even trust us enough to go to the kemana yet. No way would they trust us with that kind of magic."

Amanda stared straight ahead and forced a cough. *I thought I'd avoided having to talk about the kemana at all.*

The wizard thumped her on the back and laughed. "They trust Coulier with the greenhouse. Don't screw this up for us, got it? You're representing the whole freshman class. Get us those snakeskins for tearing down wards. I'm serious."

"They're grubs."

"Whatever."

"Grace!" Annabelle caught up to them as they stepped out of the main building and into the central field. "Hey. Did you figure out how to get those pieces connected for that maid robot for Mr. LeFor?"

"Maid robot?" Alex and Jackson exchanged a glance and snickered. "Like the kind, he's gonna dress up in the whole outfit and everything?"

"No." The dwarf girl scowled at them and shook her head. "Like our project for automated tech performance. We're making a robot that dusts, vacuums, folds laundry, *and* self-cleans at the end of the program."

"Oh." Jackson lifted his chin. "Why would anyone want one of those?"

"Are you serious?"

He shrugged.

"You know these are due in two weeks, right?" Annabelle tossed her hair out of her face. "I'm guessing by the way you guys were yukking it up with Tommy and Evan yesterday that you've already finished your project. Right?"

"Yeah. Of course." Jackson scoffed. "Tommy and I already have the perfect plan. It'll be super easy to put together."

"Oh, yeah?" Grace gave him a dubious glance. "What kind of automated tech are *you* guys gonna build that's so *easy*?"

Tommy picked the perfect moment to eavesdrop on their

conversation as he jogged out into the central field. "Robots to wipe our ass, Porter." He tossed a hand in the air as he spun to face them, grinning from ear to ear. "Automated. Makes life easier. Keeps your hands clean. Check and check. We're gonna *ace* this one, Jackson."

The other students coming out of the main building at the end of the day laughed and shouted out halfway-encouraging jokes as Tommy raced off with his friends.

Jackson scrunched up his face. "Okay, that was an oversimplification—"

"You guys haven't even started." Annabelle shook her head. "Admit it."

"I…" The wizard puffed out his cheeks. "It'll be easy."

"Can we go over these before dinner?" the dwarf girl asked Grace. "I wanna make sure they work before we have to move on to the programming part next week."

"Yeah, sure." Grace nodded at Amanda and the guys. "See you at dinner."

Alex stared after the girls and let out a heavy sigh, his face expressionless. "Must be exhausting to have to be the best at everything all the time."

"Probably about as exhausting as being in love with a married Alchemy teacher, right?" Jackson nudged the half-Wood Elf and nodded at Mrs. Zimmer standing by the side of the main building and talking animatedly with her husband.

Alex stared at them. "I can wait."

"Yeah, okay." Jackson shook his head and nudged Alex again before taking off toward the outdoor cafeteria. "Right now, I'm gonna start a line at the banquet table."

"There's still, like, an hour before dinner," Amanda said.

"Yeah. But I think I might be even hungrier than *you* today, Coulier."

"Not possible." She laughed and headed with him toward the kitchens. "You coming, Alex?"

"Nah, I'm good." Still staring at their Light Elf Alchemy teacher talking privately with her husband, Alex pulled his graded paper out of his back pocket and smacked the roll of it slowly against his other palm.

"So." Jackson stuck his hands in his pockets and shrugged. "What are *you* doing tonight? Any plans?"

"Um...so far? Pretty much just being here."

"Yeah, that goes without saying. What else?"

She shot him a sidelong glance and frowned. "Sleeping. Then waking up tomorrow to do it all over again."

Jackson choked out a laugh. "Sounds like you got it all figured out, Coulier. Hey, you know what I figured out the other night?"

He stopped halfway to the cafeteria, and she stopped with him, nodding as a group of sophomores passed and called out to her in greeting. Then she remembered he'd asked her an actual question. "What did you figure out?"

The wizard leaned toward her, glancing around the open field at the milling students before squinting at her. "There's a *hole* in the security enchantments. The ones that go up around the boys' dorm after lights out. Weird, right?"

That dragged her full attention right back to their conversation, and she smirked. "Kinda. Not *that* weird, though."

"Oh, sure. Nothing freaks *you* out, huh?" Jackson shrugged again, then ran a hand through his shaggy blond hair and tipped his head back and forth. "You guys have something like that in the girls' dorm, or am I going crazy?"

"No, we do. It's right by the back door." *Now I'm starting to think they left that hole there on purpose.* "Where's yours?"

"Second window on the top left in the first-floor bathrooms—"

Amanda barked out a laugh. "What the heck were you doing when you found it?"

He raised his eyebrows, and a tiny smile flickered across his mouth as he looked everywhere but right at her. "Taking a leak.

Getting curious at the same time. It doesn't matter *how* I found it, but I think I can get through that window. Know what I'm saying?"

"I guess." *He hasn't tried to sneak out yet.* "Good luck."

"What about you?" Jackson's gaze settled on her face again, expectant and curious as the color in his cheeks and neck darkened. "Come on, Coulier. There's no way you haven't tried getting out at night. I mean, you *have*, right?"

Amanda wrinkled her nose. "I might tell you if you tell me why you're so curious about it."

"What?" He stepped away from her and chuckled nervously. "Come on. I'm only wondering. That's all. No reason. It's not like I'm *planning* anything or…anything."

"Okay." *Not sure I can trust him a hundred percent if he hasn't even tried sneaking out on his own yet.*

They stared at each other for a moment longer, then Jackson smacked his lips. "Hey, you're gonna come watch the first Louper game tomorrow night, right? I mean, first one of the semester, obviously. The season already started, so…"

"Yeah. Probably. Didn't have any other plans."

"Awesome." He bobbed his head as if their previously tense conversation about sneaking through security enchantments hadn't even happened. "So if you're going, then maybe—"

"Hey! Shifter girl!" Summer walked briskly toward them, blowing her hair out of her face when a breeze kicked up and sent the unshaved half fluttering across her cheeks. "We gotta talk."

"Hey." Amanda smiled at Jackson, but he was scowling at Summer and didn't see it. "What's up?"

The black-haired witch stared right back at Jackson, then nodded toward the cafeteria. "Private talk, Pris. Get lost."

"Wait a minute," Amanda protested.

"No, it's cool. Don't wanna lose that first spot in line anyway."

Jackson pointed at the pavilion but kept glaring at Summer. "See ya."

Then he stormed off and disappeared behind the jutting end of the girl's dormitory that blocked half of the cafeteria from view.

"You don't have to be so rude about it," Amanda muttered.

"Well, how else is he supposed to know when to butt out of someone else's business?" Summer snickered, then her smile instantly disappeared, replaced by a wide-eyed earnestness. "We need to go back to the kemana."

She frowned. "Why? What's wrong?"

"What's *wrong*?" Summer glanced around at the other students, trying to play it off like she wasn't talking about breaking the rules again and sneaking out to steal one of the school's airboats and climb down a giant outhouse. "It's been almost three weeks. I'm dying of boredom, our classes are stupid as hell, and I need to let off a little steam."

"If you're trying to get drunk again, I'm not helping you."

"Ha! You're so funny. I've had that alchemy store on my mind. I think I can whip something up with some of the...less exciting things she has down there. Still, if you feel like distracting her this time so I can—"

"I'm not helping you break into a locked and probably warded case to get your hands on more bomb supplies." Amanda grinned at her friend. "Sorry."

"No you're not." The witch rolled her eyes. "Fine. No breaking and entering. No stealing. I gotta get out of here, okay? You get two and a half hours of private time every other day in that secret garden or whatever, and what do I have? Nothing."

"You also don't have to sift through weird-colored dirt looking for grub skins."

"Gross."

"Yeah."

"So come on. Let's go tomorrow, huh? Friday night. Everybody's doing their own thing."

Amanda folded her arms. "The Louper game's tomorrow."

"Yeah, like, right after dinner." Summer cocked her head. "Shit, are you still worried about that whole screw-up with the laser-Buddha?"

"I don't know. I'm…not sure it's a good idea to go back again right now. It hasn't been that long."

"Come on, shifter girl." The witch nudged her friend in the shoulder. "You said there would be a next time. I need one. Like, right now. Besides, nobody had a *clue* we were sneaking out last semester. I mean, except for the whole blowing-up-the-island part. And yeah, your pixie friends know, but they couldn't care less. Hell, we'll get snacks from them first, and you won't even have to charge anything to your—to *Johnny's* extra card."

Amanda studied her friend and pursed her lips. *She's pushing way too hard. Something happened.*

"Yeah, okay. Tomorrow night."

"*Yes!*" Summer slung her arm around the shifter girl's shoulders and grinned as they headed toward the outdoor cafeteria. "I knew you couldn't say no. Shifter girl like you can handle herself fine. Obviously. And hey, if that weapons store's still standing, we'll hit that first. How's that sound?"

"As long as by 'hit it,' you mean going inside to look around."

"Duh. Man, I'm starving. Hey, you think those pixies would give you, like, a menu for the week or something? You know, so we know what to expect going into it?"

Amanda laughed. "I don't think *they* know what they're gonna make until they're making it."

"Okay, whatever. Make sure you ask them for snacks tomorrow, okay? We're getting *out of here!*"

CHAPTER THIRTEEN

Mr. LeFor's class the next morning felt like an exercise in futility, mostly because he'd paired Amanda with Corey for their current project with automated tech performance. With her chin propped on one hand, she spent the first hour going over the simplest instructions with the half-Kilomea, who slowly nodded while she talked, then asked four different times what they were supposed to do.

*I should make this thing by myself so we both don't fail.*

Corey didn't object to that idea when she brought it up in a low voice. "Just...don't tell LeFor that's our plan, okay?"

She stared at him. "Why would I do that? Then neither of us would get credit."

"I don't know." The huge kid shrugged. "Everyone already thinks I'm stupid. I'm not. I just...don't like *thinking*."

Forcing back a laugh, she pulled the box of machine parts and random wiring toward her across the work table and nodded. "Yeah, that can be pretty hard sometimes. Don't worry about it. I'll make sure it's something cool."

"Awesome. You know, you're pretty okay. For a freshman."

Amanda didn't bother to remind the eighteen-year-old half-

Kilomea that he was the oldest student in the Academy's first-ever freshman class.

*He doesn't like thinking. Maybe that one's a little too hard for him to tackle on his own.*

---

Ms. Ralthorn's History of Oriceran class was more of the same obnoxiously boring lecture they'd gotten from their teacher the entire first semester. Fortunately, Ralthorn hadn't mentioned anything about shifters so far this semester although Amanda couldn't help but notice that the teacher seemed to look right at her more than any other student. Most of the time, it was with a smile that didn't look completely natural.

*I still have no idea what that secret note about The Coalition was supposed to mean.*

An hour into the class, there was a knock on the door. Ms. Ralthorn's long, drawn-out sentence sputtered to a halt, and she frowned at the door. "It's open."

Principal Glasket's head poked through the slightly open door, but she didn't bother to enter the room any more than that. "Sorry to interrupt, Ms. Ralthorn. I need to borrow Miss Coulier for a moment if you don't mind."

Chairs creaked as the students who hadn't already turned at the intruding knock now turned to stare at Amanda.

Her face instantly bloomed with heat.

"Of course." Ralthorn blinked at Amanda and gestured toward the door. "You're excused. I'm sure one of your friends won't mind catching you up on the rest of the lecture and your homework over the weekend. Go on."

Tommy snickered in the back row. "Uh-oh."

Evan Hutchinson snorted out a laugh.

Amanda ignored them both and grabbed her backpack before rising from her chair.

Grace looked up at her and whispered, "What happened?"

"I have no idea."

"Sounds like someone stepped in it this time," Tommy muttered, leering at her as she stepped down the row of desks to head for the door.

"That would be you, Mr. Brunsen." Glasket pointed at the boy and raised an eyebrow. "If you're not careful with the unsolicited commentary."

The class filled with stifled laughter as Tommy whipped back around in his desk and stared straight ahead at the front of the room.

"Now, if you don't mind," Ms. Ralthorn continued, "we still have more than enough to cover this morning, and any more unwarranted interruptions will only end up doubling your homework over the weekend."

Once Amanda slipped into the hall, Glasket pulled the door shut with a soft *click*, and the exaggerated groans from the freshmen class muted into a soft drone. "What's going on?"

"That, Miss Coulier, is a conversation to be had in my office. Let's go." The principal turned smartly and headed down the hall, her heels clicking on the linoleum floors with an echo of finality.

*I haven't done anything since that first weekend before classes. If this is about borrowing the airboat, why did it take her three weeks?*

They moved through the main building's halls until they reached the central staircase leading up to the second floor, most of which was the principal's office. The last time Amanda had been called up here, she and Summer had gotten their second round of detention.

"Am I in trouble for something?" Her voice sounded incredibly hollow in the enclosed stairwell.

"Should you be?" Glasket replied.

"I don't think so."

"Good."

"Then what's going on? Is it Johnny? Did something happen?"

"As far as I know, Miss Coulier, there's nothing for you to be overly concerned about. I'd prefer it if you took my advice and didn't continue spiraling down that train of thought." That was all the principal would say on the matter. Then they were at her office door.

Amanda's palms got clammy and wouldn't stop even when she rubbed them on the legs of her pants. *What other options are there if I'm not in trouble and it's not about Johnny?*

Glasket paused for a split second in front of her office before opening the door and standing aside for Amanda to enter. "Have a seat, please."

Amanda stepped inside and froze. There was already someone there—a woman in a forest-green suit sitting in one of the leather-upholstered armchairs on this side of Glasket's desk, a wide-brimmed felt hat of the same green shade shielding the back of her head and any other features from view. Whoever it was didn't turn as Glasket stepped inside although the principal didn't bother to close the door behind her.

"Amanda, this is Ms. Adalynn Jade. She's asked for you specifically to discuss a few...personal matters."

The woman in the chair turned enough to look at Amanda over her shoulder and offer a warm, closed-lipped smile. "Pleasure to meet you, Amanda."

The shifter girl swallowed.

It was the woman from the kemana. The woman with the red heels and the matching red leather purse that hadn't been a purse at all.

*How did she find me?*

Amanda couldn't find her voice and settled for a curt nod instead.

"I'll leave you to it, then," Glasket said.

"Thank you, Gladys." Adalynn's voice was low and calm and friendly. "We won't be too long."

"Take however much time you need. I'll be in the study next

door." The principal paused, supposedly to double-check that Amanda was okay with this. The girl couldn't pull her gaze away from the woman wearing green and sitting right here in front of her in Glasket's office. Clearing her throat, the principal backed out of the room and finally closed the door again.

Adalynn's smile widened as she looked Amanda up and down. "I have to say I'm impressed it took me this long to track you down. I'd expected it to be easier."

The shifter girl bit her bottom lip. *She never saw me that night. That Crystal probably told her who we are. That he watched us leave on the airboat.*

Slowly, the woman removed her wide-brimmed hat and set it gently down on Glasket's desk. Ruffling her fingers through the wispy bangs over her forehead and adjusting the rest of her short, no-nonsense haircut, Adalynn turned even more in the armchair and raised an eyebrow. "Now that I *have* found you, I need you to tell me where the chakra statue is."

*Crap. She definitely knows.*

"That's what you're calling it? Heck of an open chakra..." Amanda's tongue poked around against the inside of her cheek, and she swallowed again. "It's at the bottom of the swamp."

The woman raised her eyebrows. "I see. Please have a seat, Amanda. I promise I don't bite. Standing there like that makes it seem like you're contemplating darting off and disappearing again. Come."

Gesturing toward the other chair beside her, Adalynn sat back on hers and flicked her fingers through her hair again, crossing one leg over the other.

Amanda slowly approached the other chair, cast a fleeting glance at the office door, then sat. *Glasket wouldn't have left me alone in here if she thought this Jade lady's dangerous. Unless she has no idea.*

The woman drew a deep breath and folded her hands over

her knee. Here, she looked a lot more in control than she had in the kemana browsing the shelves in High Tide Ammo.

"You weren't buying a gun case for your dad, were you?"

With a light chuckle, Adalynn looked directly at the shifter girl and dipped her head. "So you *were* listening before I left the store."

"Only because I heard those guys talking about going after someone. Some Rooney guy, I think. And they talked about getting rid of *you* before you—"

"What's done is done, and I'm not interested in hashing out the details of something neither of us can change." Adalynn's gray eyes bored into Amanda, and a hot flash swept across the girl's entire body before disappearing again. "I did purchase a gun case, but you already know that."

Amanda nodded.

"You're clearly a bright girl, Amanda. Judging by your lack of surprise when I asked after the chakra statue, I can only assume you took the opportunity to look inside my purse and discover what was there for yourself."

"I was looking for a wallet or something so I could get it back to you."

"Yes. When you found something entirely different instead, I'm sure you realized your mistake."

"I didn't mean to mess anything up." Amanda shifted in the chair. "I thought you—"

"I understand." The woman's smile disappeared. "The fact remains that you inserted yourself into a rather high-priority operation three weeks ago. Fortunately for you, the chaos you and your witch friend kicked up that night before your escape allowed us to salvage what was left of the situation. So it wasn't a complete loss. We got done what we needed to get done."

"Okay…" *What am I supposed to say to that? You're welcome?* Amanda frowned. "We?"

"My partners and me. Yes."

"Wait, those wizards? I didn't mean to—"

"I want you to listen to me and keep your questions to yourself until I finish." Although she said it gently enough, the commanding blaze behind Adalynn's eyes made Amanda do exactly that. "The wizards are none of your concern, and no, I don't imagine you'll see them again anytime soon. My *partners*, on the other hand, may be a different matter altogether."

*Crap.*

"They have no idea I've found you, Amanda. Or that I'm speaking to you right now. Not yet. Dean Glasket thinks I'm here to discuss a different kind of personal information with you because that's what I've told her and want her to believe." Sitting back in her chair again, Adalynn swiped at a loose hair on the leg of her green pantsuit and cocked her head. "This is all because I've made it a habit not to share my business with those who don't need to know what it is. You, on the other hand, are a different obstacle."

Amanda stared at the tip of the woman's shoe planted firmly on the floor—almost the same as the heels she'd worn in the kemana except black and shiny instead of bright red. "You want me to find your purse. Right?"

"No, I'm afraid that would only waste both our time. If my resources haven't managed to find it by now, I'll have to accept that the chakra statue is lost to the Florida wilderness."

That made the girl look sharply up at her unexpected visitor. "Then why are you here?"

"Because you made a mistake, Amanda. However good-intentioned it might have been, and I do believe a part of you thought you were helping a stranger. At least in the beginning. However, you took something of mine that can't be retrieved or replaced. An apology isn't going to cut it." The woman's languid, carefree shrug was at complete odds with the sharpness of her tone. "The only option you have at this point is to work off that debt."

"What, for *you*?" Amanda snorted. "I'm pretty sure that's called child labor. I don't think anyone at this school is gonna let me walk out of here with a stranger to...work."

"Of course not. So we'll call it a mentorship, then. Community service hours, even. Although I assume that unlike the rest of your schoolmates here at the Academy, you don't have any experience with that."

*Sounds like she thinks she knows me.*

"Maybe I do," Amanda muttered.

"But you don't. These are your options, Amanda." Adalynn gestured toward the office door. "Either I can call Dean Glasket back into this room and explain to her exactly what happened. That you and your friend took an unsanctioned airboat trip to the kemana in the middle of the night and stole a valuable item. Or you can agree to work off this debt. Spend as long as necessary under my guidance until I'm satisfied. Then we'll leave this whole thing behind us, and no one else will ever know what happened."

"What do I have to do?"

"Whatever I tell you to. I *can* promise it won't be nearly as detrimental to your well-being or your enrollment at this school as sneaking out and getting involved in something far beyond your limited experience."

Amanda folded her arms. "What am I supposed to tell Glasket and my teachers?"

"Absolutely nothing." Adalynn's smile returned, a little more feral now. "I've already discussed the schedule with your dean, and she's already agreed to everything, as long as you're on board too. Twice a week, you'll come to me. Chaperoned, of course. It won't interfere with your classes, which I agree take precedence here. After all, you won't learn anything from this if it alleviates the need to keep up with your current responsibilities. These will be after-hours trips to join me and work off this debt you owe."

Blinking quickly, Amanda went through all the options in her head. This seemed like the best one, even though it sucked, and she tried to stall for a little more time. Because the weirdest thing about all of this was that despite sitting two feet away from Adalynn Jade in the chair beside her, she *still* couldn't smell anything.

*No scent at all? What kind of magical doesn't smell like anything?*

"I have to think about it," she muttered.

"There's no time for that, I'm afraid. The second you and I are finished with our conversation here, my offer's no longer on the table. You can take this opportunity, or you can take your chances with explaining to all the authority figures in your life that you still haven't settled into your role here as a model student. That you're still making trouble."

*This lady's blackmailing me.*

"Okay, fine." Amanda nodded slowly, scowling at the edge of Glasket's desk. "I'll do it."

"Wonderful. We start tonight." Adalynn snatched her green felt hat off the desk and placed it back on her head, adjusting it once with a delicate twist. Then she stood. "I'll let Dean Glasket know. Don't bother bringing anything with you."

The woman stood and whisked past Amanda's chair. Without another word, she left the office, her heels clicking down the stairwell before that door swung closed behind her.

Amanda sat in the chair, staring at the open door before Principal Glasket appeared in the doorway. "I'm assuming that went well."

The girl puffed out a sigh. "I guess."

"Good. You're dismissed for the rest of the day, Miss Coulier." The witch headed straight for her desk without looking at her student. "Mr. Frederick will be waiting for you behind the girls' dormitory at seven o'clock sharp. Don't keep him waiting."

Standing slowly, Amanda lifted her backpack off the floor and frowned. "Who's Mr. Frederick?"

"Well, for tonight and the foreseeable future, I suppose, he's your chaperone." Glasket gestured toward her office door and didn't look up from the paperwork on her desk.

Feeling like she'd stepped into a particularly sticky patch of mud, Amanda turned and headed for the door.

*Great. I'm gonna spend my Friday night doing community service for a lady with no scent who hires wizards to blow up weapons stores.*

# CHAPTER FOURTEEN

History of Oriceran was her last class of the day, which let out right before lunch. The thought of spending the rest of the day doing nothing but waiting around for 7:00 p.m. didn't make it feel like much of a Friday though.

Amanda reached the outdoor cafeteria as the pixies finished laying out a huge lunch on the banquet tables without ever having to leave the kitchen's confines. The last platter of baked chicken appeared at the end of the table, and she looked up to see Fred through the window as she shuffled that way aimlessly. The large pixie shot her a wink and a thumbs-up, then disappeared on the other side of the window.

The obnoxious alarm signaling the end of class blared across the campus, and Amanda went through the motions of piling her plate with food as the rest of the student body filtered out of the buildings, laughing and shouting at each other and racing for the cafeteria. She picked the closest picnic table and sat, tuning out the other conversations growing louder around her as the students demolished the lunch spread and formed groups. She barely tasted the food and couldn't get the image of Adalynn Jade's predatory smile out of her head.

*That lady knows something else. Something about me. Why else would she think I'm not like the other kids here? That I've never had to do community service before?*

She didn't notice her friends coming to join her until Grace sat beside her on the bench and bumped her with her shoulder. "Okay, seriously. What's going on with you?"

"What?" Amanda blinked at Grace, Jackson, and Alex, all of whom were already in their seats and staring at her in concern.

"You got pulled out of class," Jackson said. "Glasket didn't look super happy."

"She didn't exactly look pissed, either," Grace added. "Honestly, she looked more scared than anything else."

"Really?" Amanda returned her attention to her plate and lifted a forkful of pasta salad to her mouth. "I didn't notice."

"Except for you went up to her office with her." Alex shrugged. "Plenty of time to notice what she looked like and figure out what was going on, right?"

"So?" Grace frowned. "Everything okay?"

"Yeah, it's fine." She couldn't tell her friends about any of it. Mentioning Adalynn Jade meant she'd have to explain how and why she'd been at the kemana in the first place three weeks ago. Even if they could keep *her* secret, she didn't trust herself to talk about the whole thing without mentioning Summer.

*Not gonna throw her under the bus because things got a little weird.*

"Then you weren't in trouble for anything?" Grace popped a grape into her mouth, her eyes wide.

"No. Glasket wanted to check in on how the greenhouse is going."

"She called you out of class for *that*?" Jackson snorted. "Didn't think she liked you enough to save you from that level of boredom."

"Yeah, well, I think she was busy the rest of the day or something. I don't know. Everything's fine." Hating herself for lying right to their faces, Amanda crammed the last of her lunch in her mouth and stood, taking her plate with her. "I have to get back out to the greenhouse anyway. I think I almost have my pound of grub husks for Zimmer."

Grace wrinkled her nose. "Ew."

Alex blinked at his plate, swallowed thickly, then pushed away the rest of his lunch and said nothing.

Jackson turned on the bench. "Hey, Coulier!"

She'd already reached the trash can and pretended not to be able to hear him over the drone of a hundred other magical kids shouting and laughing and chewing.

*I need to be alone so I can figure this out.*

---

The next four hours were a lot easier to handle than she'd expected, probably because she was alone in the greenhouse with no one and nothing to disturb her.

"Only me and the grubs." Amanda dug through the end of the final gardening trough, letting the clumps of dirt sift through her gloved fingers and looking for any last shed grub skins. "I can tell a couple of hundred gross little polka-dot worms about this whole mess. You guys can't say a word to anyone."

She pointed at one such grub burying its bright-purple head in the soil, its back end flopping up and down as it wriggled farther beneath the surface.

*I really hope they can't talk.*

Picking out an almost completely whole grub skin from the last of the dirt—which was a lot darker and nicer-looking after three weeks of magical-insect fertilizer—Amanda went to the workbench and the starter binder to double-check.

There was nothing in the short description of the energy grubs about any ability to communicate. The entry in the *Magical's Guide to Magical Greenery* didn't have any information to refute that, either. It did, however, have a final one-line note beneath the cramped paragraph in small print dedicated to the magical fertilizing energy.

**Not a sentient species but still prone to become invasive if not consistently harvested and disposed of. For best disposal practices for the energy, see Chapter 23: Sustainable Magical Ecosystems on page 274.**

"Oh, good. They can't talk, they can't think, and they'll turn into a mindless fertilizing machine and kill everything I plant in here if I don't get rid of them fast enough." She slammed the thick hardback shut and dropped the remaining grub skin into the five-gallon bucket where she'd been keeping them.

It took longer than she expected to weigh all the skins on the tiny scale she'd found in the metal cabinet, which wasn't large enough to weigh the bucket on its own, let alone a bucket filled with flecks of transparent purple and orange bug husks. After three rounds of adding up the figures—because they kept changing every time—she finally stuck everything back in the bucket and called it good.

*Not my fault if they don't give me a big enough scale. Sixteen-point-two ounces is gonna have to be good enough for Zimmer.*

After putting everything back in the cabinet, locking it, and spraying down the troughs of dirt and grubs a final time with the hose attached to the wall, she grabbed the bucket and her backpack. Then she headed out of the greenhouse as she had every other day since this became her stand-in for Illusions class.

The second the greenhouse door shut behind her and she headed down the hall toward Mrs. Zimmer's office, a silver light seeped up out of the soil in all five troughs. The light climbed above the dirt and sent the energy grubs scattering deeper beneath the surface. If Amanda had been there to seen it, she would have thought the light would spill over the sides of the trough and flood the room.

Instead, the silver light sank back beneath the dirt and flickered out once the grubs stopped moving. A large mound in the center trough jerked, shuddered, and grew.

---

Mrs. Zimmer wasn't in her freshman Alchemy classroom or her office, so Amanda left the bright orange five-gallon bucket on the teacher's desk and scribbled a quick note.

**16.2 ounces. Ms. Calsgrave said you wanted this.**

Then she grabbed her bag and headed out for dinner.

The outdoor cafeteria was packed again with the entire student body, and apparently, she'd misjudged the time. The line at the banquet table had shortened to only two students waiting for the chance to get their food, and everyone else was sitting down and digging in. Amanda piled her plate high with honeyed ham slices and green beans and some kind of ambrosia salad without thinking about what she was doing.

*There's no way I can eat all this. I'm not even hungry.*

Still, she had a feeling there wouldn't exactly be a chance to grab herself a late-night snack while she'd be serving the first night of her sentence with Adalynn Jade.

She found Jackson and Grace sitting at their usual table, but Alex was nowhere to be found.

"Whoa." Grace lowered her fork. "You don't look so hot."

"I'm fine." Amanda sat and scowled at her plate. "What time is it?"

"Uh…" Jackson scrunched up his face. "Six? Maybe. Hey, they're almost done setting up all the chairs in the field for the Louper game. If we go now, we can snag the best seats."

"I can't. Sorry."

Her friends exchanged a confused glance. "Why not?"

"Glasket has me doing an extra assignment. It's probably gonna take me all night." Amanda looked up at the wizard and shrugged. "I found out right before dinner."

*How did I get so good at lying without thinking about it?*

"Are you kidding?" He thumped his hand down on the table. "She can't do that. It's the weekend!"

"She's the principal," Grace muttered.

"So? The weekend's for *us*. And Louper matches. Whatever happened to school spirit?"

"Sorry. I'll be able to catch the next one, though. You guys have fun."

"Man…" With an aggravated click of his tongue, Jackson stood and grabbed his paper plate. "You *sure* it's gonna take you all night?"

"To be on the safe side, yeah." Amanda looked up as the wizard turned away from the table and saw Summer standing by the trashcan, scowling at her.

"Okay, fine. Grace." Jackson spread his arms. "Wanna grab one of the best seats in the field with me and watch our team—"

"Sorry." The blonde witch shook her head. "Annabelle has this thing about not doing any homework on the weekends, so…I kind of agreed to work with her tonight on the last parts of our tech project. Our Louper team's not all that great anyway. You know that, right?"

All the energy seeped out of Jackson, and he heaved an exasperated sigh. "I *know*. Henry needs to work on his balance, and if Carlton had picked literally *anything* else as his avatar, maybe we'd have a chance. But a Willen? Seriously? Who wants to be a Willen, even in a Louper game?"

Amanda snorted. "Maybe he thought it'd help him find the flag."

"Yeah, when it's shiny. It's not always." Shaking his head, Jackson waved both girls off and headed toward the central field. "Guess I'll go yell at the players who can't hear me by myself. See ya."

"See ya."

Grace stood and drained the rest of her drink before giving Amanda a sympathetic frown. "You sure everything's okay?"

"Yeah. I'm... I don't know. This semester isn't exactly turning out the way I thought it would."

"I get it. Honestly? I'd take a greenhouse by myself over trying to make my shoelaces look like diamonds any day of the week. Maybe you'll get to grow something fun."

"Maybe. Good luck with your robot."

Grace rolled her eyes and passed the trash can on her way back to the girls' dorm, tossing her plate inside without stopping before she disappeared around the corner of the kitchens.

Summer was still standing there, glaring at Amanda and looking way more pissed off than usual.

*Now she's gonna ask about going to the kemana tonight, and I'll have to tell her no too.*

Summer stormed toward the picnic table and slid onto the bench opposite the shifter girl. "Did I seriously hear you say you have an extra assignment you're supposed to be working on *all night?*"

"Yep."

"Hey. We had plans."

"I'm sorry, Summer. It came up this morning—"

"No, you're trying to give me the slip, aren't you?" Summer pounded her fist onto the picnic table. "Because you're too scared of getting in trouble—"

"I already am!"

The last few stragglers at dinner paused their conversations to look at the shifter girl. Some of them seemed a little too eager to watch Amanda lose her cool and maybe do something stupid. Like shift in the middle of dinner.

Summer ignored them all and folded her arms. "What do you mean you already are?"

Dropping her fork with the bite she probably wouldn't have eaten anyway, Amanda sighed. "She found me."

"Is that supposed to mean something to me?"

"The woman from the kemana, Summer. With the red purse and the you-know-what inside it."

The witch snickered, then realized her friend wasn't joking. "Wait. What?"

"Yeah. That's why Glasket pulled me out of class this morning. I don't know *how* she found me, but she was here, at the school, and I got a personal escort to a cozy little meeting with her. She knew we took the purse—"

"Whoa, whoa. Don't lump me in there with you, shifter girl. *You* took that purse all on your own."

Amanda finally met the other girl's gaze and raised her eyebrows. "I know. But we both touched that laser statue or whatever it is, and I'm pretty sure we're both to blame for dropping it in the river."

Summer swallowed. "Did you tell her that?"

"No. She didn't mention you other than saying the *chaos* we stirred up gave her people a chance to salvage the operation or whatever."

"Oh. Good. Then you're off the hook."

"I'm not doing an assignment for Glasket tonight. I'm going to meet that lady and work off my debt to her for taking her purse and trying to be a decent person. I don't know how long I'll have to do this, but it's twice a week. Glasket apparently is super okay with me leaving campus to be an indentured servant for a stranger." It all poured out of her in a rush before she drew a deep breath and let it out slowly.

*Okay. That felt better than confessing to a bunch of worms.*

Summer stared at her. "You're not screwing around."

"No. I'm serious. I have to do this, or we're *both* in trouble."

"Hey, so we're clear, if that purse lady didn't say anything about me, don't try to pull this off as some kind of favor you're doing me, all right? I don't owe you anything. I didn't get caught."

Amanda frowned at the other girl. *She still hasn't figured out how to say thank you and be even kind of nice. Why are we friends again?*

"Don't worry. I know you don't owe me."

"Good." Summer stood and knocked on the table. "Sucks to be you, shifter girl. Guess we'll have to wait 'til tomorrow to head out into the swamp. Don't try to make any more excuses, though, okay?"

Amanda didn't have anything to say to that, but it didn't matter. Summer was already walking away, kicking at clumps of grass with her combat boots and swinging her arms as if she didn't have a care in the world.

*She's like two completely different people. Hard to remember I like her when she's such a jerk.*

Now, Amanda was glad she'd be heading out to meet with Adalynn by herself. She didn't think she could handle being cooped up in a car with Summer for however long it took to get wherever she was going tonight.

# CHAPTER FIFTEEN

At 7:00 p.m., it had already been dark for almost an hour. Thanks to the first Louper match of the semester being broadcast in the central field for the whole school to watch, Amanda wasn't stopped by any other students or even her friends looking for her. So far, she'd managed to hold them off with a white lie that didn't quite feel like a white lie. It felt like she'd lied to Summer too because she wasn't sure she'd be up for sneaking into the kemana again tomorrow night. If that was still a possibility after whatever Adalynn Jade had in store for her tonight.

A tall, dark silhouette stood out against the rising moon behind the girls' dorm, and Amanda shoved her hands into the pockets of her zip-up hoodie as she approached. She wasn't trying to be sneaky or particularly quiet, but the man leaning against the wall of the building jolted when he turned and saw her there.

"Lord love a duck! You 'bout scared the life outta me." The wizard's southern accent was a little more pronounced than Johnny's.

Hearing it here—at the Academy where everyone else was from somewhere *not* Florida and definitely not the Everglades—

made Amanda wish she were back at the bounty hunter's cabin instead.

*Maybe even at Darlene's with Arthur and Dale and the other old-timers. They didn't care what I am. Couldn't spook them this easily, either.*

"Sorry," she muttered. "I didn't mean to. Are you Mr. Frederick?"

"Ha! I suppose that's one way to call a fella by his name. Naw, you can call me Shep."

Despite her trepidation about her impending trip to see the scentless Ms. Jade, she wrinkled her nose and shot him a small, curious smile. "What's *that* short for?"

"Huh? Nothin'." The wizard removed the newsboy cap from his head and ruffled a hand through thinning light-brown hair, leaving it sticking up in all directions. "My daddy gave me Frederick, but Shep's the name my mama gave me, and I aim to use it the way she intended. Ancestors watch over her. I ain't all that much a fan of all this yes-ma'amin' and no-sir business either. So don't even think 'bout callin' me anythin' else, ya hear? You're Amanda, then, am I right?"

"Yep."

Shep looked her over and squinted. "We're makin' a bit of a trip tonight, girl, and you ain't got nothin' but the clothes on your back. If you need to grab somethin', I don't mind waitin'."

"No, I'm good. Thanks."

"All right, then." He nodded toward the north end of the Academy's campus and took off that way. "Best be headin' out. I'm sure you got no trouble keepin' up through a bunch of wilderness now, huh?"

"I can keep up."

"Good." He cast a final glance at the main field flickering with the light of the projected Louper match, then shoved his hands into the pockets of his loose, faded khakis and took off. "Two nights a week as I heard it. That right?"

"I guess."

"That a set schedule, then? Friday nights and what else?"

Amanda shook her head as she followed him across the grass, shrugging against the light and slightly crisper than usual breeze rustling through the swamp around them. "I don't know. This is the first night, so…"

"Aw, I'm sure you'll hear more 'bout when and where and how when you need to hear it. I ain't tryin' to pry, mind. I like bein' 'vailable and stickin' to my schedules is all."

"Yeah. As soon as I know what's happening, I'll let you know."

Shep chuckled and shook his head, casting her a sidelong glance as she caught up to him. "Well, bless your heart. Shoot, you ain't the one gotta keep me in the know, girl. Dean Glasket's got me on salary, and I'll get everythin' I need to know from her. Might've jumped the gun a little on askin' you now. I get the curiosity somethin' awful, 'specially at night. It ain't my job to know all the details. I know that much. I'm here to do what needs doin' by a fella with my kinda knowledge of the area, and I ain't fixin' to overstep my bounds. Hope I ain't scared you off too much already. Seein' as we'll be gettin' to know each other a lot more'n not for however long you gotta be makin' these special trips."

"It's pretty hard to scare me, so don't worry about it."

"Ha! I bet. More'n one little birdie told me 'bout what you jumped to at that dance y'all had in the fall. Personally, I ain't a fan of hogs. Wild, unpredictable little devils come blastin' through a fella's property and messin' with damn near everythin' in sight. No, I reckon you ain't the kinda girl gets scared much at all. No, sir."

Amanda tried to hide a smile as the sounds of shouting Louper spectators faded behind them. *He sounds like Johnny, sure. If Johnny ever enjoyed friendly conversation.*

Shep rattled on in his thick accent about growing up in Louisiana and moving to the Everglades when he was Amanda's age. "Been here ever since, and it ain't all that different from home. S'long as I ignore the differences, hear?"

When she frowned up at him, the wizard let out a whistling laugh through his teeth.

"Yeah, that's a brain-twister right there, and don't I know it. Almost there, girl. You're gonna love this part, lemme tell ya. Hell, *I* love it, and I've been drivin' and errand-runnin' for all kindsa funny folks comin' up on thirty years now. Just know you ain't lost your mind and started seein' things. I can promise you it's all real."

Only when he paused to gesture toward a very familiar stand of cattails did Amanda realize where they were.

The very same hole in the Academy's wards around the campus property shielded by an illusion. The one she and Summer had been sneaking through for weeks to get to the dock and the school's small fleet of flat-bottom airboats.

*Is this some kind of test?*

She swallowed and tried to smile at Shep. "Okay."

"Okay." His grin flashed at her in the low light of the rising moon. "Follow me is all."

Then he stepped toward the cattails and disappeared through the illusion.

Amanda drew a deep breath and followed him. The wizard was still grinning when she emerged on the other side, and what had previously only looked like thick swamp underbrush gave way to the long wooden dock stretching out into the river and the mounted wooden signs pointing toward the Everglades kemana. "Wow..."

"That's what I keep sayin', girl. Every time I come down here. I tell you what, those teachers of y'all's really know what they're doin' with good strong illusions like this'un here. I didn't believe it myself the first time I saw it. I said to myself, 'Shep, if you ain't workin' for some of the most talented magicals this side of the Mississippi, you ain't doin' it right.'" His whistling laughter split through the low hum of insects and the lap of swamp water against the airboats' hulls. "Sure. Wow is right. Come on, now. Don't wanna be late for this here important meetin' of yours, do we? Keep up."

She couldn't help turning around to check this side of the illusion. This whole thing felt like one giant prank, although Principal Glasket didn't seem remotely like the practical-joking type. No one else was there—no sight or smell or sound of anyone but her and this man who seemed content to chauffeur a teenage shifter around the Everglades.

She stared at the dock as Shep clomped down it toward the water, and the only thing she could think to say was, "I thought you were the driver."

"Oh, sure. Drive the cars, sometimes even a truck when supplies need to come in. I tell you what, operatin' one of these here airboats is loads easier than all the rest. Now, I know the idea of skippin' 'round through this damn swamp seems 'bout as easy as findin' a needle in a haystack, but I tell you what, girl. Best part of my job when I get to hop on one of these. I always fancied I'd be some kinda captain on the bayou in my younger days. This here's 'bout as close as I ever got to it." He stopped at the end of the dock and turned with wide eyes. "Well don't stand there. Come on. We gotta head out."

"Right. Yeah, I'm coming." She blinked away her disbelief and shuffled down the dock, pretending to see all of this for the first time. Pointing at the wooden sign for the kemana with the crookedly painted letters, she added, "So you're the one who takes all the upperclassmen to the kemana, right?"

"You bet." Shep untied the closest airboat, and Amanda didn't wait for his invitation before she hopped onto the deck with a *thump*. "Well, hey. Look at you. Now, I don't mean no disrespect, girl. None at all, but I…" He jammed his hat back onto his thinning hair and let out a low whistle. 'I gotta say I ain't seen any shifter anywhere hop right up onto a deck of any boat without lookin' like they wanna pounce on the water and tear it to bits."

*Crap. Am I supposed to be acting afraid of the river?*

Amanda shrugged as the wizard stepped onto the airboat and made his way to the controls. "I guess I've been on more boats than the average shifter. Maybe."

"Ha! You got an answer for everythin' too, don'tcha? All right, Amanda. Then I reckon you ain't gonna flinch and wobble your way overboard once we get movin', then, huh?"

She laughed and turned to face the bow. "No. I don't usually wobble."

Shep's whistling laugh cracked across the water before he started the fan, and the roar of the blades drowned out all other sounds as they slowly took off from the dock and headed out into the swamp.

"Where are we going, exactly?" she shouted over the whir.

"That same kemana, girl. I tell you what. Whatever it is you got goin' on out there and need me to chaperone ya for, you oughtta count yourself lucky for it. Freshmen ain't allowed out here, period."

"Yeah, I know."

"Uh-huh. 'Course you do. Now, you might get yourself a little excited to go spreadin' the word to all your other friends in your class at that school. Sayin' how you got the exception to make these trips to the Everglades kemana before the rest of 'em. Dean Glasket did want me to remind you to keep all this on the hush-hush and to yourself. Understand?"

Amanda turned to look at him and nodded. "Don't worry. I can keep a secret."

"Uh-huh. Reckon you can. That's good."

This whole thing suddenly felt way too surreal, and she lowered herself to the deck to sit cross-legged in the center of the bow. A mist of saltwater sprayed up and peppered her face, and she closed her eyes to inhale the salty air.

*This is what I get for sneaking off campus and into the kemana. A personal trip off campus and into the kemana. I bet Adalynn thinks it's hilarious.*

Now she had a feeling that whatever the woman wanted from Amanda to "pay off her debt," it wasn't going to be anywhere near as easy as Adalynn had made it sound.

*No way is it community service. I can't believe I got stuck in this mess.*

# CHAPTER SIXTEEN

"Now, another word of advice," Shep said as the airboat's hull thumped against the bank of the tiny island with the warped wooden outhouse standing up in the center like a splinter. "You seen the way out here with your own eyes, but don't go tryin' to get out here on your own and find your way without me now. You hear?"

"Wasn't even thinking about it," Amanda muttered.

"Good. 'Cause, see, there's an enchantment on that part of the Everglades we set out from. Right there at the school." Shep hopped off the boat and tied the rope around the same tree stump Amanda had used three weeks ago. It took everything she had not to stare at it. "Only folks got a certain little permission spell, the way I see it, can find their way out here from the dock. I know you don't scare, and you don't wobble, girl, but I reckon even a little spitfire shifter like yourself ain't gonna find your way out here on your lonesome. Not until you get brought down here next year with the rest of your class, understand?"

"Totally. Yep." She rubbed her mouth in an attempt to keep it shut. *This feels like a super screwed-up dream.*

"All right. Come on, now. We made good time, but I ain't

fixin' to keep whoever's waitin' on ya waitin' any longer." The wizard trudged up the bank of the island with his hands in his pockets.

To Amanda's utter disbelief, he walked right past the outhouse and toward the overhanging tree branches on the other side of the island. She pointed at the narrow wooden building. "What's that?"

Shep's whistling laugh split through the evening silence. "If you gotta use the necessities, girl, lemme highly recommend against sittin' on that there john. Lotta folks won't be too happy bout it."

"Why not?" *Man, this is a hard game to play.*

"Leads right down into the kemana, that's why. Reckon someone oughtta put up an Out of Order sign on the thing, but everyone who comes out here already knows."

"Oh." Frowning at the outhouse as she passed it, she asked, "Then what's it for?"

The wizard snorted. "Overflow. Now come on and stand right here by me. I promise you ain't seen nothin' like this before. Get ready."

When she joined him on the other side of the island, Shep reached up for the lowest-hanging branch of a large oak stretching down over the dry land. He gave the branch a sharp twist, eliciting a loud *crack*, and a pale golden light illuminated in a circle around them on the ground.

"Welcome to the Everglades kemana, girl."

Amanda was about to ask him what they had to do next, but the sudden wind forced itself down her throat, and her gut raced up to meet it as the entire circle of dirt and grass beneath them dropped like a stone into the underground city.

She couldn't catch her breath, and if her feet hadn't been somehow magically glued to the platform dropping at a frightening pace, she probably would have tried to get off. Five seconds later, they stopped falling with another quick gust of air and stood solidly on the ground in the kemana. The island platform was gone, and the ceiling had closed—if it had ever opened in the first place.

"Hoo-wee!" Shep snatched the cap off his head again and smacked it against his knee, cackling in delight. "Gets me every time! I tell you what, girl. I don't most of the time get to come down here like that with the other kids gettin' ferried down the river. My job's to stand watch over them airboats and count heads when the kiddies float back up to head home. But if I ain't damn tickled by that drop! Come on." He gently nudged Amanda's shoulder as she fought to catch her breath. "Almost there."

Swiping the wind-tossed clumps of hair out of her face, Amanda scowled up at the kemana's ceiling. *So we climbed into a wooden toilet for no reason. I think I still like that way better than dropping through the ground.*

She puffed out a heavy breath and stumbled after Shep now that her feet could move again beneath her.

The kemana was at least twice as crowded as when she and Summer had been here in the middle of the night, which meant it was also twice as loud. The raucous laughter from groups of magicals ending their workweek or celebrating a Friday rose from every alley and storefront and open space around the kemana's crystal. The echoes reverberated in the huge underground city, and Amanda blinked furiously against the noise pounding in her head.

A gnome sitting on a stool and picking a banjo with blinding speed winked at her before blowing into the harmonica mounted to a special neck holder resting on his collarbones. A group of witches in ridiculously tight jeans and gaudily sparkling belts with puffed-up hair toasted one another with glowing pink drinks that fizzed and hummed. A Kilomea pushed a cart filled with dirt and wiggling purple beetles across the floor, glaring at the shifter girl until one of the beetles leapt over the side and ballooned to ten times its previous side.

"Aw, no you ain't!" The Kilomea lurched after the beetle and swung a huge, hairy fist into the glistening carapace. The bug screeched, making Amanda duck and spin around to stare at the spectacle. Apparently, a good punch was all the thing needed to shrink back down again before the Kilomea scooped it up. He glanced at his cart, shrugged, and popped the beetle in his mouth instead.

"Amanda!" Shep shouted over the din, waving her forward. "Come on, now. This way."

She hurried after him, weaving through the crowds, and couldn't get rid of the nagging feeling that everyone down here was watching her. That they recognized her and knew exactly who she was and what she'd done the last time she was here.

*Don't be dumb. Nobody knows. Nobody cares. If you were in even more trouble, it wouldn't have been Adalynn Jade sitting in Glasket's office. Maybe one of the bouncers from down here instead. Or Johnny.*

That last thought made her gulp, and she ducked under a magically floating banner that shouted the message painted across it in giant gold letters. "New Year, New You! Step into Bartholomew's Beauty today and become the best magical you were meant to be! All consultations fifty percent off through the end of February!"

Amanda grimaced at the banner's shrieking, childlike voice nearly splitting her eardrums, spun, and searched for Shep. The wizard didn't particularly stand out in the crowd of magicals letting loose on a Friday night, and she thought she'd lost him until she saw his newsboy cap waving in his hand above the crowd.

An Atlantean woman, arms laden with shopping bags, hissed at her when the shifter girl almost knocked her over. The black snakes on her head hissed as well, and Amanda dodged out of the way before hissing back. The Atlantean ignored her and kept walking, but now the shifter girl felt another tingling buzz of a shift wanting to break through.

*No. Not here. Not tonight. No wolves and no fighting random magicals because everything's too loud.*

"Look at ya." Shep tittered when she reached him. "Wide-eyed and bushy-tailed and starin' at everythin' like you was a newborn babe. You never been down inside one of these before, have ya?"

Amanda shook her head. Opening her mouth felt like too much of a risk.

"Well, we ain't here to sightsee. That'll come soon enough when you get down here with the rest of your friends for one of them school trips. My job's to take ya where ya need to be *now*, and nowhere else." With a quick sniff, he turned and headed down an alley between a smoke shop and a store claiming to have the best flyfishing lures money could buy—the kind any catch in the Everglades would find impossible to resist.

*Because magic. Magic makes everything possible. Except for a shifter.*

The farther they moved down the alley, the fainter the buzzing conversations, shouted deals made, and raucous laughter became. Even when the background noise of the kemana became a low buzz behind them and Amanda could hear their footsteps again as she followed Shep down the steadily darkening space between buildings, the alley still didn't end. It seemed to stretch on forever.

*Definitely didn't see something like this the last time.*

Before she knew it, the alley had become a tunnel, leading steadily down and farther below the Everglades swamp and the island serving as the kemana's entrance. Shadows moved independently across the tunnel walls, though there were no floating lights or even regular bulbs or lanterns or torches to light the way. The light seemed to come from the tunnel walls itself, which brightened and dimmed depending on which shadows moved across the rough-hewn rock.

They weren't Amanda's and Shep's shadows either, but there was no one else here in the tunnel with them.

"Are you..." She cleared her throat to get rid of the cobwebby feel in it as they kept walking. "Are you sure you know where we're going?"

"Trust me, girl. Ain't no part of this kemana I ain't been down more'n enough times to remember." The wizard swallowed thickly as the tunnel took a descending hairpin curve. "Might be there's a few parts less savory than others. But instructions is instructions, Amanda. I ain't fixin' to go 'gainst what Dean Glasket asked of me."

*Even if it means escorting her only shifter student down into the creepy bowels of the kemana where the walls move. Awesome.*

The tunnel finally opened into a second massive cavern right below the main thoroughfare of the kemana. There was no crystal down here. No dim yellow glow from the magic-sustaining artifact. This lower level of the underground city was much darker and much quieter because there were far fewer magicals down here than above. None of them looked at the wizard and the shifter girl making their way across the shadowy version of another marketplace. Most of the other magicals here huddled together in muttered conversations, exchanging clenched handfuls of whatever they dealt in down here.

Amanda had a feeling it wasn't money and harmless trinkets. The air was thick with the scent of concentrated magic—the kind she'd only smelled a handful of times before, and all of them before she'd met Johnny.

*Smells like all the dark magic sank to the bottom of the kemana. And everyone here looks like they're doing drug deals. Only not with drugs.*

A huge Azrakan with asymmetrical horns circling his head kicked himself off the wall of a shop—the sign over the door simply reading: 'Untouchables'—and approached the newcomers. A forked tongue flickered between his lips as he sneered at them. "You lost, wizard?"

Shep froze and looked up into the Azrakan's beady, glittering black eyes.

For a moment, Amanda thought her chaperone was going to tell her to run, that they'd made a mistake and tonight wasn't the night she wanted to be down here with a guy who'd said himself he was *only the driver* for the Academy of Necessary Magic. She got ready to shift if she had to.

"You *look* lost," the Azrakan growled, exposing stunted, worn-down, stained front teeth.

"Naw." Shep sniffed and didn't flinch away when the other magical loomed over him. "But I'll put a helluva hex in yer hide if you don't *get* lost, ya hear? Our business down here ain't none of yers."

A low chuckle escaped the Azrakan, and he blinked lazily at Amanda before stepping out of Shep's way and returning to his spot against the store's wall. Shep nodded toward another narrow alley two storefronts down and waved Amanda forward with him. "Stay close, girl. Almost there."

She couldn't imagine a reason why someone as jovial and well-meaning as Shep Frederick would have to come down here on his own to deal with the kind of magicals hovering in front of shop doors and peering from dark corners.

*I don't have any business being down here either. But here we are.*

On the other side of the last storefront they passed, Shep stopped in front of two large, iron double doors with vines etched all around the border. He knocked twice, and the echo filed the entire cavern with a hollow, metallic *thump*. Then he glanced at Amanda to give her a thin smile and a wink.

A heavy *clink* came from the other side of the door, followed by the scraping of a lock being pulled back before only one of the iron doors creaked and groaned open. A Kilomea stood on the other side, eyes glittering in the dim light rising from the walls of the kemana's lower, darker level. He squinted at Shep. "What do you want?"

"Girl's here to see Ms. Jade." The wizard gestured toward Amanda, and she obediently approached the slightly open door. "She's expected."

"Uh-huh." The Kilomea glanced up at the rest of the dark and eerily quiet marketplace before waving Amanda inside. "Move it."

She headed toward him but stopped when she realized Shep wasn't going anywhere. "Wait, what about you?"

"Don't you worry your pretty little head on my account, Amanda." He nodded with a kind smile. "I ain't goin' nowhere. Be right outside these here doors when you're done with your business in there. Best I stay outside for now, huh? Go on."

"Okay." She hesitated before finally slipping through the crack between the six-inch-thick iron doors. The Kilomea glared at her the whole time, and she glowered right back before his massive, hairy hand tugged on the iron handle. The door whispered across the ground and shut again with an echoing *thud*.

There was nothing on the other side. Only a stone closet with barely enough room for the Kilomea between the double doors and the stone wall, let alone a teenage shifter. He whipped a black bag toward her and nodded. "Put it on."

"What?"

"Your head. Don't make me say it again, or you're not getting where you need to be right now."

"Are you kidding?" She eyed the heavy black sack. "You want me to put a bag on my head?"

"Ms. Jade's orders."

"No way."

With a low growl, the Kilomea snapped the bag open in both hands and tried to put it on her.

Amanda slapped his hands away and ducked, snarling. "Don't touch me."

"Then quit being a pain in the ass." He narrowed his eyes at her, and she finally snatched the sack from his hairy fist before slowly tugging it over her head.

*This is nuts. All I wanted was to have a little fun, find the kemana, try to be a decent magical and keep a lady from losing her purse. Now there's a bag on my face like I'm in some kind of gang movie.*

The thought sent a jolt of realization through her.

*Oh, shit. Is Adalynn some kinda mob boss?*

"No peeking," the Kilomea growled.

She heard his feet shuffling slightly away from her in the tiny box of space that couldn't even be called an actual room. He snapped his fingers, a flash of dark blue light illuminated through the weave of the bag, and the temperature dropped by at least five degrees.

Amanda sucked in a quick breath.

*What happened?*

"Now," the Kilomea grumbled.

"Now *what?*" she snapped through the bag.

"Take it off and get moving."

"Is this some kind of joke?" She whipped the bag off and glared at the huge magical's unwavering sneer. "I just put this stupid thing on, and we're still..."

*Oh.*

No, they weren't still inside the tiny closet space behind the iron double doors. Now, she stood inside a huge circular room decorated like some kind of Victorian study—all dark, glistening wood, expensive upholstery covering wingback armchairs and sprawling settees, and an actual crystal chandelier hanging from the stone ceiling.

Amanda spun to see this circular room had no doors whatsoever.

*No way in or out except for his fancy trick when there's a bag over my head. What did I get myself into?*

"You'll have to excuse the theatrics," Adalynn Jade said from across the study. The fire in the hearth crackled and threw sparks over the lip of stone and onto the intricate area rug in front of it.

The black bag slipped out of Amanda's hand when she

whirled and saw the woman standing behind a large mahogany desk on the other side of the room. "What?"

"Teo enjoys the spectacle," the woman continued in her low, calm, almost crooning voice. "I have to admit that there's a certain air of mystery and gravitas that comes with the whole thing. It's all a precaution, Amanda. Safety and anonymity, of which I'm sure you already recognize the importance."

The shifter girl blinked. "There aren't any doors."

Adalynn gave her that same intelligently feral smile. "No. Not the kind you're used to. Thank you, Teo. That'll be all for now."

With a grunt, the Kilomea stooped to snatch the black bag off the floor, then gestured for Amanda to step into the room. She didn't move. The hulking magical rolled his eyes, snapped his fingers with the same dark blue light she'd seen through the bag, and disappeared.

That finally made the girl move, and she staggered backward toward the closest wall of the study. "Did he—"

"Teleport? I suppose you could call it that. We have an intricate transportation system down here, but that's something we'll cover much later. *If* you behave."

Amanda stared at the woman, who'd changed out of her forest-green pantsuit and now wore straight-legged beige slacks and a flowing white shirt with long sleeves and a deeply plunging neckline.

*Yeah, she looks like a mob boss. Like all those assholes who showed up for the Monsters Ball and tried to buy me like some kind of rare painting.*

"Don't look so surprised, Amanda." Adalynn chuckled and gestured toward the leather armchair in front of the glistening mahogany desk. "You agreed to this. You're already twenty minutes later than I anticipated. I can make an allowance for the first time since all of this is new to you and must come as a surprise. Next time, I highly recommend lighting a fire under those swift shifter feet of yours. I don't like to be kept waiting."

"I wasn't trying to be late."

"Oh, I know. Be sure your chaperone knows not to waste my time again. Have a seat."

Amanda took a moment longer to study her surroundings. Shelves of dark wood lined the walls. Large books, jars of powder and liquid, and something that looked a lot like frog legs bobbing inside liquid, spinning orbs of glass, and a whole row of stone figurines carved in the same style as the laser-Buddha filled them.

*This is gonna be a long night.*

# CHAPTER SEVENTEEN

Adalynn sat behind her desk again before Amanda crossed the circular study toward the indicated chair. When she did sit, thumping heavily down onto the leather upholstery, the woman didn't look up from the stack of papers she studied on her desk.

For at least ten minutes, they sat there in silence with nothing but the crackling fire and the occasional shifting log to make a sound. Amanda wiped her hands on her pants and tried to peer over the edge of the desk to see what was so important.

*Doesn't like her time wasted, but now I'm sitting here doing absolutely nothing. Hypocrite.*

"Keep your eyes to yourself, Amanda," Adalynn muttered, not looking up from the papers as she picked up a tortoiseshell fountain pen and scribbled a sprawling signature across the bottom of four different sheets of paper. "I don't appreciate prying eyes."

"I thought I was here to 'pay off a debt,'" Amanda muttered.

The woman slowly looked up at her. "I have even less patience for attitude."

The girl shrugged. "You probably should've thought of that before you blackmailed a teenager into coming down here to sit and watch you do paperwork."

Adalynn signed one more paper, then laid down her fancy pen, tapped the stack of papers against the desk, and set them aside. "The more time I spend on this planet, the more I wonder how much humans on Earth really knew about Oriceran and magic and our origins before the reveal of it all brought our worlds together."

*So she* is *a magical. Why doesn't she smell like anything?*

Amanda leaned forward in her chair. "What *are* you?"

"The phrase would have been more appropriate as 'Curiosity killed the *shifter.*'"

Wrinkling her nose, the girl stared right back at the woman's piercing gray eyes. "It hasn't killed me yet."

"No. Not you. You're a tough one. I'll give you that. It's why I like you. At least enough to offer you this opportunity." Adalynn sat back in the leather-upholstered office chair, the back of which rose two feet above her head. "It *has* killed several others. Curiosity. There are some out there who believe too much of it is a bad thing. Bad for business. Bad for politics. You name it."

Amanda steeled herself and wouldn't look away from the woman's gaze. "So this is about you punishing me because I got too curious?"

"Not at all. *I* am not of the same mind when it comes to whether or not too much of a good thing exists." Adalynn folded her hands in her lap and tilted her head. "I didn't bring you here so I could beat the curiosity out of you, Amanda. It's too deeply ingrained in your blood, and I have no interest in surrounding myself with empty shells. Your curiosity is what's helped you survive this long, isn't it?"

The girl shifted in her seat again. "You don't know what I've had to survive."

"Hmm. Not the way you do, of course. You lived it. Keep that curiosity. Maybe understanding how it got your parents and your sister Claire killed will help illuminate the importance of—"

"What did you say?" Amanda's hands clenched into fists.

Adalynn's smile widened. "You heard me. Now, I think it's time you heard the truth."

"You…" The body-wide tingle of her shifter magic—the kind that made it possible for her to change her form at will—raced through her and drowned out all other thought. Amanda leapt from the armchair and lurched toward the desk, snarling. Her eyes flashed silver, and she caught a brief glimpse of her outstretched hands sprouting wiry gray fur as her fingers shortened. Then a brilliant white light blinded her to everything else.

It felt like a baseball bat the size of her entire body had hit her.

She flew backward, clipping the arm of the chair before toppling onto the floor. The urge to shift still raced through her, but the pain that came with it made it impossible to go full wolf.

"I'll thank you not to lose your head during our time together, Miss Coulier. Don't try that again."

"Why?" Pushing herself up off the floor, she shook off the dizziness and glared at Adalynn Jade. "Because you know I can rip you apart if I tried?"

"Hardly." The same white light blazed at the woman's fingertips. "I stopped you as easily as if I were swatting away a fly. Because *you* are the one without control."

"Wow." Stretching out the kink in her neck, Amanda stared at the woman now standing behind the desk. Finally, she had a reason to stop pretending to be the good girl she'd thought everyone wanted her to be. "Is this the part where you offer to teach me how to harness my shifter strength? That because you could blast me back with a little white light means you know all about being a shifter and how to *be* in control?"

Adalynn dipped her head with a coy smile. "Those are *your* words. Not mine."

"I'm not standing here in a room with no doors to say, 'Yes, please. Teach me how to be better.' I don't even know what the hell you are!"

"*What* I am doesn't matter. What I can tell you is all you need to worry about right now." The woman sat calmly in her chair again and nodded. "Sit."

"No. Not until you tell me why I'm here. You said it was to pay off this debt because I ruined whatever *operation* you had going on with those wizards, and now you're bashing me around the room with spells and saying it's because I don't have *control*. What do you want from me?"

Adalynn's smile disappeared. "It's certainly not to take you on as a charity case. I can tell you that much."

"So put me to work then. I have no problem with it. Yeah, I took your purse and dropped that weird statue-weapon into the swamp. It was an accident, but I get it. I have to pay for it. So quit being all mysterious and make me *pay* for it already." She was panting by the time she finally spat it all out, with her hands balled into fists.

*She knows what happened to my family. She knows who I am. What does she want?*

"You misunderstand the purpose of our meetings, Amanda." Adalynn spoke as calmly as ever and ran her hand slowly across the surface of her glossy desk. "That was my fault. I misconstrued my reasons for seeking you out. Intentionally."

"What?"

"Sit. I'll tell you why you're here."

Amanda approached the chair with halting steps and lowered herself into it. The hard leather creaked beneath her weight. *This thing feels like no one ever sat in it before now.*

Adalynn nodded. "Be honest. If I'd shown up at your school and told you I wanted you to meet with me here twice a week so I could help you, would you have agreed to come?"

"Nope." She didn't even have to think about it. "I don't need help."

"That's exactly why I wanted you to believe this was a debt *you* owe to *me*. Because that stubbornness of yours is inherited. You don't want help, but your moral compass is still intact. You stole from me, whether intentionally or otherwise, and your desire to right that wrong is almost as strong as your curiosity. I can't speak for your sister Claire, and we'll never know whether she followed so perfectly in your father's footsteps, but you most certainly did."

"Stop." Amanda's hands clenched again into fists, and she buried them between her thighs and the tight, creaking edges of the leather upholstery. "You don't know anything about my family."

"In some ways, that's very true. I was, however, *very* close to the opportunity. Unfortunately, your family's time was cut drastically short. You're still here, though. I had to find some way to tug at that sense of honor you carry. And your curiosity." The woman tilted her head. "You're not here to work off a debt to me, Amanda."

The shifter girl swallowed, fighting to steady her breathing.

*None of this makes sense.*

"But I ruined your operation and lost your magical statue."

Adalynn chuckled and gestured at the shelf with at least a dozen similar stone figurines lined up on its surface. "Those are expendable."

"So what, then? My family's dead, and you didn't get what you wanted from them, so I'm working off *their* debt to you. Is that it?"

"As entertaining an idea as that is, no. Your parents and your sister didn't owe me a thing. It's quite the opposite." Adalynn swiped at her wispy bangs again. "After everything that happened last spring, I feel more than a little responsible for the dark turn your life *almost* took. It most certainly would have been much worse for you if the bounty hunter hadn't been assigned to your case. Which I'm assuming quite a few federal employees already recognized."

Amanda shook her head. "I have no idea what you're talking about, but you're really starting to creep me out. Even more than showing up at my school and making me put a bag over my head to get inside this room."

"I'm the one paying off a debt, Amanda." The woman spread her arms, and this time her smile was tight and not nearly as amused, tugging at the corners of her mouth until her whole face looked stretched way too thin. "To your family. To you. That's why you're here."

Scowling, Amanda slumped back in the armchair and slowly shook her head. "You're nuts."

"Maybe. I also have a finely tuned moral compass. Your father came to me for help last March. He wanted to make some changes in the way he ran his business. That included his relationships with his clients and a rather large and eclectic list of contacts within and beyond the financial sphere. Also, his relationship with his twin daughters, who up to that point had been raised believing they could never truly be themselves within any sphere of society or life in general. Does any of this hit home for you?"

There was nothing Amanda could say at that moment that would add to the conversation. She couldn't believe what she was hearing, and it took her a moment to find her voice again. Fortunately—maybe—Adalynn Jade was a patient woman, whatever kind of magical she happened to be. She gave Amanda all the time she needed before the girl finally managed to whisper, "You knew my dad?"

"Yes. Not as well as I would have liked but enough to know that Bruce Coulier was more than a shrewd businessman. He was a good man. A good *shifter*, as rarely as anyone uses that phrase nowadays. I truly am sorry for everything you've had to go through since you lost your family."

"Why are *you* sorry?"

"I suppose you could say I feel somewhat responsible. I made your father wait longer than I could have before our first scheduled meeting, which never took place. If I'd been less concerned with my agenda and had paid more attention to a magical coming to me for help, I..." Adalynn closed her eyes, which Amanda figured was as close as the woman ever got to showing intense emotion. "I can't help but think your family might have been better prepared that night if *I'd* been better prepared to provide Bruce with what he asked of me. So, in light of what's occurred between last May and now—specifically having found *you*, Bruce Coulier's daughter who seemingly disappeared off the face of this planet shortly after being abducted and auctioned off at a Monsters Ball in Manhattan—I have something of an opportunity to make amends. When you and I are finished, I will have paid off the debt I owe *you* for not having done my job."

The tension slowly seeped out of Amanda's clenched fists and her hunched shoulders as she stared at the woman. "It's not your fault. *You* didn't kill my family."

"No. But I may be able to help you find the magicals who did."

# CHAPTER EIGHTEEN

Adalynn Jade's confession hit Amanda harder than the blow of that white light that had knocked her out of a shift. She couldn't breathe. She couldn't move.

*I'm finally gonna be able to take those assholes down. Whoever they are, I'll find them. And I'll make sure they pay for all of it.*

"Who?" The question came out of her as a barked command.

Adalynn lifted her hand in a signal for the shifter girl to wait. "I said I *may* be able to help. That's a road best taken further in the future when you understand the rest of—"

"Tell me who they are!" Amanda slammed both fists down on the leather armrests and stood. "Then we can stop all this stupid playing around and sneaking me into a kemana. Then you won't owe me anything—"

"That's enough!" A halo of light blazed around Adalynn Jade's head, distorting the features of her pleasantly symmetrical face until it looked like her entire head was stretching out like taffy.

Or maybe that was a side effect of the powerful magic pressing down on the shifter girl with such force that she knew she couldn't possibly fight it. Knowing it and wanting to fight it anyway were two entirely different things. Amanda snarled and tried to shift, but the woman's magic instantly cut off her ability to do so, as if someone or something had seized the wolf inside her by the throat and shoved it back into the recesses of her mind. Her body betrayed her, and she slammed back down into the armchair with a *thud*.

The halo around Adalynn's head disappeared, and the woman drew in a slow, deep breath. "I don't enjoy doing that, Amanda. It's in both our best interests for you to stop fighting me on this. It's not my intention to start a war with you, but I promise you I will win every time."

Amanda drew in a shaky breath and puffed it all out again through loose lips. "What was that?"

"We'll file that away for now with your other questions about my personal history. Tonight, I wanted you to know why I'm so pleased our paths have crossed." For the first time, Adalynn looked a little nervous when she swallowed and folded her hands one more time in her lap. "I hope you're still as curious about the rest of this as you've been since our meeting at the Academy this morning. I want to help you, and whether or not you want my help in return, I think you already know you need it."

"No, I don't."

"Shifters are notoriously compulsive, so take some time to think about it. If you're ready for the next step, I expect to see you here again at eight o'clock on Tuesday night. *Sharp*. There's no room for excuses once you and I get started."

"Wait. What?"

"That's it, Amanda. You may go." Adalynn raised her hand and pointed at the space on the opposite side of the study where Teo the Kilomea had teleported the teenage shifter into Ms. Jade's presence. The dark blue light flashed again, and Amanda spun in her chair to see the rest of the Kilomea's figure flicker into existence. "We're finished here for tonight, Teo. Please escort our guest back out to her chaperone at the front gates."

"That's *it*?" Amanda jumped up out of her chair, and this time, the woman didn't pull out any other fancy tricks for controlling a young shifter. "I haven't even been here twenty minutes."

"Yes, well, you would have been here longer if you'd been on time. You're not the last item on my to-do list, Amanda, but I do have other business that needs my immediate attention tonight." The woman glanced up at her, then nodded toward Teo. "He may look like it, but I promise he doesn't bite. Enjoy your weekend."

"But—"

"You heard her, kid," Teo grumbled. "Let's go."

She stared at Adalynn for a moment longer, but the strange woman without any scent acted as if she were already alone in her study.

*This is insane. And I'm going along with it. Right?*

Teo grunted. "Long night for everybody. Hurry up."

With her mind whirling in a chaotic storm of a billion thoughts that didn't make any sense at all, Amanda shuffled across the study floor and stopped in front of the Kilomea, holding out her hand.

"What? You want a cookie or something?"

"Don't I need the bag?"

He smirked around his protruding eyeteeth. "Not anymore."

The dark blue light encompassed them both when he snapped his fingers. Then they stood in the same tiny, cramped space behind the iron double doors. Teo pushed on one, and it creaked open with that same heavy, metallic squeal. "See ya next time, kid."

"Yeah. Okay." Amanda slipped through the door as if she were sleepwalking, barely registering the smile lighting up Shep's face when he turned and saw her emerging into the kemana's darker underbelly.

"There you are. Lookin' a little worse for wear, sure. Not as bad as I'd have reckoned after walkin' through a set o' doors like *them*."

"Wait." Amanda turned toward Teo. "Do *you* know what—"

The iron door whispered across the floor again and let out another hollow metallic *bang* as it settled back into place against its twin. And that was it.

"All right, then." Shep whipped off his newsboy cap and ruffled his thinning hair. "Reckon it's time for us to make our great escape. Don't mention to any of these fellas down here I called it that, huh? I can handle myself fine if things need handlin'. For the both of us too, girl. Just that I'd prefer not havin' to in the first place. So step lively now and keep close 'til we're at least up top by one level."

With a final glance at the closed iron doors etched with flowering vines, the wizard shoved his hat back down onto his head and took off toward the tunnel leading up to the main thoroughfare. The dark, muttering, sneering magicals down here in the lower level cast them warning glances, but no one headed after them or tried to engage.

*They might if we were here way later. Like, if Summer and I had found* this *part of the city instead...*

The thought of Summer running around down here trying to make friends made Amanda shudder. She had a feeling the young witch would be incredibly more successful with that down here than up above.

Shep didn't say a word as they climbed the long, winding tunnel turning back and forth on itself. Amanda figured there was a reason for it—not that the wizard was particularly afraid but because he didn't want anyone overhearing whatever they might have discussed. She didn't either.

When they exited the alley between the two storefronts and headed back down the avenue toward the magical lift she could only assume would take them back up to the island the way it had dropped them down here, the shifter girl finally got hold of her mind. At least enough to ask, "Do you know anything about Adalynn Jade?"

"Hmm?" Shep cast her a sidelong glance and shrugged. "Other'n the part where it's my job to bring you down here twice a week so you can have a little sit-down with her? That...that *is* all y'all were doin', right?"

Amanda nodded slowly. "Yeah. Only a talk."

*If I say anything else about it, there's no way he won't tell Glasket. And I'm pretty sure she'd never let me leave again if she had any idea what was going on.*

"Good. Good." He gestured toward the glowing circle on the ground beside the kemana's curving stone wall. "Sure, girl. I know a thing or two 'bout Ms. Jade."

"Like what?"

Shep stepped into the glowing circle and glanced around, but none of the magicals spending their Friday night out in the Everglades kemana paid any attention to the old man and the girl leaving early and calling it a night. "Now, keep in mind not everythin' ya hear is the straight-and-narrow truth, yeah? Most of it's rumors. 'Course, makes sense if Dean Glasket flipped the green light on you comin' all the way out here to meet with that Ms. Jade, and I ain't tryin' to put ideas in your head—"

"It's okay, Shep. Really. Just tell me."

"Uh-huh." Squinting at the wall, he reached out to poke a darker circle of stone.

Amanda's stomach dropped into her gut and sank to the tips of her toes as they sailed upward toward the cavern ceiling. She might have cried out as they neared the solid layer of stone above them if she'd been able to make any noise at all. Then they were through, standing on the same grass in front of the same tree branch overhanging the island.

She drew in a sharp gasp and stumbled out of the circle.

Shep's whistling laughter followed her. "Sure. Takes some gettin' used to, but once that's outta the way, you'll learn to enjoy the ride."

"Probably not..." She braced her hands on her thighs and bent over, giving her stomach time to settle back where it belonged in her body instead of flopping around all over the place.

"Count yourself lucky, girl. You'll be gettin' more practice'n the rest of those kiddies at the Academy." He headed briskly across the island, past the outhouse, and toward the airboat moored to the thick, heavily glossed tree stump on the bank.

"Shep."

"Yeah?"

"You never answered my question."

"Oh. Huh." A slightly nervous chuckle escaped him, and he shook his head as he untied the rope before coiling it up around his shoulder as he hopped up onto the airboat. "Well now, I suppose I didn't quite get that far. What is it I was fixin' to say? You remember?"

Eyeing him suspiciously, Amanda hopped up onto the boat with him and watched the wizard pretend to pay more attention to starting up the fan's propellers. *He doesn't want to say. Which probably means I need to hear it.*

"You were about to tell me what you've heard about Adalynn Jade."

"Oh. That." The throttle control stick turned in his hand, the fan kicked up, and they glided smoothly across the river on their way back to the Academy. "Some folks say she's some kinda sorceress. Ain't the same thing as a witch, you know. Least not as far as I can tell. I ain't exactly sure I believe all that hullabaloo, mostly 'cause I ain't seen Ms. Jade up close 'n personal enough to watch her do any kinda magic anyhow. Then there's the folks who say…"

"Who say what?" She shoved her hands into the pockets of her zip-up hoodie and tried not to look as annoyed as she felt. *Why can't anyone simply* tell *me something straight-up?*

"Well, there's those who say Ms. Jade's one of them magicals you don't wanna mess with if you can help it. A Quickwing." When he saw her confused frown, Shep wrinkled his nose and clicked his tongue. "That's an old word for it, girl. Might be you recognize the same thing if I called her a boss."

"Like, of her own company or something?" Amanda didn't think that was what the wizard meant. His next unsure chuckle confirmed that for her.

"Magical Mafia ain't exactly a legitimate business, girl, but sure."

"No way…"

Shep shot her a quick look again and smirked before returning his attention to steering them safely upriver. "I'm only sayin' things other folks repeat. Can't take it with nothin' but a grain o' salt, understand? I ain't got proof, and if I were you, I sure wouldn't risk my hide tryin' to go lookin' for none."

Amanda snorted. "Sounds fun, but I'm not sure proving my principal is sending me off for meetings with a mob boss would do any of us any favors."

"Smart girl. Don't you spend your time thinkin' too hard on it, huh? Unless that Ms. Jade does somethin' you can't in good conscience go without tellin' somebody."

*Like throwing me across the room with a spell while her face stretches out? Or sending two wizards into High Tide Ammo to rough up the guys running the store?*

"Yeah, okay." She faced the bow and studied the moonlight rippling across the surface of the river. "You have any idea what she is?"

"Besides what we already covered?"

"I mean what kind of *magical* she is. I know it's a weird question, but I…I can't tell."

"Huh." He squinted at her. "Well, no, I ain't tried to pin that down before. Does it make a difference one way or t'other?"

"I guess not."

*If Adalynn can tell me who killed my family and help me find them, I guess the rest of it doesn't matter at all.*

"Tuesday."

"What's that now?"

Amanda cleared her throat. "I'm supposed to come back here Tuesday. And be in her office at eight. Does that work?"

Shep burst out laughing. "Well, it's gonna have to work, ain't it? Sure. I'll get you back to those doors on Tuesday. No problem."

# CHAPTER NINETEEN

Amanda spent the next day alone in the greenhouse, sifting through the dirt and watering it, and getting ready for the first batch of Everthorn seeds she could now officially plant. Ms. Calsgrave had let her choose where to start—it was either Everthorn or Pale Mole's Moss, which was easier to keep alive but took a lot more preparation. She was ready to finally have something to show for the work she'd been putting into the greenhouse.

*I need something to show for anything I've been doing in the last few weeks. And an excuse to stay away from Summer.*

It worked for the entire day, but then the black-haired witch found her after dinner anyway and couldn't contain her excitement. "You ready, shifter girl?"

"Nope."

"Very funny."

"I'm serious, Summer." Amanda tossed her plate in the outdoor cafeteria's trash can and glanced around. "We can't go back to the kemana tonight."

The witch scowled at her and folded her arms. "Why the hell not?"

"Because that's where I was last night." They stared at each other, and Amanda shook her head. "Not a good idea to go playing around down there when a lot of magicals saw me last night. It's...too close to home, you know? I can't keep sneaking out there *and* get escorted twice a week with Glasket's permission."

*Not to mention that if Summer and Adalynn end up going head-to-head, I won't be able to stop it. Not a pretty thought.*

"You've gotta be kidding me." Summer rolled her eyes. "You promised."

"No, I agreed before I knew what I'd have to do to 'pay off this debt.' You can go by yourself if you want. I can't stop you." Amanda shrugged. "I don't owe *you* anything, either. So good luck."

"You..." Summer turned quickly to stare after the shifter girl walking away and leaving her alone in the center of the cafeteria. Then she scoffed. "Every magical for themselves, right? Yeah, I thought so."

Of course, Amanda heard what was probably supposed to be muttered under her friend's breath, and she couldn't help feeling a little bad. Still, she had to shake off the feeling as she headed back to the girls' dorms. *I've already gotten in way too much trouble trying to be friends with Summer Flannerty. It's fun, but now I need to focus. School and figuring out what the heck Adalynn can do to help me is more important. As long as she's not trying to jerk me around too.*

For the first time this semester, Amanda crawled into bed before Lights Out at 10:00 p.m. and stayed there through the night. She was already half-asleep when she thought she heard Summer's door open and shut and the witch's footsteps whispering down the hall. She didn't care.

*I need sleep, and if Summer wants to keep breaking the rules all the time, that's her choice.*

Waking up that Monday to the obnoxiously blaring tune of *Shake Your Tailfeather* was a lot easier after not staying out all night. Although now Amanda felt a little itchy after going so long through the spring semester without shifting. She brushed the feeling aside, got dressed for the day, and headed out to the cafeteria for breakfast.

All the other students shuffled through the dorms' halls and out toward the kitchens and the banquet tables. Summer didn't try to approach her at all, and that was fine with the shifter girl. Grace looked exhausted when she joined Amanda at the table with only a bowl of oatmeal.

"I stayed up way too late with Annabelle finishing our maid robot," she muttered, staring into the cream-and-brown-sugar-drowned oats. "Like, I tried to tell her we had to get to sleep, but she wouldn't stop *talking...*"

Amanda fought back a laugh. "The project isn't due for, like, another two weeks or something, isn't it?"

"Yeah." The blonde witch thumped her chin into one hand and slowly spooned up her first bite with the other. "Last time I partner with an overachiever on Annabelle's level. That's for sure."

Alex joined them with a plate of bacon and a side of one hard-boiled egg to go with it. Jackson joined them shortly after, his plate laid out neatly with four steaming biscuits and nothing else.

Grace frowned at his plate. "That's not breakfast."

"Sure it is." The wizard broke open one of the biscuits and noisily inhaled the steam through his nose before slathering the pieces with butter. "I don't know what those pixies did to these things since last semester, but they've gotten even better. Like, I don't think there's anything on either planet as good as these."

"You're gonna crash hard later with nothing but biscuits," Alex muttered.

"Oh, yeah? And a whole plate of bacon's gonna do you any better?"

"Yep." The Wood Elf nodded toward the other end of the pavilion, where Corey sat alone at the table with half his plate of only hardboiled eggs already wolfed down. "That's how Corey got so big."

Amanda barked out a laugh. "I don't think it's the eggs and bacon, Alex. I think it's the Kilomea part."

"He works out."

Grace and Amanda exchanged an amused glance, and the witch leaned forward over the table, smirking. "Since when did you care about working out?"

"Since whenever I want." Alex shrugged and shoveled two slices of bacon into his mouth. "Just trying to build muscle. He has some pretty good tips if you can ignore all the grunting and spitting."

"He does spit when he talks." Amanda nodded. "Even when he's whispering."

"He works out?" Jackson gulped down his biscuit and frowned at Alex. "Where? There's no gym."

"You haven't seen his room, have you?" At the wizard's blank stare, Alex shook his head. "It's basically a one-guy gym."

"You two hang out in his room to work out?" Grace asked.

"No. I'm building mine." The Wood Elf didn't say another word on the subject and focused instead on the rest of his breakfast.

Amanda wrinkled her nose, watching his complete lack of enjoyment in cramming down what had to be at least a whole pound of bacon. "I'm not sure *bacon's* gonna help with the muscle-building."

"Well, we can't all be shifters with built-in strength," Alex muttered around a mouthful.

"Or Kilomeas, right?" Grace laughed and found her energy again to start eating the oatmeal.

Whatever energy the freshmen had that morning was instantly expended with Mr. Petrov's Combat Training class to start their day. So far, not a single one of them had managed to finish running the obstacle course still rigged with the magi-tech guns that swiveled and launched minor attack spells at any student who made it past the rope ladder at the start of the course. Amanda, though, was determined to make it to the end. After all, she'd spent two weeks running her replica of this course in Johnny's back yard.

*He's probably already taken it apart by now. That back yard's getting crowded.*

She went after Blake, who hadn't been able to make it past the first quarter of the course before getting blasted off the platform. The shy, quiet girl picked herself up off the ground where she'd landed, groaned, and dusted off her pant legs.

"Every single time, Cameron," Petrov growled. "There's a pattern! If you haven't figured that out by now, either you're completely incompetent, or you *want* to be knocked off."

The girl glared at their teacher as she shuffled back to the end of the line.

"Try ducking *right* next time. Understand? Right." The bald teacher pumped his right fist in the air, then shook his head. "Never thought I'd have to give hints like this. All right, Coulier, you're up. Get going."

He pointed at the magical floating timer in the air, and the numbers returned to zeros across the board.

Amanda took off running before the timer started the count. Then she was climbing the rope ladder, reviewing the rest of the course in her mind before she reached the top platform.

The other freshmen cheered her on, which they'd gotten in the habit of doing for everyone trying to complete Petrov's impossible course. It was the only thing they could do not to write the entire class off as completely hopeless.

She crouched on the first platform and waited for the first

swiveling gun to point her way. The second it fired a burst of orange energy, she leapt to the other side of the platform and launched herself onto the first set of monkey bars. Then she waited again.

"Go! Go!"

"Get across! Keep moving!"

She ignored her classmates' shouts and waited for the second and third swiveling gadgets to come her way. Apparently, no one else had figured out by now that Petrov's special "obstacles" worked on a timer—five seconds between each blast. Amanda was ready for them.

The first fired a green blaze that hit the monkey bar where she dangled and sent a surge of crackling green energy across the metal. She'd already moved to the next and paused again to wait for the second blast. Only once did she have to backtrack on the bars, but after the third gadget launched its attack, she raced across to the other side, swinging wildly.

Jackson's mouth fell open. "Is she even *touching* those things?"

"Doesn't look like it, huh?" Grace folded her arms. "She's gonna finish."

"Yeah, but if she does, what does that mean for the rest of us?"

The witch wrinkled her nose. "Nothing, I hope."

Amanda dropped to the next platform after the monkey bars and headed across the suspended bridge. The freshmen had decided on their own time that Petrov had enchanted the bridge to thump around way more than any of their weight warranted— except for Corey, of course. She'd found a pattern to this too. Instead of scrambling across the bridge as she had all through last semester, she darted and paused six different times, riding the undulating waves of the loosely attached wooden planks beneath her feet.

A crackle of purple energy blazed along the handrails, which more than half the class still forgot about if they even got to this part. She crouched in the center of the bridge and ducked before the handrails ignited with doubled energy and met in the middle above her head.

"Holy crap." Alex slowly cocked his head. "She's gonna do it."

The second the magical wall disappeared above her, Amanda leapt to her feet and launched herself across the second half of the bridge. The class erupted in cheers that quickly morphed into gasps of horror when the swinging metal beam on the other platform crashed toward the shifter girl's head.

Amanda ducked the swing, spun in her crouch, and darted back and forth across the next platform between the intermittent bursts of white light spewing from opening panels in the platform's surface.

She was almost there. The end was right in front of her—six feet, that was it.

Then she realized she had no idea what tricks waited in those last six feet to throw her out of her groove. She faltered.

A wall of blazing white light rose at the end of the final platform, shimmering and throwing off sparks. It looked exactly like the halo of light that had flared up around Adalynn Jade's head when the woman had forced Amanda back into her seat—forced her out of a shift and snuffed out all her instinctual magic.

The instant memory made Amanda falter, and she skidded to a stop in front of the wall of white light. At the same time, the platform rumbled, and two unseen panels slid away from each other right beneath her feet like an automatic trap door. She felt the wood move beneath her but wasn't fast enough to jump away.

She dropped right through the trapdoor and landed on her feet in the grass with a quick *thump*. The other freshmen screaming for her to get to the end of the course let out a collective groan of disappointment.

"You almost had it!"

"Hey, now we know what happens at the end!"

Jackson ruffled his unruly mop of dirty-blond hair and

snorted. "You know what? I'm starting to think this thing is completely impossible, and the sergeant doesn't wanna tell us."

Grimacing, Amanda stomped her foot in the grass and stalked out from beneath the platform. Her classmates' disappointment faded into the background when she looked up at Mr. Petrov. The teacher had left his folding lawn chair in front of the training building's open door and now stood halfway between the building and the course, his arms folded. A tiny smirk spread across his lips.

"That was definitely...something, Coulier."

She gestured toward the trap door now swinging its way back into place. "Are you sure this thing is even possible to finish?"

"I don't know. You tell me."

She spread her arms.

"You expecting a cookie or something? Getting farther than anyone else doesn't mean anything if you didn't finish. Get back in line."

Amanda rolled her eyes, wiped the sweat off her forehead, and stomped back toward the line of freshmen waiting for their turn to fail miserably on the impossible course. Some of the other kids clapped her on the back and offered encouragement, and she nodded and tried to smile. It didn't exactly come across as genuine.

"Listen up!" Petrov let out a piercing whistle. "The rest of you should take this as a lesson. Coulier almost made it. *Almost*. When you're out in the field and being shot at by actual deadly magic and maybe even real guns, almost doesn't cut it. This week is the last chance any of you get to try to run this thing on your own. Next week, you start running this course in teams. Pris. Go."

The teacher waved at the timer to reset it again, and Jackson hissed out a sigh before taking off for one more attempt at *not* getting shot off the course halfway through.

Blake turned and gave Amanda a small, sympathetic smile. "That was really good."

"Thanks, I guess."

"If anyone's gonna finish this thing, it'll probably be you."

Amanda laughed and nodded at the back of Corey's head, which rose more than a foot above the other kids at the center of the line. "Unless Corey ends up bashing the course to pieces on his next run through."

The other girl clamped a hand over her mouth to stifle a laugh. "That would be good for all of us."

Amanda returned her attention to Jackson, who'd now made it halfway across the monkey bars before the next magical jolt flickered beneath his hand. He shouted and dropped like a stone. "This thing is impossible!"

"Porter," Petrov shouted, ignoring his student's frustration. "You're up!"

---

Thankfully, the rest of their classes that day didn't reveal any surprises. Amanda headed off to the greenhouse in the main building instead of joining the rest of her class for Illusions with Ms. Calsgrave. The teacher met Amanda's gaze out in the hall and nodded before the shifter girl kept moving.

*Yep. Works out well for everyone. I get to spend two and a half hours with a bunch of dirt, and she gets to forget she can't teach a shifter how to cast illusions.*

The greenhouse was exactly the way she'd left it that weekend, except for the tiniest green sprouts of the first Everthorn shoots already poking up out of the soil. Despite her frustration with not finishing Petrov's course, the sight of actual plants in that first trough made her smile.

"We're finally getting somewhere."

She didn't see the shimmering silver light rippling across the surface of the dirt when she turned to head toward the metal cabinet.

# CHAPTER TWENTY

When it was time for her second visit to Adalynn Jade's weird office in the dark underbelly of the Everglades kemana the next day, Amanda had no idea how she felt about the trip. Shep was his usual chipper self when they met behind the girl's dorm as before, and he didn't stop talking until they reached the alley in the kemana's upper level that eventually led toward the descending tunnel.

Then he stopped and cast Amanda a quick sidelong glance. "You seem quieter than normal, girl."

That made her laugh. *We've only done this once. How does he know how much I normally talk?*

"I'm tired," she said. "But I'm fine."

"Oh, sure. Reckon it don't help none to be out here at night toward the middle of the week. You got early risin' to do in the mornin'. Don't you worry 'bout it, girl. We're on time tonight. I made sure of that. I'll still be waitin' for ya by them doors when all's said and done. Best you put what we talked 'bout last time outta your mind, understand? You focus on whatever business you got down there and leave it at that."

"Sure. Let's go."

With a heavy sigh, the wizard led the way down the tunnel. Amanda squinted as she followed him. *So now he's suddenly worried about what I think of this whole thing? Well, we're all doing what someone told us to, and I'm gonna figure out exactly what Adalynn Jade is.*

The process of getting her through those huge iron doors was exactly the same. Teo still met her there with an expressionless nod and a grunt. Once he pulled the huge door shut behind her again—with Shep waiting dutifully on the other side, this time with a rolled-up magazine pulled from his back pocket to pass the time—Amanda immediately extended her hand toward him in that tiny space behind the doors. "Hand it over. I'm ready this time."

"Huh?" The Kilomea leered at her, his wiry eyebrows lifting comically. "What do you want?"

"The bag. I need it to get to Adalynn, right?"

Teo burst out laughing and nudged her hand aside. "Nice try. You're done with that one, shifter girl."

Hearing Summer's constant nickname for her coming out of a grown magical's mouth made her wrinkle her nose. "Then why use it the first time?"

His laughter died into a slow, careless chuckle, and he snapped his fingers without answering.

This time, Amanda was ready to head forward toward Adalynn Jade's huge mahogany desk and sit in the stiff and creaking leather armchair to get down to work—whatever that happened to be today. Except for when the dark blue light around her and Teo faded, they weren't standing in Adalynn's doorless, windowless study.

The drone of conversation and shouted haggling, laughter, music, and the buzz of concentrated magic coming from the giant crystal filled the air around her. A second later, she realized exactly where they were—up top, in the kemana's main level. More specifically, they'd teleported to the alley that led back to the old-timers' shivering, boiling machine against the kemana wall filled with whatever ingredients the squinty, grimacing old locals decided to use to make their moonshine.

Amanda grimaced and clapped a hand over her nose, which did nothing to ward off the sting of the thick alcohol scent in the air. She glanced up at Teo and shrugged. "I heard if you get even one gesture wrong or don't pay enough attention, a spell can backfire. Do we need to try again?"

The Kilomea grunted and turned down the alley toward the moonshine setup. "Don't be a smartass."

*So this is how I learn more about my dad and Adalynn, huh? I wasn't into moonshine with Summer, and I'm still not trying to be a part of all that now.*

She paused when she saw Adalynn at the end of the alley, talking in low voices with the old-timers protecting their giant fermenting machine and pouring ingredients into various openings, and eyeing anyone who so much as glanced down the wrong alley. The woman wore a purple sleeveless dress that stopped above her knees. It looked more like a shapeless sack with holes cut into it, but somehow, Adalynn Jade made it look fashionable.

*It's probably way more expensive than it should be.*

Adalynn nodded as she accepted the jug of slightly brown liquid one of the wrinkled old Elves handed over, then patted the guy on the shoulder and turned to head toward Teo and Amanda. A smile flickered across her mouth when she saw the shifter girl staring at her, and she handed the jug to Teo without stopping. "Right on time. Just like I told you."

"I would've been earlier if I knew we were supposed to meet up here."

"I didn't bring you on as that kind of assistant, Amanda. Don't expect me to share my itinerary with you beforehand. Or ever." Adalyn waved at the jug in Teo's hand. The Kilomea snapped his fingers, and the jug disappeared as the woman headed down the alley toward the main thoroughfare of the kemana. "Stay close and keep your eyes open."

"Wait. What?"

"Move," Teo grumbled.

"Hey, Shep's...down there waiting for me." Amanda hurried after the strange woman who could morph and magically control a shifter's impulses and who still had no scent. "We should tell him—"

"Your chaperone is exactly where he needs to be." Adalynn pulled a cream cloth from the pocket of her shift dress and used it to quickly wipe her hands before stuffing it back into her pocket. "When your time with me is over tonight, you'll meet him where he is and return with him to the Academy as agreed. Now, we don't have time for me to answer even this many questions. If you want to learn what you obviously came back here to learn, your mantra for the next few hours is Eyes Open, Mouth Shut. Understand?"

Gritting her teeth, Amanda stared at the woman's profile. *Fine.*

Adalynn shot her a sidelong glance and smirked. "Excellent. Do try to keep up. We have a lot of stops to make."

She exited the mouth of the alley, and Teo followed closely behind. He chuckled as he passed the shifter girl. "Watch and learn, kid. Don't try anything stupid."

Amanda growled low under her breath and swiftly followed after her new... She had no idea *what* to call Adalynn. Mentor was the wrong word. Benefactor might've worked—she'd heard the term tossed around by her dad when she used to listen in on his business meetings—but so far, Adalynn Jade hadn't *given* her anything.

*More like a jailer. Except she's trying to keep a promise to my dad by having me here. What the heck did he want from her?*

For the next hour, Amanda and Teo followed Adalynn Jade around the kemana like two hired goons would have followed any number of the crime-lord magicals Johnny Walker had put away behind bars over the years. The woman stopped randomly in individual storefronts and spoke softly and quietly to the magicals running the shops—a shoe store, a nightclub, four different food trucks operating twenty-four-seven underground. Each of the business owners smiled and nodded at whatever she said to them. Random items were exchanged at each stop, though they were all either wrapped in cloth or tucked into gift boxes or hefted into Teo's arms in varying bag sizes.

None of the magicals meeting with Adalynn looked particularly surprised to see her. While the exchanges were short and quiet and a little tense, the business owners looked more excited than anything else to be speaking to the woman.

*I would've called this some kind of shakedown, but they don't look scared at all. They look happy.*

The last stop they made was at a food truck selling what Amanda guessed was the closest one could get to Greek food in the middle of the swamp. Adalynn didn't pay for the food she handed both Teo and Amanda, and the gnome running the food truck grinned and constantly nodded when he gave the woman a larger box from underneath the order counter.

"Enjoy your week, Grisham."

"Enjoy the spanakopita, Ms. Jade." Adalynn turned without looking at the shifter girl shadowing her. The box disappeared when Teo snapped his fingers and sent it off to wherever he'd teleported everything else.

Finally, Amanda couldn't hold back her curiosity. "What are we doing right now?"

They headed back to another alley between buildings, for the most part, ignored by all the other magicals going about their business in the kemana.

"Eat your spanakopita, Amanda." Adalynn nodded at Teo, who

opened a side door in the alley that should have led right inside the tailor's shop. Instead, the shifter girl was ushered right into Adalynn Jade's study.

When Teo followed them and shut the door, the door disappeared, and they were once again standing in the circular room without any windows or doors. Every single parcel, package, and bag Adalyn had taken from the business owners in the kemana was now piled on top of a huge trunk on the side of the room, and the woman smiled at her cache.

"Thank you, Teo. I'll let you know when we're finished."

The Kilomea snapped his fingers and disappeared.

Amanda's head spun. "I thought this room was underground. I mean, even *more* underground than the main kemana—"

"My office is nowhere near the kemana." Adalynn sat behind her desk and delicately finished her meal before wiping the corners of her mouth with a napkin. "It's safer for everyone that way."

"For all the magicals you shook down out there, or for *you?*"

The woman's sharp gaze bore into Amanda, and she gestured toward the empty chair in front of her desk. "I'm not sure exactly what you're insinuating, but please. Do have a seat and explain it to me."

The scent of the freshly made spanakopita in her hand made Amanda's mouth water, but she couldn't quite bring herself to eat it. She did, however, make her way slowly to the chair. "We're not in the kemana?"

"No."

"Then why does Shep have to bring me *here* twice a week?"

"Well, for now, Amanda, this is where I have business."

"You mean like shaking down all those magicals for whatever's in those boxes." She nodded toward the chest covered in all the mystery gifts.

Adalynn's eyes widened. "You think it was a shakedown?"

"Yeah. Are you some kind of mob boss?" The second it was out of her mouth, she regretted asking it.

*I'm letting Shep's gossip get to me. But what else was that out there?*

"I can assure you, Amanda, every magical I spoke with tonight is a completely willing party in our common arrangement. Those plotting their moves in High Tide Ammo three weeks ago, however, were not part of the arrangement."

"That didn't answer my question."

Adalynn's mouth twitched in a small smile. "No. I'm not a mob boss. Nothing I do within this kemana or any other is illegal. Our rules run these underground cities of ours—*magicals'* rules. No, I'm most certainly not at the top of the food chain although I do have ties to certain…organizations. Both known and unknown."

"Like the bastards who killed my family."

"Language, please." The woman crossed one leg over the other and sat back in her ridiculously tall desk chair. "A foul mouth doesn't make you any tougher than you already are. Nor does it make you seem older, more mature, or more capable. I don't want to hear you speak like that during our time together. Do you understand?"

The paper tray in Amanda's hand crunched when her grip tightened on it automatically. "Do you work for the magicals who killed my family?"

"No."

"You said you know who did."

"I said I might be able to help you *find* them, Amanda. There's a difference. Your food's getting cold."

"I'm not hungry."

A thin laugh escaped the woman. "I highly doubt that. You're a teenage shifter. Eat, and I'll tell you what you witnessed in the kemana tonight. I have no interest in trying to have a conversation with a girl who's even more bullheaded and unpredictable on an empty stomach."

Amanda glared at her.

*She thinks she knows me. She thinks she knows shifters and who my parents were and how to help me. I don't have any other choice but to find out, do I?*

She crammed the entire spanakopita into her mouth in one gigantic bite, then crumpled up the paper tray. Her point probably would've been a lot more effective if she didn't have to spend two whole minutes chewing, but the spanakopita was a lot bigger than she'd thought. When she finally swallowed it all down in a loud gulp, Adalynn looked at her again. "So what were you doing with all those magicals if you weren't collecting payment or protection money or whatever?"

"I was accepting gifts. Nothing more."

"For what?"

The smile disappeared from the woman's face. "From having still managed to correct the problem in that weapons store three weeks ago. The magicals within the Everglades kemana wanted those two idiots out of business. They came together as a community and enlisted my help. You and your friend almost botched that completely, I might add. Fortunately, I only work with individuals who know how to pivot and adapt to changing circumstances. That's what I thought of you when we met, but now you seem to have it in your head that I'm a negative influence and someone with whom you'd rather not spend your time."

Amanda wiped the grease from her mouth with the back of a hand. "Maybe that's because I have no idea what you are."

"What I am has nothing to do with what I can show you, Amanda. Or with the connections I can make for you and the final pieces of your puzzle I can help you put together. If the time ever comes when you need to know that specific detail, you'll know. Until then, I suggest you focus on what's in front of you instead of the answers you don't have."

The girl's fist came down on the armrest. "I don't even *know* what's in front of me! All you said was that you brought me here so you can pay off a debt to my dad, but I have no idea what that is or why I should trust you. Or why I came back at all."

"Because your curiosity has had very little outlet over the last few months. Maybe even your entire life." Adalyn set both hands firmly down on the surface of her desk and leaned forward. "Because you're all alone at that school of yours, through no fault of your own. And because I may quite literally be the only magical you have access to who can help you reach the next stepping stones of your potential. Yes. To repay an obligation I feel I owe your father. And a little bit because I like you."

Amanda shrugged. "Why? You don't even know me."

"That's true. We've only had two meetings so far, but I still recognize in you what I've recognized in so many others. Namely shifters."

"So you think we're all the same, then?"

"In some ways, you *are* all the same. However, it takes a certain kind of shifter to be open to the possibility that there's far more than meets the eye." Adalynn cocked her head. "You can't honestly tell me you haven't given in to the fate everyone else seems to expect from you. That you're nothing more than an unpredictable magical with the ability to shift your form but good for very little besides muscle and acrobatics."

"I can do more than that."

"I know. I also know quite a few of your kind who believe the same and have accomplished what the rest of both worlds previously thought impossible. Shifters who want more, as you do."

Amanda couldn't decide whether to laugh at the woman or sit quietly and wait for more of the story to show itself. "I don't know what you want from me. I already tried doing magic. It worked with a soul stone, but I had to give that back to the dead magical it belonged to in the first place."

Adalynn raised her eyebrows. "You stole a soul stone?"

"No. I…borrowed it. With a friend."

"Ah. Well, I'm sure that was quite the adventure. I'm talking about more of an alliance, do you understand?"

"Nope." The girl folded her arms. "I don't understand anything you tell me."

"Well, at least we're finally getting honest with each other. I told you I have connections with certain organizations, Amanda, and I meant it. Have you heard of The Coalition?"

*The Coalition. On the note Ralthorn gave me. How the heck does Adalynn know about that?*

"Yeah, I've heard of it."

"Good. I intend to fulfill my obligation to your father. He wanted access to The Coalition, and I wasn't able to give it to him. However, I can set up a meeting for *you*. If you think you're ready."

"Of course I'm ready. But I don't..." She frowned, trying to put the pieces together.

"You don't know who they are." Adalynn chuckled. "The Coalition is a coalition of shifters, Amanda. Of those like you who were tired of being shoved into the background because they can't perform magic like *everyone else*. Trust me. There's much more to being a shifter than you've been shown in your short life. I need to know that you can keep this to yourself. Understand?"

"Yeah. Yeah, I can keep it to myself. What does that have to do with me being here with you twice a week? All those packages you picked up from the kemana?"

"It doesn't. I wanted to see how you'd react. There's a reason secret societies are difficult to gain access to. Once I know you *can* keep a secret, especially after today, I'll be able to connect you with The Coalition."

"That doesn't—"

"Teo."

The Kilomea shimmered into existence.

"She's ready to go. Please give her chaperone my regards on the way out."

"Wait." Amanda stood. "Why won't you—"

Teo snapped his fingers, and the dark blue light shimmered around them both before they returned to the tiny space behind the iron doors.

"—tell me what I'm…" Amanda blinked and turned to scowl at the Kilomea. "You couldn't let me finish my question?"

"It'll have to wait 'til next time." He opened the door, and there was Shep, rolling up his magazine to stick it in his back pocket again. "Ms. Jade sends her regards, wizard."

Shep looked startled by this but nodded vigorously as the Kilomea practically shoved Amanda through the doors. Then the iron closed again with an echo.

"So." Shep took off his cap to scratch his head, then tugged it back on again. "How did it go this time?"

Amanda glared at the iron doors. "I have no idea."

"Well, I reckon that's usually a sign you're headin' in the right direction." He chuckled and gestured back down the alley. "Time to get back up topside, girl. Couple of fellas down there by the extra-dark shops sound like they're about to get into the kinda tiff I ain't fixin' to stick around for. Come on."

Trying to make sense of the huge waste of time Adalynn had dragged her through, Amanda stalked off after her chaperone to head back to the kemana's main level, the surface of the island, and the airboat back toward the Academy.

*I hate mysteries. I still have no idea who or what she is.*

Even then, she didn't think she'd be able to refuse any future invitations from Ms. Jade.

*The Coalition. That's who I've needed to find all along. If they can't help me find who killed my family, I'll have to look elsewhere.*

# CHAPTER TWENTY-ONE

That meeting Adalynn held over Amanda's head didn't happen over the next few weeks. The shifter girl went through the motions of her classwork, dealt with Summer's permanent cold-shoulder, and lied to her other friends about where she went every Tuesday and Friday night. All while learning nothing from Adalynn but how to organize files she wasn't allowed to read, even when Amanda said she'd settle for figuring out how the heck this teleportation spell Teo always used worked. None of her questions were answered, including where Adalynn's office was, if not inside the kemana itself. Still, she couldn't abandon her agreement with the woman who was either an actual mob boss of some kind or who knew the right people. Maybe for the wrong reasons.

The rest of her focus went to her new flowering plants in the greenhouse. The shoots were growing with remarkable speed, and even though Amanda couldn't entirely focus on her school-work when she had to leave campus twice a week without being able to tell anybody, at least she had something positive to show for her efforts.

Valentine's Day rolled around, which Principal Glasket

thought was an excellent opportunity to announce the upcoming Spring Fling dance at the Academy the next month. "Any student who would like to be a part of the decorating and preparation process for the dance should speak to Ms. Calsgrave. She's heading the entire setup this semester. Those who offer significant contributions will get first pick of the school-sanctioned events they wish to head next year. Yes, we do still expect you to dress up. Dates are optional, of course."

Grace snorted as the principal dismissed the impromptu assembly at the end of the school day. "So you're hanging around for the party, right?"

Amanda stared at her with wide eyes. "What party?"

"The Valentine's Day party?" The blonde witch gestured toward the kitchens, where paper hearts fluttered around the outdoor cafeteria under a constant-motion enchantment. "I'm pretty sure it's nothing but cookies and candy. BethAnne said she thought the pixies were making everything for dinner in the shape of hearts."

"Oh, great." Jackson rolled his eyes. "So we're having heart-shaped meatloaf? I mean, what else can you put in a cookie cutter and shape like that?"

"Pretty much anything they want." Grace laughed. "Pixies, remember? I'm pretty sure there's no rule in cooking that says magic can't be involved."

"Hey, if a chicken doesn't look like a chicken on my plate, I don't wanna eat it." Jackson smirked at Amanda. "Unless *you* do, Coulier. You can be the taste-tester."

"Well, I'll be here for dinner." She shrugged. "I can't stay for the party."

"Why the heck not?"

"It's Friday…"

Jackson rolled his eyes. "That's right. You're off to your secret meeting with some secret whoever. Why can't you tell us what that whole thing is anyway?"

"It's a personal thing." Amanda caught sight of Summer walking toward the cafeteria, where the pixies would set out dinner on the banquet tables in the next fifteen minutes. The black-haired witch glared at her but didn't say anything. *I have no idea why she's still pissed at me.*

"Okay. Personal thing. Sure." Jackson clapped his hands together. "You handle your thing every Friday night for the rest of the semester, and I'll eat your share of the cookies."

Alex shook his head and took off toward the kitchens.

Grace put a sympathetic hand on Amanda's shoulder. "Well, maybe they'll set out some cookies *before* the party."

"If they don't, you should save some for me."

The witch laughed. "Sure. Late-night snack. I'll stick them under your door."

"Sounds good to me."

All the other students were still in the outdoor cafeteria when Amanda met up with Shep to start their trip to the kemana. The pixies had laid out a ridiculous spread of cake and cookies and candy, and from what Amanda could hear as she and her chaperone headed toward the northern border of the school, some of the kids had made up some kind of magical spin-the-bottle game.

*Like anyone's gonna follow through with that. I'm kind of glad I have an excuse to get away from all that.*

"So. You got any Valentines today?" Shep muttered.

She laughed and wrinkled her nose. "No way. I never understood this anyway."

"Yeah, me neither. Figured I'd ask. I had me one of them cookies, though, and I tell you what. Those pixies know what they're doin' when it comes to sweets. Good thing it's Friday. Reckon all the other kids'll be spikin' 'n crashin' on all that sugar in the next hour. Whew. Somethin' I'd rather not have to witness if you ask me."

"Yeah." Amanda glanced over her shoulder when a round of shrieking laughter came from the cafeteria, followed by an explosion of someone's magically set-off fireworks that were probably supposed to be shaped like hearts but looked like giant red and pink blobs.

---

Her visit with Adalynn wasn't any more of an improvement, either.

"You keep saying I'll get to meet these Coalition shifters." Amanda finished labeling the last of the three dozen potion vials the woman had told her to go through, then closed the lid on the box that looked like a miniature treasure chest. "But something tells me you wanted a free office assistant."

Adalyn sipped the cocktail in her hand and smiled. "You're not wrong about that. These things take time. The more I can tell them about you, the more I can *vouch* for you, the more likely they are to agree to this meeting. Plus, they've been busy the last few weeks. You'll meet them when it's time."

*Right. When it's time. She better not be lying about this whole thing.*

"I know you have difficulty with patience, Amanda," the woman added as if she could read the girl's thoughts from the other side of her circular study. "Do trust me on this. When you can sit here and sort through my personal belongings *without* asking me why, you'll be ready to meet them."

Amanda rolled her eyes but didn't say anything else until her few hours with Adalynn Jade were over. Shep was right there waiting for her when Teo let her back through the iron doors that didn't lead to the woman's study in the first place.

---

When she got back to her dorm room a little after 10:00 p.m. that night, all she could think about was flopping down on her bed and getting a decent night's sleep. *Who knew doing busywork for absolutely no reason could be so exhausting?*

Her door encountered a little resistance as she opened it into her room, and whatever was on the other side whispered against the floor. Amanda stepped inside and smirked at the paper plate of cookies shaped like hearts, cupids, and arrows. Most of them had already fallen off the plate because they hardly fit all together under the door. With a tired chuckle, she stacked the cookies onto the plate again and took them with her to bed. Of course, she had to try at least *one*.

And of course, trying only one turned into trying all half-dozen as she sat on her bed and stared blankly at the far wall of her dorm room. *Thanks, Grace. Late-night cookies are exactly what I needed.*

Sucking the rest of the strawberry frosting off her fingers, Amanda froze when she saw the folded piece of paper on the floor. Frowning, she got up to investigate. The handwriting wasn't recognizable at all, but then again, she hadn't paid attention to anyone's but her own. At first, she thought it might've been another note left by Ms. Ralthorn.

*Maybe she found out more about The Coalition and realized she'd given me nothing to go on with the first one. Why would she slip it under my door?*

It wasn't from Ms. Calsgrave or any other teacher. That much was clear.

**Meet me behind the kitchens tomorrow night. 11:00. You know how to get out.**

No signature. No clue as to what this little meeting was supposed to be about or why it had to be arranged through a note slipped under her door.

Amanda took the note back with her to her bed and peeled off her clothes to change into her pajamas.

*It wouldn't be Summer. Besides the fact that she's still pissed at me for not breaking all the rules with her anymore, she wouldn't leave me a note. She'd only tell me tomorrow.*

With a shrug, she wiggled under the covers and turned off the lamp on her bedside table. It didn't matter who left the note. Right now, she needed to get some sleep.

*And practice "being patient."*

She snorted and rolled her eyes. As if Adalynn Jade knew anything about what shifters needed.

The next morning at breakfast, none of her friends knew a thing about the anonymous note left under her door. Grace owned up to shoving a plate full of cookies into Amanda's room but had no idea about the note's sender.

"Secret admirer, maybe?"

Amanda crunched on a strip of bacon. "Don't secret admirers usually write something that's, you know…admire-y?"

"Maybe it was Summer," Alex suggested.

"No, Summer doesn't leave notes."

"You think someone's trying to get you in trouble?" Grace smirked over her glass of orange juice. "I mean, everyone knows at this point that you've figured out how to sneak out of the dorms after Lights Out."

Amanda's eyes widened. "Seriously?"

"Yeah. Isn't that how you and Summer got detention the first time last semester?"

Jackson shrugged and muttered, "Not to mention getting all the extra food from the kitchens."

"How does everyone know about that?"

Grace laughed. "Well, it was only rumored until two seconds ago."

Alex burst out laughing, and they all turned to stare at his uncharacteristic amusement. The Wood Elf shook his head, tossing his dark ponytail back over his shoulder. "You wouldn't hold up very well in an interrogation."

"I'm not being *interrogated*." Amanda couldn't help but laugh with him. "You guys are my friends."

"That's what *you* think."

"What?"

Alex's laughter stopped abruptly, and he got up from the picnic table to take his plate to the trash. "I'm kidding. It's good to know you'd tell us stuff even if you weren't facing torture and dismemberment."

Then he walked away without another word.

"Jeeze." Amanda scratched her head. "Does he seem way more morbid than usual to you guys?"

"I think it's 'cause he might be failing Alchemy," Jackson muttered, staring after Alex as he left the outdoor cafeteria. "Which might be because he's failing at *not* being in love with Zimmer."

"Or maybe Alchemy's hard," Grace offered with a shrug. "I haven't been able to get the measurements right for the transmutation of...whatever the heck we're supposed to be turning those lava rocks into. I'm pretty sure Zimmer's given us an impossible assignment to make some kinda point, but I have no idea what that point would be."

"That we're freshmen," Amanda muttered. "And that we have to *be patient*."

Grace and Jackson stared at her. Then both shook their heads. "That's not right."

"Why would *that* be the lesson?"

"I don't know. It's what's on my mind, I guess." Amanda stood to take her plate to the trash. "I'll see you guys later."

"What are *you* up to today, Coulier?" Jackson called after her.

"More gardening. Gotta get *something* right, you know?"

"Shifter with a green thumb." He chuckled. "Is that normal?"

Grace wrinkled her nose at him. "How should *I* know?"

CHAPTER TWENTY-TWO

Amanda spent almost the entire day in the greenhouse, leaving only to join the rest of the students for lunch again in the cafeteria before taking another long shift with the center trough full of her fast-growing Everthorn plants. Already, the things were almost eight inches tall and now sprouted tiny royal-blue flowers in clusters between the heart-shaped leaves.

"At least I can grow something in here. So I won't fail Illusions class." She scoffed. "Growing plants for Illusions credit. That's ridiculous."

Still, she found a certain kind of meditative rhythm in caring for the plants here. Watering them, sharing her thoughts out loud as she tested the dampness of the soil and occasionally brushed her fingers against the undersides of the glittering blue petals unfolding now with incredible speed.

*I could get used to this whole greenhouse thing. Maybe Calsgrave's onto something here.*

Then she locked up before dinner, smiling at the flowers that seemed to glow happily back at her from the plants sprouting in a neat line down the length of the center trough.

There was a little talk among the other students at dinner about who wanted to help set up for the Spring Fling dance and who would ask whom to be their date. Most of the upperclassmen, the seniors especially, seemed to think having school dances every semester was a waste of time. Still, Amanda heard them muttering to each other about how to make the dance even *more* epic than their last attempts at Homecoming first semester.

*They think they're too cool for all the regular high school stuff, but they're still excited.*

That night after Lights Out, Amanda sat on her bed with the anonymous note in her hands and considered whether or not she wanted to go out and meet whoever had sent it. There was no way it could have been from anyone outside the school, like Adalynn Jade or one of her *employees.* That would've been too juvenile for the woman. So it had to be a student, right? Unless one of the teachers was trying to catch her sneaking out again, but that didn't make sense. The teachers were doing everything they could to *help* Amanda as the Academy's only shifter student.

When 10:55 p.m. flashed across the alarm clock on her night-stand, she tossed the note onto her bed and stood. "Screw it."

Her curiosity was too strong to ignore.

She padded across the room and paused in front of her door, listening for sounds of movement or anyone else out and about in the girls' dorm. Nothing.

*Probably not another prank to get me outside for a surprise party. They already did that for my birthday.*

It was as easy as every other time she'd snuck out. The halls were empty. The low lights in the common room that never entirely turned off at night glowed in greeting when she reached the bottom of the stairs. And the hole in the security enchant-ment around the building's back door was still there— the sulfuric stink of the wards gave way to the salty, slightly sweet nighttime air.

Amanda went through her usual process—propping the door open with the tin bucket from the broom closet, shifting, and carrying her clothes in her jaws before leaping through the door's narrow opening. Then she shifted back again and quickly tugged on her clothes before searching the darkness on campus.

*At least whoever left the note wasn't trying to catch me in the act out here.*

The swamp around the school buzzed with the soft drone of year-round insects, and the occasional nocturnal animal rustled in the underbrush as she made her way toward the kitchens. The pixies were still awake—they always seemed to be awake, or maybe they needed very little sleep. Fred's large form passed behind the closest window, casting a shadow across the grass outside. He didn't look out to see the shifter girl sneaking toward the back of the kitchens in the thick darkness.

Amanda held her breath as she rounded the back corner of the building and stopped. "*Jackson?*"

He jumped in surprise even though she'd only whispered his name. Then he turned toward her with a sheepish grin. "You came."

"Yeah." A surprised laugh escaped her. "*You* left that note?"

"I mean, I had Blake slip it under your door for me." He ran a hand through his shaggy blond hair and shrugged. "Now I have to do her homework for the next week, but it was worth it. Right?"

"Um...I guess."

"This is so cool." The wizard's eyes lit up under the stars, and he cast the kitchen building a glance before pointing toward the edge of the swamp lining the campus. "We should get away from the buildings, right?"

"Sure. What's going on?"

"I did it!" Jackson hunched his shoulders and immediately

lowered his voice. "I finally figured out how to sneak past the enchantment. Looks like you had no problem with it either, huh?"

Frowning, she walked beside him away from the kitchen, both of them casting wary glances around the campus to be sure no one else was out and about and could see them. "I mean, yeah. Good job, I guess. Why did you have to send me a secret message to get me out here, though?"

"Well, because...I mean, it's secret, right?" They stopped by a thick stand of cattails shielding them from view—if anyone had been looking—and the wizard's excitement at sneaking out and finding Amanda out here with him faded into wide-eyed nervousness. "I wanted to talk to you about..."

He frowned when she swiped her hair out of her eyes and stepped toward her. "What's that?"

"What?"

"On your forehead." Jackson gently brushed his fingers against her head, then frowned at his hand. "Blue dust?"

"Oh." Amanda dusted off her hands and smiled. "It's from the greenhouse. The flowers bloomed really fast. I guess I didn't notice they left a bunch of dust everywhere. Is it still all over my face?"

He studied her intently, then shook his head. "No, you're..."

"Jackson? You okay?"

The wizard frowned and stared at nothing over her shoulder.

Amanda took a step back and eyed him warily. "Hey. You look like you're gonna be sick."

"What? No. I'm not sick. I'm—" He lurched forward a little, exactly like someone who was trying not to be sick but couldn't control their stomach. "I'm—"

"Whoa. Maybe you should go get some water or something—"

"I want you to go to the Spring Fling dance with me as my date." The words rushed out of him in a single breath, and he froze. "Wait. What?"

Not knowing what else to do, Amanda turned and scanned the edge of the swamp. *Is this a joke?*

"I didn't say anything..."

"Yeah, I know. I didn't mean to say *that*." Jackson clamped a hand over his mouth and started breathing heavily. "I don't know what happened. That was weird. Why would I *say* that?"

She laughed softly. "Because you wanted to ask me? Wait, is *that* why you wanted me to meet you out here?"

"No." Jackson's eyes widened even more, and the look he gave her seemed a lot like desperation. "I wasn't planning on asking you in the first place. I guess... Well, it's out now, so... What do you think?"

He grimaced at her, and she shrugged.

"Yeah, okay. I mean, I wasn't planning on going with anyone or having a *date*, exactly. But we can go together as friends."

"Yeah. As friends. Okay." A hesitant smile broke through his confusion, and he wiped his blue-dusted fingers on his jeans. "Cool. I guess that worked out, then."

"Okay. So, are you gonna tell me why you asked me to meet you out here, or—"

"Um...I'm gonna go back to the dorms." He clapped a hand on her shoulder and nodded as his usual carefree grin returned. "Thanks for coming. Now I know it works."

"What?"

"The hole in the enchantments, Coulier. And slipping notes under your door by promising to do all Blake's homework for a week. See ya."

Without waiting for her to say anything else, Jackson darted off across the grass toward the kitchens and the boys' dorm on the other side of the girls'.

Amanda was left standing there all by herself beside the cattails, and she huffed out a laugh.

*What the heck was that?*

A faint tap of what sounded like glass on metal rang across

the campus, followed by a grunt. That could only have been Jackson sneaking back through the hole in the enchantments—in the window of the first-floor bathrooms.

She shook her head. *That was even weirder than finding Summer out here every time I snuck out last semester.*

After drawing a deep breath of the crisp night air, she stepped between the cattails to hide before she shifted. Then the small gray wolf padded through the other side of the reeds and moved silently through the swamp.

*Might as well go for a run while I'm here. It's been forever.*

---

Neither Amanda nor Jackson ever noticed that someone else had snuck past the security enchantments in the dorms that night too. Summer had followed them, staying upwind in the brisk night air now that she understood the way things worked when a shifter girl snuck out at night.

The black-haired witch had almost blown her cover completely when Jackson had staggered back toward the boys' dorm, looking sick and excited at the same time. Fortunately, neither of the other students had bothered to pay that much attention to who else might be out there. Standing upwind on the *other* side of the kitchens had kept Summer hidden the whole time.

She saw Amanda vanish into the cattails, saw the brief flash of a wiry gray tail darting into the swamp five seconds later, and scowled.

*I see how it is, shifter girl. Hanging out in the kemana all the time with some lady who says you owe her for stealing her stuff. Sneaking out with that* wizard *now.* Summer flipped a middle finger at the cattails where Amanda had disappeared, then headed back across the campus. *Fine. If you're done being friends, you should've said so.*

## CHAPTER TWENTY-THREE

At the end of February, they got their grades back from Mr. LeFor on their automated tech projects, AKA magical robots. Amanda hadn't expected to get amazing marks on her last-minute idea for a robotic butler that helped pick out clothes, which Corey hadn't had a single hand in helping her with. However, LeFor looked especially pleased when he tossed the graded rubric down in front of them at their table. "Inventive. I have to give you that. Daily application could've been a little more fleshed out, but overall, not bad. If you two want to team up again for another project, I'm fine with it. It'll be interesting to see what else you come up with."

Then the teacher moved on to deliver grades to the other students. Corey had his face buried in both huge hands the entire time, and he peeked between two of his thick fingers. "What'd we get?"

Amanda stared at the write-up with a slowly growing smile. "B-plus."

"What? Lemme see." He snatched the paper out of her hand and scrunched up his face as he went over the notes LeFor had left under each rubric item. "Whoa. That's, like, way better than any grade I've ever gotten."

"Yeah, *we* did a pretty good job, right?" She nodded toward LeFor and tried to give her "partner" a subtle hint that they weren't entirely off the hook yet.

"Totally. B-plus. Huh." Corey scratched his head. "What did we make again?"

"A robot that picks out your clothes, remember? Pretty easy to put together. Not a lot of daily application, apparently. Because...nobody needs help picking what to wear, I guess?"

"Yeah, yeah. Right. Hey, you wanna do my other projects for me too—"

"Shh!" She scowled at him and shook her head. "No. Don't ask me that again. Just...I don't know. Find a different partner next time."

"B-plus! Woo!" The half-Kilomea thrust his hand into the air and waved their graded rubric around with a goofy grin. "I got a B-plus!"

Amanda met Grace's gaze and shook her head. The blonde witch gave her two thumbs-up. Beside her, Annabelle pored over their graded rubric for the project and scowled. "Not enough originality? Are you kidding me? We had that maid robot cleaning *toilet bowls* at the end! How is that not original?"

Grace leaned toward the dwarf girl and muttered, "We got an A-minus. That's good—"

"No, it's not. *Minus*, Grace. That's not the best we could do." Annabelle shoved the rubric into her backpack and folded her arms. "Don't worry. I'll talk to Mr. LeFor after class about our grade."

"Oh, great." Grace scratched the back of her head and leaned away from her partner.

"Mr. LeFor," Tommy shouted. "How come we didn't get a grade on ours?"

He and Jackson frowned at the teacher, who backtracked across the workshop-slash-classroom to eye their paper.

"Oh. You did get a grade. I didn't write it down." LeFor pointed at their paper, and a large red D appeared at the top. "I'm not entirely convinced of the practicality of your project, boys. I, for one, wouldn't put my trust in any piece of tech designed to deal with more...sensitive parts of my anatomy."

"What? Are you kidding?" Tommy spread his arms. "I've wanted one of these my entire life."

"Well, next time, Mr. Brunsen, try coming up with something that might be more effective and useful for *others*, not only yourself."

Jackson elbowed his partner in the ribs and pointed at their rubric. "Dude, we didn't fail. D's still passing."

"True. We get to keep the Asswipe4000, right?"

Mr. LeFor pinched the bridge of his nose as the class exploded with laughter. "By all means, Mr. Brunsen. Keep it and lock it up in your room. For all our sakes."

"All right!" Tommy and Jackson high-fived each other, and the other students kept laughing.

Amanda smirked at the wizard as he joked around with Tommy and their other friends at the back of the class. He looked up at her once and immediately blushed before ignoring her for the rest of the time.

After her next Illusions class spent in the greenhouse that week, she met up with Ms. Calsgrave for a progress report. "The Everthorns are doing well."

"Really?"

"Yeah. Already flowering like crazy. Petals everywhere. So I can probably start growing something else soon, right?"

Calsgrave shrugged as she closed the door to her office and headed down the main building's hall. "I think that could be the next step, sure. I'll come to take a look next week, and we can go over everything together. I might have a use for those flowers in mind if you don't already."

"No." Amanda shrugged. "I'm trying to grow stuff. Looks like I did a pretty good job."

"Absolutely." The teacher glanced down at the shifter girl's hands coated in blue dust. "It's good to see you getting your hands dirty without getting into trouble, Miss Coulier."

"Oh. Yeah. Thanks." Amanda wiped her palms off on her jeans.

"Mrs. Zimmer's incredibly happy with the grub skins you brought her. I'm sure you'll see those pop up as some kind of new reagent in your Alchemy class. She wanted me to ask you what you had planned next that can be grown and harvested for materials in her class as well."

Amanda smirked. "So you *did* give me the greenhouse so I could grow ingredients for the school."

"That's only part of it." Calsgrave winked at her as they stepped outside into the afternoon warmth. "The rest of it was nothing more than a feeling I had about you."

"Really? What kind of feeling?"

"The way you put all the pieces together last semester. The visit from your familial spirits. Knowing our…disgruntled incorporeal visitor was looking for that stone to be returned and wasn't on a mindless rampage across campus. Herbalism is more than gardening and growing plants and harvesting them for certain physical attributes. It's also about putting the different pieces together. If you want a certain outcome, you have to start from scratch with identifying and growing certain plants. So far, I think you've got the hang of it. So think about what you'd like to plant next, and next week, we'll talk about putting those Everthorns to good use."

Feeling unusually productive and optimistic, Amanda grinned and headed toward the outdoor cafeteria for lunch.

Her friends joined her at the picnic table. They talked about everything but the upcoming Spring Fling dance, mostly because Jackson kept pulling the conversation away from that particular topic every time Grace brought it up.

"What's wrong with you?" the blonde witch finally asked him, leaning forward across the table. "You suddenly don't like dances, or what?"

"I mean, I never really had a thing for them in the first place." Jackson shrugged and avoided Amanda's gaze altogether. "What about this whole stupid thing with running Petrov's course in *teams* now? Like, how are we supposed to make sure everyone else on our team finishes when *none* of us have been able to run the whole thing on our own?"

"We should ask Corey to carry us all across," Alex muttered.

They burst out laughing.

"What? He's strong enough."

"And have the guy crash down off the platforms with all of us in his arms?" Jackson punched his friend in the shoulder. "I don't think so. I'd rather be shot down by *all* the sergeant's magical guns than smashed under Corey's weight. And all that hair." The wizard shuddered. "No thanks."

"We should tear the whole thing down," Grace muttered, resting her chin in her open palm. "Then we wouldn't have to keep killing ourselves to fall off and be sore all day."

"Hey." Amanda grinned. "That's not a bad idea, though."

"I was *kidding*."

"Yeah, but maybe you're onto something. Think anyone would be down to tear the thing apart? Like, maybe at night or something?"

"And risk Petrov screaming at us the next day for breaking his stuff?" Grace shook her head. "No thanks."

"Good luck trying to get the whole freshman class to sneak out of the dorms at night anyway." Alex crammed a large forkful of salad into his mouth. "You know, enchantments and everything."

That made Jackson look up at Amanda, and his eyes widened before he cleared his throat. "Yeah, well, we can dream, right? I'm outta here, guys. Gonna fit a nap in before History."

"Why?" Grace laughed. "You could nap *in* history. Ralthorn doesn't notice."

"Yeah, but I'm not trying to fail *every* class." Jackson stood and went to throw his trash away.

Alex shot him a glance over his shoulder. "What's *his* problem?"

Amanda shrugged. "The dance is coming up. Then finals for the end of the year, right?"

"Ugh. Don't remind me." Grace rolled her eyes. "We haven't gotten a *hint* about what's gonna be on the finals. How are we supposed to study if we don't know what we're studying *for*?"

"A test on everything we've learned this year." Alex stared at the witch as if she'd grown an extra pair of eyes. "That's what finals *are*, right?"

"We still need to know what to study. What about you, Amanda? You feel like you could ace the finals without knowing what they're on?"

"I have no idea. I mean, one final's about finishing the obstacle course. For Illusions, I'd keep...what? Growing stuff in the greenhouse?"

"True. You have it easy, don't you?"

Amanda scoffed. "Hardly."

"Well, at least you get to leave twice a week for your secret meetings you won't tell any of us about." Alex's voice echoed inside his plastic cup before he chugged down the rest of his water. "Still not gonna say anything about it, huh?"

"I can't, guys. Sorry."

"Yeah, we know." Grace stood. "Hey, you wanna compare

notes from Ralthorn's last class before we have to sit down and take more?"

Alex and Amanda both stared blankly at her.

"Nope," the Wood Elf said plainly.

"Not even a little."

Grace folded her arms. "You guys don't take notes, do you?"

They both shook their heads.

"Okay, fine. I'll go find Annabelle, then. See ya."

Alex focused on the rest of his lunch and muttered, "Is that supposed to give you better grades? Taking notes?"

"Only if we have a note-taking class."

# CHAPTER TWENTY-FOUR

Amanda's next trip to the kemana was a lot more eventful than she'd expected. Shep dropped her off in the usual spot outside the iron doors, and Teo's glittering blue teleportation spell whisked her away to land inside Adalynn Jade's circular study.

She was so used to the process at this point that she went straight to the metal folding chair and the wobbly card table set up for her on the side of the room. "So what am I doing tonight? Polishing your silver?"

Adalynn chuckled behind her desk and deposited a stack of papers into one of the large drawers before sliding it gently shut. "That would be an excellent idea if I owned any silver. Maybe I'll have you work on the crystal instead. Or *crystals*, specifically."

Amanda paused beside her chair to look at the woman. "Are you talking magical crystals or the kind that has to be so clean someone could eat off it?"

"Who says they're mutually exclusive?" The woman smirked at Amanda's confused frown, then stood from her desk chair. "You won't be cleaning or organizing anything tonight, Amanda. I have something much different in mind."

"Great." The shifter girl plopped into her chair and huffed out a sigh. "Let me guess. Picking up packages. Going around to all the shop-owners in the kemana to tell them you're still here and they can give me any message they have for you. Yeah, I know, we're not technically in the kemana right now, but they don't know that, do they?"

"Sometimes, you're remarkably perceptive." Adalynn stepped around her desk and leaned against its edge. "Tonight, I'd say you're getting ahead of yourself."

"Okay, so what am I doing, then?"

"How about a meeting?"

Before Amanda had the chance to ask what kind of meeting or with whom or even whether Adalynn was serious, a flash of dark blue light came from the other side of the study behind the large mahogany desk. When it disappeared, a woman with long, thick red hair stood in its place. Her loose-fitting jeans, light jacket, complete lack of makeup, and heavy brown boots made her look even more out of place in Adalynn Jade's study than Amanda.

After so many weeks of smelling nothing but herself and the occasional musty scent Teo left behind during his brief visits to the room, the smell of another shifter here with them was overwhelming.

Amanda leapt out of her chair and stared at the red-haired shifter woman. "Who are you?"

The woman turned her head to shoot Adalynn an unamused glance. "You haven't told her."

"I was waiting for the right moment." Adalynn spread her arms. "If I'd brought this up any sooner, we'd both be too bombarded with questions to get started."

"What's going on?" Amanda muttered.

Adalynn gestured toward her and raised an eyebrow at the woman. "See? Amanda, this is Fiona Damascus. She's an emissary from—"

"The Coalition," the girl whispered.

Fiona chuckled wryly. "Well, at least you've told her *that* much. It's nice to meet you finally, Amanda. I've been looking forward to this for quite some time."

"Wait. What?" Amanda cocked her head. "I thought you were—"

"Well, now that we're all here, I suppose it's the perfect time to sit down and have this little meeting we've all been anticipating so much, yes?" Flashing the shifter woman a winning grin, Adalynn gestured toward the empty leather armchairs in front of her desk. "Have a seat, Fiona. Amanda, come join us."

Fiona didn't take her gaze off the shifter girl as she slowly made her way toward the armchair Amanda had been sitting in for every conversation she'd had across Adalynn Jade's desk. Adalynn herself returned to the tall leather office chair, and Amanda's feet shuffled beneath her as she crossed the room.

*She's been looking forward to this for quite some time? What kind of game is Adalynn playing here? She said The Coalition was busy and couldn't make it any sooner.*

This thought made her scowl at Adalynn as she plopped down into the chair beside Fiona.

"Oh, don't look so disappointed," Adalynn crooned. "This is what you wanted, isn't it?"

"Yeah, but—"

"Amanda." Fiona sat back in her chair, folded her arms, and smirked at the girl. "Tell me what you know about The Coalition."

"What?" She looked back and forth between the women staring at her. "Nothing. She wouldn't tell me anything."

"I assumed that was better left up to you." Adalynn nodded at Fiona. "Straight from the shifter's mouth, as it were."

The red-haired shifter playfully rolled her eyes. "Of course you did. She obviously knows *something*—"

"Coalition of shifters," Amanda blurted. "Started because you were all tired of everyone else saying shifters aren't really magical. I mean, no, we can't cast spells and stuff, but we aren't…*not* magical."

Fiona's hazel eyes narrowed above a slowly growing smile. "Keep going."

"That's it. Or…I don't know. Maybe that The Coalition is a secret society, and you guys are trying to either figure out some way to prove we're more than instinct-driven wolves who tear out throats. Or maybe you're trying to do real magic." Amanda shrugged. "Or maybe you're like the shifter mafia, which makes sense if Adalynn knows you so well."

The shifter woman burst out laughing. "You told her you were a gang boss?"

"Absolutely not." Adalynn swiped at her wispy bangs and chuckled. "She came to that conclusion all on her own."

"Yeah, well, you didn't exactly deny it."

"Why don't we focus on what we can *all* agree on?" Fiona raised an eyebrow at the shifter girl. "That we want this meeting to happen and that *you* are up for the challenge of continuing forward afterward. Am I correct?"

"I guess it depends on what that challenge is supposed to be."

"Well, let me start by saying we're all incredibly grateful Ms. Jade found you when she did. We tried to locate you after we received word about your family. Let me extend The Coalition's full condolences to you for that, Amanda. Truly."

"Okay." *A sorry wrapped in a bunch of fancy words doesn't really mean anything almost a year later.*

Fiona nodded. "Of course, we didn't fully understand what had happened to you after the fact. How or why you'd disappeared that night—"

"I didn't disappear." Amanda's fists clenched in her lap. "I was kidnapped. The assholes who killed my family and kidnapped me were gonna sell me on the black market to the highest asshole bidder. So call it what it is."

Fiona and Adalynn exchanged a quick knowing glance, then

the shifter woman hummed. "I suppose you've been through enough to earn that one. Calling it what it is. Now I'm here to tell you exactly what Bruce Coulier wanted from The Coalition and why we wish to continue pursuing what we never had the chance to begin with your dad. If, of course, you still want to hear it."

Amanda glanced at Adalyn, who simply cocked her head and offered a small, deferring shrug. "I do. I had no idea my dad knew anything about other shifters, let alone The Coalition. He barely even let Claire and me go out for runs unless we were camping out in the middle of nowhere."

"That was probably part of why he came to us before the end. Your dad was a good shifter. A good husband and dad and all-around family man. As I understand it, even his squeaky-clean record in finances still brought him several unsavory clients. Those who threatened him if he refused to make certain investments for certain entities that went against everything he'd built the foundation of his firm on. Everything he believed in."

"You mean he wouldn't launder money, so they killed everyone but me. Is that it?"

Fiona's eyes widened. "You sound like you've heard all this before."

"I haven't, but I know enough about shitty people *and* magicals to put two and two together."

Adalynn cleared her throat. "We discussed the use of strong language—"

"It's fine." Fiona raised a hand toward the woman without looking away from the scowling shifter girl. "She had a right to speak her mind this way. I'm not interested in censoring a twelve-year-old girl who—"

"Thirteen."

"What?"

"I turned thirteen in December." Amanda swallowed the lump in her throat. *I always wanted to know what happened to Mom and*

*Dad, didn't I? Why they're all gone, and I'm still here. So why is it so hard not to get up and walk away?*

"Of course. Happy belated birthday, then." Fiona ran a hand through her hair and shrugged. "Did Ms. Jade tell you that your dad had reached out to us through her?"

"Yeah, that he tried." Amanda shot the scentless woman on the other side of the desk a condescending glance. "She was too busy to pay attention, so I guess you didn't get the message until it was too late."

"That's...an oversimplification. Although partially accurate, I guess." A frown flickered across Fiona's eyebrows. "We didn't receive those messages from Ms. Jade until about a week after your family's tragedy. We'd heard *you'd* survived, Amanda, but it was impossible for us to step in and do anything about it. Which you don't have to understand. Just know—"

"You don't have to apologize for that." The shifter girl shook her head. "It all worked out in the end anyway, and I'm pretty sure the magicals who *did* step in and do something about it were the best ones who could've found me. So you're off the hook."

"Right." The shifter woman tried hard to hide a smile. "Then I'll stop trying to be gentle."

"Sounds good."

"Bruce wanted The Coalition to take you and your sister under our wing. To expose you to strength in numbers of our kind, which isn't the traditionally thought-of *shifter pack*. Though I suppose you could call The Coalition something of a brotherhood. We're trying to change the way the rest of both worlds view us, Amanda. Your dad knew he'd gotten sucked in too far over his head with his refusal to give in to the kind of thugs who were blackmailing him and threatening his family's wellbeing. I can only assume he wanted his final act to be for you and your sister. To deliver you both to us so we could teach you what he couldn't. Ms. Jade was merely the go-between for setting up this kind of agreement, and yes, unfortunately, she delivered your dad's request too late."

"And now...what?" Amanda shrugged. "You feel guilty for three dead shifters and another one who was almost sold into slavery, so you want me to be a part of your brotherhood now? That doesn't make up for the fact my family's *dead*."

"It most certainly does not," Adalynn interjected. "However it is, at the very least, a good start in actively honoring their memory."

For a moment, Amanda didn't know what to say.

*I don't wanna be the little girl who gets to join a secret shifter society so everyone else can finally clear their conscience. That's not my job.*

"I already have new guardians," she muttered, glancing back and forth between the women. "I don't think I could get any better ones, even if they were shifters."

"You're referring to Johnny Walker and Lisa Breyer, aren't you?" Fiona nodded. "I'd have to agree with you there. They've done an excellent job with the resources at their disposal."

"What's that supposed to mean?"

The shifter woman shrugged. "Well, they're not one of *us*, for starters."

"You can't turn me against them—"

Fiona barked out a laugh. "That's the last thing we're trying to do. Joining The Coalition doesn't mean you have to give up anything or turn against anyone. It's adding a little more knowledge and support base under your belt."

"You want me to join you." Amanda folded her arms. "Why?"

Both women sighed, and Adalynn glanced down at her manicured nails before picking at the edges around them. "I did tell you she was skeptical."

"Yes, you did." Fiona still stared at the girl. "You think we're trying to right our wrongs and nothing else. Is that it?"

"That's what it sounds like, yeah."

"Amanda, we know where you go to school. We know where

you live when you're not at the Academy of Necessary Magic and spend your breaks between semesters at the bounty hunter's cabin in the swamp. We know what you've been involved in over the last ten months since your life was turned upside-down." Fiona spread her arms. "We could use a bounty hunter in our ranks. If you're willing to learn the ropes."

"I'm not a bounty hunter yet."

"No, but you will be. Until you graduate with more practical knowledge under your belt, The Coalition can help with the hands-on experience side of things. What do you think?"

Despite her reservations, Amanda couldn't help a small smile. "I might be interested."

"Is that a yes?"

She grinned. "Okay, fine. Yeah. It's a yes. I have one question."

Fiona chuckled. "I'll try to answer it the best I can."

"Can shifters do *any* kind of magic?"

The red-haired shifter turned to share an amused glance with Adalynn, then stood. "That one will have to wait for a later time. I look forward to our next meeting."

She stuck out her hand toward Amanda, and the shifter girl wrinkled her nose. "Can't even answer *that* question. Figures."

She stood and took Fiona's hand anyway. The woman's grip was tight and a little painful, but it made Amanda smile all the same.

"Then that settles it." Adalynn stood from her desk chair and nodded at Fiona. "I'll oversee all the arrangements."

"I wouldn't trust anyone else to do it."

"Thank you for your time, Fiona."

The shifter woman walked toward the back of the circular study, and when Adalynn snapped her fingers, Fiona Damascus disappeared in a blaze of dark blue light. Then the woman turned her attention back to Amanda. "Well. I'd say that went fairly well."

"You couldn't have told me all this from the very beginning?"

"I told you this was about your ability to hone your patience, which you did. Now, if you can *keep* your grip on it, I imagine you'll learn everything you want to know about The Coalition and your abilities."

"So..." Amanda glanced around the study. "Are you finally gonna tell me what *you* are?"

Adalynn's thin smile didn't look all that amused. "Your time's up early tonight. You know the drill."

Teo appeared in another burst of blue light, and Amanda snorted as she joined him and got ready to be teleported to the fake room behind the doors.

*I have no idea what the drill is. But it looks like I'm finally about to find out.*

# CHAPTER TWENTY-FIVE

Her other visits to Adalynn Jade's study in the next few weeks didn't include more meetings with Fiona Damascus or any other emissary from The Coalition. Apparently, Amanda's new shifter friends still had to finish *preparing* to bring her on board, whatever that meant. The only thing she got out of Adalynn was to keep being patient.

*They picked the wrong kid for being patient. Or the wrong magical race. Since when did shifters start preaching patience and waiting all the time?*

Fortunately, she had other things at school to grab her attention, like deciding what to cultivate next in the greenhouse and how in the world she was going to pull off going to the Spring Fling dance with Jackson as *just friends* when she knew that wasn't what he wanted.

"How do I even know that?" She tipped the watering can over the Everthorn flowers and leaves for the fifth time the morning of the dance. The blue petals shimmered and sparkled under the water as if they were responding to the shifter girl's thoughts voiced aloud. "Maybe he does wanna go as friends. But he was acting so *weird* about the whole thing—"

A knock sounded on the greenhouse door, and Ms. Calsgrave stepped inside before Amanda could tell her it was open. "You know, I'm happy to see you spending even your free time on the weekends in here."

"Well, I mean, that's probably the only way to get these things not to die, right?"

The Illusions teacher chuckled. "You're dedicated. I like that. I came to see how things are coming along now that you've... Oh, *wow*."

Amanda set the watering can on the workbench at the end of the center trough and grinned. "Pretty great, right? They came up way faster than I expected."

"They're beautiful. These are...Everthorns, you said?"

"Yep. Picked them right out of the binder, and we had the seeds, so..."

"Yeah. You went all out. Only the energy grubs as fertilizer?"

The shifter girl shrugged. "I mean, unless you count love and attention as an actual fertilizer too."

Calsgrave smirked. "Well, you never know. I only stopped by to see the progress in here, but now that I'm looking at the flowers, I think these would be perfect for the dance tonight."

"What?"

The teacher shook her head and blinked rapidly, pulling her gaze away from the sparkling blue petals. "It fits the theme. Something along the lines of 'Midnight Magic.' You know, dark blues, black, artificial starlight. Miss Porter volunteered to handle the starlight illusions, and I have to say I'm pretty impressed with what she's done so far. *These* flowers would be perfect as decorations. Maybe even corsages to hand out to the other students."

Amanda wrinkled her nose. "Is anyone even gonna *want* a corsage?"

"We'll make it optional. If no one wears them, we can pin them up around the dancefloor. Have any plans for the day besides the dance tonight?"

"Not really. I was gonna hang out in here and, you know, be an herbalist."

Calsgrave chuckled. "Then why don't we prune off some of the biggest flowers and work on making some decorations? There's something…extra about these blossoms."

"Yeah, okay." Turning toward the green metal cabinet on the other side of the greenhouse, Amanda hid her smile from her teacher and focused on grabbing an extra pair of gloves and two sets of gardening shears.

*Something extra, huh? Maybe it's because a shifter's growing the plants in here. Hey, perhaps* that's *my extra magic.*

The thought made her snort.

"Everything okay?"

She closed the metal cabinet doors and returned to her teacher, who still gazed at the Everthorn's blue flowers as though caught in some kind of trance. "Everything's good. Never thought I'd be on a decorating committee for school dances, but whatever."

Calsgrave took the extra gloves and the pair of shears and smiled at her student. "I like your perspective on it. Now, is there anything I should know before I start cutting away at these—"

The harsh snip of Amanda's shears cut through the greenhouse, and two fully bloomed flowers dropped into her hand on the ends of their long, delicate stems. She grinned. "Nope. Looks like it's totally safe."

---

They worked together for the next two hours to trim the fully opened flowers from the long row of Everthorn bushes filling the center trough. Ms. Calsgrave seemed way more excited about the process of weaving the flowers into strands of gold and silver ribbons to make the corsages, chattering away about whatever popped up into her head. Amanda ignored most of it, probably because she didn't understand most of the *spiritual lingo* that made up most of her teacher's blabbering.

*Let her talk, I guess. Everybody needs to get stuff off their chest, and it's not like I have anything better to do right now.*

When they finished, they had almost fifty shimmering corsages laid out on the longest workbench sitting against the wall of windows. Shimmering blue dust coated everything—the wooden benches, the outside of the troughs, the baskets Calsgrave had fetched to hold the finished decorations, and their fingers.

"Well, if they aren't happy with these, then I'd have to say *they're* the problem," Calsgrave muttered.

"Who?"

"Kids." The witch blinked rapidly, then looked up at Amanda with a sheepish smile. "I'm sorry. Did I say that out loud?"

Amanda laughed and dropped the last corsage into the basket. "Yep. I get it though. A bunch of magical kids running around the school can't be the easiest thing to deal with."

"Trust me, Amanda, it's one of the hardest things I've ever done with my life—" Ms. Calsgrave clapped a hand over her mouth and gasped. "I need to stop talking."

"Are you okay?"

"No. I mean, yes. I'm..." The teacher abruptly stood and scooped up the basket filled with ribbon and twine and flowers. "I'm going to take these out to the central field and find the perfect places to hang some of them. The other students can wear the rest if they want. If anybody complains, they'll have to suck it up and deal with it. Bunch of ungrateful little—*what?*"

Now Calsgrave looked terrified by what had come out of her mouth.

"Please forget I said any of that."

"Secret's safe with me." Trying not to laugh, Amanda mimed zipping her lips shut, then pointed at her teacher's face. "You have some petal dust all over your mouth, though."

"Oh my goodness." Rubbing vigorously at her face with the sleeve of her light sweater, Calsgrave hurried into the hallway. "See you at the dance. Great job with the greenhouse. And I... I don't..."

The woman frowned, blinked rapidly, and took off down the hall.

Amanda raised her eyebrows and slowly gazed around the greenhouse. "I guess teachers get nervous about dances too. Maybe she should garden more."

That made her laugh, and she worked on cleaning up the rest of the gardening tools and the extra leaves and stems picked off the Everthorn flowers. When she was almost finished, the sound of breaking earth and dirt toppling onto the floor made her turn around.

"What the actual heck is that?"

A massive mound of dirt rose at the end of the trough, making the last Everthorn plant shiver above the surface. Then another wave of soil exploded and toppled over the edge onto the floor. The grub emerging from the mound of dirt was twenty times its regular size, its purple and orange spots shimmering with an extra layer of silver light. The thing let out a squeak that sounded like a baby bird, then started gnawing furiously on the closest plant.

"No!" Amanda leapt toward the end of the trough and smacked the grub's gelatinous hide. The thing trembled under the blow like a giant pile of Jell-O but kept munching the flowers and leaves of the plant in front of it. "Hey. Cut it out!"

When she smacked it again, the grub turned its weirdly eyeless head toward her and belched a spray of purple light and shredded leaves. It smelled like the fake grape flavoring in the medicine she and Claire used to get when they were little. The chewable kind.

Amanda grimaced and turned to look around the greenhouse. She barely avoided being pushed into the other trough beside her when the grub flopped out over the side and plopped onto the floor. The sparkling purple kept spraying from its mouth. Some of it landed on one of the adjacent trough's legs, and the shifter girl smelled charred wood.

"No, no, no. I am *not* letting this place burn down because one giant worm got too…giant." She raced down the aisle as the grub kept spewing magic and sparks that caught on the undersides of the wooden troughs. Then a low, rumbling growl rose from the thing's throat.

She snatched up a full-length shovel and spun with it in hand to see the grub launching itself across the floor toward her. With a surprised shout, she swiped at the creature with the head of the shovel. A sickening *smack* filled the room, and the giant magical worm rolled over and over under the other two troughs. It picked itself up and inched its way toward the open greenhouse door leading into the hallway.

"Hey! No you don't!"

Amanda darted after it and reached the doorway first, where she managed to kick the grub back a foot. It yelped, then opened its shimmering mouth and attempted to spew magical sparks at her again.

She swung down fiercely with the shovel. The sharpened end sliced into the grub's flesh and split it open down the middle. Neon-orange goo and more sparks splattered all over the floor and bit into her sneakers. The air in the greenhouse was thick with that weirdly fake grape smell, and a burst of purple glitter sprayed up from the thing's belly before it finally fell still.

"Ew." Amanda stood over the giant split grub with the shovel in one hand and wrinkled her nose. "How the heck did you even *get* that big without me noticing?"

She shut the greenhouse door just in case, then headed toward the workbench with the starter binder lying open on its surface and the *Magical's Guide to Magical Greenery* right beside it.

She shot a few glances over her shoulder, but the monster worm was well and truly dead.

"Where was it even *hiding*?"

After looking up everything she could find on the energy grub one more time, Amanda didn't read anything particularly new in either the binder or the encyclopedia. But the entry she remembered reading stuck out even more now.

**Not a sentient species but still prone to become invasive if not consistently harvested and disposed of. For best disposal practices for the energy, see Chapter 23: Sustainable Magical Ecosystems on page 274.**

"Invasive. Why can't they simply write 'the things grow to the size of a cocker spaniel and spew magic at you?'"

Still, she looked up the ways to dispose of said grubs on page 274. Fortunately, all it took was salt. There was a whole plastic tote full of the stuff on the bottom shelf of the metal cabinet. Once she'd dumped almost half of it on the giant grub lying split-open inside the door, she shrugged and decided to leave the mess there for now.

*Never said how* long *to cover it in salt. If this thing isn't* disposed of *by tomorrow, I'll ask the kitchen pixies for more.*

With that, she put the plastic tub away, locked up, and dusted her hands as she left the main building. Time to get ready for the Spring Fling dance.

---

Grace and Annabelle tried to convince Amanda to let them dress her up again for Spring Fling as they had for Homecoming, but she refused. "I'm not a big fan of dresses, okay?"

"Oh, why not? You looked so *good* in that one last time."

"Yeah, and then it got shredded up by some wild boar tusks." Amanda shrugged. "Sorry about that. Again."

Annabelle burst out laughing. "Nobody cares about a

shredded dress. You know what I *do* care about? Dressing up for a school dance. Come on, Amanda. *Please?*"

"Not this time. Thanks, though."

The dwarf girl looked her up and down and grimaced. "You're not gonna wear *that*, are you? Look at all this… What even *is* that? You get into a box of glitter or something?"

"Oh, jeeze." Amanda dusted off her pants in the middle of the dorm's third-floor hallway. "It's from the stupid flowers."

"What flowers?"

"They're part of the decorations for tonight, I guess. You know, from the greenhouse. It was Ms. Calsgrave's idea. I helped her put them together and make the corsages—"

Annabelle shrieked in delight. "We have *corsages?*"

Amanda blinked. "Yep."

"You should've said *that*. Grace, help me do the rest of my hair. Then we get *corsages*."

Grace laughed and headed into Annabelle's room after her. "Do you have a date for the dance?"

"No. That doesn't matter!"

The blonde witch turned back toward Amanda and shrugged. "What about you?"

"Going with friends."

"Uh-huh. Sure. I guess we'll see when we're all out there on the dancefloor. So you better—whoa!"

"Come on!" Annabelle jerked Grace into her room, and their laughter filtered out into the hall as the dwarf girl instructed the witch exactly how to do the rest of her hair.

Amanda headed down the hall toward her room, smirking at Annabelle's shouted instructions and Grace laughingly telling her it was impossible to do it *exactly* the way she wanted.

*Being dressed up for one dance was enough. This time, I'm doing my thing.*

# CHAPTER TWENTY-SIX

Amanda ended up wearing a black skort Lisa had bought her for her birthday, which had at first made her crack up laughing until the half-Light Elf had explained it. "Hey, you can dress up with one of these if there's an occasion, but it won't stop you from being able to run if you have to."

Thinking about that made the shifter girl smile as she pulled the rest of her dark hair into a ponytail and headed down the hall toward the stairs.

*I didn't come to bounty-hunter school to dress up all fancy and go to a dance. I can't back out now, though. Jackson'll lose it.*

The other girls raced out of the girls' dorm with her, fawning over each other's dresses and hair and whatever little jewelry they had to put on for the occasion.

"Anyone know what the theme is for this one?"

"I heard it had something to do with black magic?"

"What? Is that even a thing?"

"It might be *tonight*?"

"Ms. Calsgrave was walking around with a huge basket of flowers…"

"That doesn't mean anything about a *theme*."

Amanda tugged down the hem of her black tank top and tried not to look too smug about it. *Midnight Magic. I guess they're not technically wrong.*

"Come on, Amanda." Grace raced ahead of Annabelle, wearing a silver, shimmering dress with thin spaghetti straps. "You're gonna love it."

"Hey, I heard you had a hand in the stars—"

"Shh." The blonde witch clamped her hand over Amanda's mouth, then immediately pulled away. "Sorry. It's supposed to be a surprise, okay?"

"Yeah. Got it. Good job on the *surprise.*"

Grace grinned. "Thanks."

The students made their way from the dorms to the central field, which was like last semester's grand reveal of the dance theme—sectioned off by the archway and the shimmering veil of fabric enchanted with an illusion to keep anyone from seeing the other side until they stepped through the arch. Amanda and Grace walked through together, and the witch's glinting smile of pride lit up with Amanda's widening eyes.

"Whoa." Amanda tossed the end of the veil aside and looked up to see one of the small bouquets of Everthorn flowers tied to the outside of the arch. A shimmer of glittering blue dust rained down when the fabric brushed against the flowers. Or maybe that was the shimmer of the entire central field.

The decorating committee had transformed the entire dancefloor and setup of snack and drink tables into some kind of dark, star-studded universe. Huge orbs that could have been moons or other planets glowed in the dark and hung at various heights over the dancefloor. A low illusion of billions of sparkling stars hung maybe twelve feet over the central field, casting a flickering silver glow over everything.

"*You* cast that illusion?" Amanda muttered.

Grace shrugged. "I mean, I had some help. It came together

pretty well, right? Oh, hey. Are *those* the flowers you were talking about?"

The witch pointed at a table inside the archway, where the basket of Everthorn-flower corsages lay beside a sign that read, "Enjoy the Midnight Magic."

"Yeah. That's them."

"Wow, you *grew* these?" Grace took off toward the table and struggled to wait patiently while the other girls ahead of them grabbed their corsages first.

"It was easy. I didn't know anything could grow that fast."

"Well, whatever you're doing, keep doing it. These are great." Grace snatched up two corsages and handed one to the shifter girl. "Here. Put it on. Then at least you'll look a *little* dressed up. Oh, jeeze. What's with all the blue dust?"

"Comes off the petals." Amanda finished slipping the loose ribbon wrapped around the flower stems over her wrist. "It adds to the ambiance, maybe?"

"Sure." Grace shrugged and ran her shimmery-dust-coated fingers through her hair, leaving behind faint blue streaks in all the blonde.

"I *like* it," Leah said as she passed, eyeing Grace's hair longingly. "Where'd you get that stuff?"

"From the *corsages*."

A large group of girls flocked toward the table and the basket to put the ribbons over their wrists and run the flower dust through their hair or on their faces. Amanda snorted. "That's one way to get them excited, I guess. Hey, I'm gonna—"

"Go check out the snacks? Yeah, I figured." Grace shot her a thumbs-up. "Have fun. Oh, hey! Find me when the Lady Gaga song comes on!"

Amanda strolled through the throng of kids spreading out on the dancefloor. *I don't know any Lady Gaga songs. I guess she'll have to find me.*

A navy blue tablecloth studded with twinkling stars draped

the banquet table on the far end of the dancefloor. The platters were stacked high with puff pastries made to look like glowing planets, and delicately thin cookies dyed a dark blue and cut into intricate swirls. She grabbed one of these and crunched down on it—blueberries and cinnamon.

"Figured I'd find you here first," Jackson said before cramming a puff pastry into his mouth. "Oh, *crap*, this is good. Have you tried one of these?"

Amanda shook her head and ate the rest of the spiral. "You should try these too. If you like blueberries."

"As long as it doesn't taste like a glass of milk, I'm in."

They moved down the table together, trying the star- and planet-shaped snacks as they went. Jackson kept glancing at her with wide eyes before reaching past the shifter girl to snag another handful of something else the kitchen pixies had whipped up for the dance.

*He's nervous. Even though we're supposed to be here together as friends?*

"So." Jackson swallowed heavily. "I would've picked you up outside the dorm, but I had to finish some stuff. Sorry."

"It's fine." Amanda wiped cookie crumbs off on the sides of her skort. "I mean, probably wouldn't be if you had to pick me up to come to a dance, but good thing we all live a five-minute walk away, right?"

"Yeah." The wizard chuckled nervously. "Not like you need a ride for a date that's not a date either, right?"

"Right." She tried to smile, but it felt way too forced. *This isn't going very well, date or no date. I don't even know what the difference is at this point.*

"So Grace did the whole stars-in-the-sky thing, huh?" He pointed at the illusion overhead.

Amanda crammed another cookie in her mouth and nodded.

"Hey, what's that?" Jackson reached for her wrist as she lowered it from her face. His fingers brushed against the flowers and came away covered in blue dust. "These are *your* flowers, huh?"

"Oh, yeah. They make a mess, but everyone else here seems to like the glittery effect."

The wizard wrinkled his nose. "I can't stand glitter. It gets everywhere, and then you have to deal with it all over you for the rest of your *life*."

She laughed. "I don't think it lasts that long."

"Isn't the *guy* supposed to give that weird wrist-bouquet thing to the girl at these dances?"

The rest of her cookie went down the wrong way and almost made her choke. "What?"

"You know, 'cause you're my date to the dance, right? So I'm supposed to do all this stuff for you. You're stealin' my thunder. You know that?"

Amanda stared at him, then Jackson's eyes widened, and his mouth popped open like he'd had no idea what was coming out of it.

"I said all that for real, didn't I?"

"Uh…yeah." She pulled the corsage off her wrist. "Didn't mean to screw it up. You can give it to me and pretend that happened from the beginning if you want."

He stared at the bundle of flowers and ribbons, then shrugged. "You want me to give you flowers?"

"I didn't say that—"

"I mean, I totally will if you want me to. If that's what you like or whatever. I mean, girls like flowers, right? Even shifters? I have no idea—" The corsage flew from Jackson's hand and toppled onto a plate of cookies when he clapped both hands over his mouth. "What the hell is going on?"

"It's okay. Really." Amanda grabbed the corsage and two cookies with it, then handed one to her friend. "I didn't think you'd be so nervous."

"I don't know *what* I am! What's wrong with my *mouth*?"

She was about to tell him nothing, that they were all trying to figure out how *not* to make a school dance weird. Then someone screamed on the other side of the central field—an angry scream.

"You've *never* been my friend! All you do is take my stuff and use it for yourself! What do I get out of it? Nothing. 'Cause you suck!"

"Um...Caroline?" The junior girl getting a full-on tongue-lashing from her friend shrank into herself and smiled nervously at everyone now staring at them. "Can we talk about this later—"

"No. I don't want to talk about it later, Becca! You're the worst friend I've ever had."

"Wait a second." Becca tried to grab her friend's arm, but Caroline swung out of the way and pushed the other junior away. A burst of blue dust spewed from the corsage on her wrist and made Becca blink heavily.

"Don't touch me!" Caroline spun away and stormed off across the dancefloor.

The other students made way for her as she headed toward the archway and the shimmering veil hanging from it. Becca looked like she was about to cry, then noticed the other students staring at her. "What's *your* problem, huh? You're all jealous! And this dance sucks!"

Her hands lifted toward her mouth, and she frowned in confusion before storming off the dancefloor too.

"That was weird," Jackson muttered.

"Yeah." Amanda slowly bit down on another cookie. "I thought maybe this dance would be less eventful than the last one..."

"At least it's not a bunch of wild pigs."

Another girl broke into huge, wailing sobs in front of the stage. It was Candace, her face contorted in surprise and pain. "Why would you *say* something like that?"

"Because no one's ever said it to your face, and you need to hear it." George Harland shrugged her off when she tried to grab his hands. "No. You can't cry about it and make me feel bad. Maybe if you spent less time worrying about the way you look and more about, you know, being a good person, people would feel bad for you."

"I don't need your pity, George Harland."

"Good. You don't have it."

"Well, you're a stuck-up, selfish—"

"Dude, back off!" A fight broke out at the table beside the archway, where the basket of corsages was almost empty. Another senior shoved Jimmy against the table and shook one of the last corsages at him. "I was here first, you little twerp. It's not like *you* have a date. You're eleven!"

"You're an asshole!" the tiny Jimmy shouted back before attempting to fight the other senior over the corsage. It was the most any of them had heard the small kid say all semester.

"What is going on?" Amanda gazed at the central field, which was quickly sinking into chaos.

Girls broke down crying and ran through the crowd. Brandon Everly stood stock-still in the center of the dancefloor, staring in horror as Jasmine pulled down the strap of her dress and showed him a scar normally covered up by clothing. "I thought I was gonna *die* that night, Brandon. Do you hear me? I have no idea who was chasing me through the park, and now every time I walk alone in the dark, I think I'm gonna get attacked again…"

"It wasn't me. I promise," a sophomore boy howled above the music. "My sister thought I stole her money and told me to leave, and I *did*. I didn't even try to explain what happened, and now I don't even know if she's alive!"

"I have dreams about killing everyone on the entire planet!"

"I hate wearing deodorant!"

"I have no idea when my birthday is, and I've been changing it every year!"

Jackson dropped the half-eaten cookie in his hand. "Um… Everybody's losing it."

"Yep." Amanda blinked and gazed from one student sinking to the ground in her dress and sobbing uncontrollably to the group of sophomore guys getting into a shouting match over absolutely nothing as their "dates" tried to pull them away from each other.

*What's going on?*

Annabelle jumped up onto the table beside the archway and snatched up the last corsage from the basket. "You're all *losers*! And I *still* can't get straight A's even though I'm smarter than all of you!"

She chucked the corsage at a group of freshman girls gaping at her. A puff of blue dust coated all of them when the ribbon-wrapped flower bundle hit the closest girl in the head. Then they shouted back.

"You're literally the shortest girl here!"

"And you have the *biggest* ego. Give it a rest, Annabelle!"

"Oh, no." Amanda looked down at the corsage in her hand and rubbed her fingers together, sending a shimmer of blue dust down to the ground at her feet.

"Time for us to split, probably," Jackson said behind her. "Hey, if you wanna get away from all this, you and I could go find somewhere private that—"

"Maybe stop talking before you say something you'll regret." She shook her head at him and took off toward the stage, where the teachers had gathered to enjoy the dance and now stared in shock at the entire student body losing it on the dancefloor. "Sorry. I gotta go... Sorry."

She darted around another fistfight breaking out, and when her corsage crashed against one of the boys' shoulders with another puff of glittering blue flower dust, she chucked it as far as she could away from the central field.

Principal Glasket had taken the stage now and tried to get the students' attention with an amplifier spell instead of waiting for one of LeFor's magical microphones. "Everyone needs to settle down, please. This is the Spring Fling dance, not a fighting ring—"

"Nobody likes you, Glasket!" someone shouted and tossed a shoe at the stage.

"That's *Dean* Glasket—"

"You're not a dean, either. Who even uses that anymore?"

Amanda raced toward the stage as the principal got over the shock of hearing her students' opinions shouted out in her face. "Dean Glasket? Hey, sorry. Can we—"

"Mr. Harland!" the principal shouted, pointing across the field. "Keep your hands to yourself! What is going *on?*"

"Dean Glasket?" Amanda slammed her hands down on the stage and stared up at the angry principal. "I think there's—"

"Not right now, Miss Coulier. I'm trying to deal with a... I don't even know what this is." Glasket kicked the randomly flung shoe off the stage. "All of you need to get ahold of yourselves *right now!*"

"I can't do this. I can't do it." Mr. Petrov gripped both sides of his bald head and spun with wide eyes as if he saw ghosts everywhere. "I don't even *like* kids. I don't know why I took this job in the first place. All I ever wanted to do was have a nice, quiet farmhouse somewhere. An apple orchard. Nice little stream babbling away in the background. But no, I'm here. Teaching a bunch of kids with authority issues how to climb a damn jungle gym!" He ripped off the loose necklace of ribbon and Everthorn flowers from around his neck and chucked it at the ground. "I'm outta here!"

Ms. Calsgrave stepped quickly out of the way as the Combat Training teacher sprinted across campus toward the training field. Her wide eyes settled on Amanda. "What's going on?"

"I think it's the flowers." Amanda pointed at the necklace on the ground. *Weird that he was wearing this in the first place, but whatever.* "I think there's something wrong with—"

"Oh! Oh, no!" Calsgrave's hands flew up to her mouth. "I

didn't mean to put an enchantment on the corsages. I wasn't even thinking."

"Ms. Calsgrave, I don't think it was you. But—"

"Look out, Amanda." Alex brushed past her, clipping the shifter girl in the shoulder. "I got something to say."

"Alex, wait."

He didn't. Instead, the half-Wood Elf dropped to one knee in the grass in front of Mrs. Zimmer, who watched the chaos at the dance and didn't notice him until he grabbed one of her hands in both of his. "You're the love of my life."

"I'm sorry?" Zimmer scowled down at him. "What are you doing?"

"I don't care that you're married. He's a douche. I know I'm only fourteen, but I'll—"

"Whoa! Okay." Amanda leapt after him and hauled Alex to his feet. "Bad timing."

"There's never a good time for that." Zimmer shook her head. "Don't ever say anything like that again."

"We were made for each other—"

"Stop talking." Amanda spun Alex around and shook him by the shoulders. "You're saying all the wrong stuff. Go...eat some cookies or something."

"Will that make her love me?"

"Sure. Go." She cringed as he shuffled away toward the table.

"Miss Coulier."

Amanda spun to find Principal Glasket hovering in front of her. The scowl on the witch's face told her everything she needed to know. "I need you to join me in my office. Right now."

"Yeah, okay."

"You too, Ms. Calsgrave."

"I'm so sorry, Gladys," the Illusions teacher whined. "I had no idea."

"Save it for my office." Glasket stormed off toward the main building, and Amanda glanced over her shoulder to see Mr. LeFor take the stage.

"Okay, everybody. Pack it up!" he shouted. The music cut off abruptly, followed by a bright blaze from the floating decorative planets now acting as spotlights. "The dance has been canceled. All students back to the dorms."

"Why?" someone yelled back. "Because you never want us to have any fun?"

"Because all of you are acting like a bunch of crazies who've lost their minds. Let's go."

The students groaned, broke down crying, or burst out laughing at private jokes. Some of them, Amanda saw, were already realizing that what they'd been saying for the last twenty minutes wasn't what they'd intended to say out loud.

*Like Jackson and Ms. Calsgrave. Crap. What did I do?*

# CHAPTER TWENTY-SEVEN

Principal Glasket paced back and forth in her office, scowling in irritation and glancing at Amanda every thirty seconds. Clearly, she was trying hard not to bite the shifter girl's head off.

Amanda sat in the chair in front of the principal's desk, waiting for Ms. Calsgrave to return. *I have no idea what's going on.*

"I didn't do it on purpose," she muttered.

"I know that, Miss Coulier. That doesn't excuse the oversight. On any of our parts."

"Ms. Calsgrave helped me cut the flowers and put the corsages together. It was her idea—"

"I told you we would *not* have this conversation until Ms. Calsgrave returned." Glasket stopped pacing and studied Amanda's small flush. "Once she does, we'll be able to—"

The office door flew open, and the Illusions teacher stumbled inside, her hands covered with comically thick leather gloves and the *Magical's Guide to Magical Greenery* tucked under her arm. "Sorry. Sorry, I thought there was more resistance on this door."

She shut it again carefully behind her, and Glasket spread her arms. "Well?"

"Well... First, I guess I can say that if we'd had a little more time to prep the greenhouse before handing it over to Amanda, we might've gotten the labels down a little more effectively."

"Meaning what, exactly?"

Calsgrave hurried toward the desk and slammed the gardening encyclopedia down. She had to whip off the gloves to turn to the pages she wanted. "Meaning anyone could have made a simple mistake like this. I know, I know. Not simple with the side effect of the flowers. But honestly, Gladys—"

"Dean Glasket."

"Sorry. Honestly, *I* couldn't even tell the difference." Calsgrave finally stopped flipping through the pages and tapped the image of an Everthorn with the dusty, dark-blue flowers. "She didn't plant Everthorn. It was Dreamscape."

Glasket's mouth fell open. Then she looked at Amanda. "You had no idea?"

"No. I picked the first thing that looked cool in the starter binder and planted it. Wait, what's Dreamscape?"

Calsgrave shrugged. "It's very similar to Everthorn. Except for its magical properties, which all depend on how it's cultivated and by whom."

Amanda stood and hurried toward the desk to get a better look at the picture in the book. "No, that's what I planted."

"It's not. Dreamscape flowers in clusters of four. Everthorn has clusters of five. Other than that, they're almost completely identical to look at."

"We had seeds for this Dreamscape as well?" Glasket asked.

"Yep. The seeds look the same too, apparently. So those were mislabeled." Calsgrave shot the principal a sheepish smile. "At least we found the issue."

"Which is?"

"Well, the Dreamscape takes on the *aura* of the gardener, I guess you could say. Whatever the caretaker is thinking or feeling when, you know, nurturing the plants, that's what properties the flowers themselves take on. And they amplify the intention."

Glasket leaned against the edge of her desk and frowned at Amanda. "What exactly were you trying to achieve when you planted these, Miss Coulier?"

"What?" Amanda looked sharply up from the open page in the encyclopedia. "I was trying to grow some plants instead of wasting my time trying to cast illusions I'll never be able to cast." She glanced at Calsgrave and shrugged. "No offense."

"Absolutely none taken."

"That doesn't explain why every single student on this campus has suddenly lost their ability to filter what comes out of their mouth." Glasket tossed her hair out of her face. "Anything else you can remember about your time spent in the greenhouse?"

"I was gardening?" Amanda tried to stick her hands in her pockets, realized her black skort didn't have any and folded her arms instead. "I really like it, by the way. So I hope this doesn't, like, get rid of my greenhouse privileges or whatever."

"Try to focus, okay?" Ms. Calsgrave attempted an encouraging smile. "Maybe it had something to do with *why* you like it so much?"

"I mean, yeah. It's peaceful. I'm alone. The grubs were doing well, and the plants started growing. No one else is in there with me, so I can think out loud without anybody... Oh."

"Do share, Miss Coulier," Glasket muttered.

"I was talking to the grubs. And the plants."

"Oh, is *that* what's under that giant pile of salt?" Calsgrave asked.

"A giant grub, yeah. I'll clean it up later."

"I don't see how that has anything to do with the disastrous Spring Fling dance we've had tonight," Glasket interjected.

"Yeah, except it does. Not the giant grub, but everything else." Amanda grimaced at the principal. "Sorry. I was talking out loud in the greenhouse about everything that was going on. Because I didn't think I was supposed to talk to anyone *else* about it. That I couldn't tell anyone, you know?"

"I'm not sure I follow."

"All the stuff with…" Amanda shot Ms. Calsgrave a sidelong glance. "Ms. Jade."

"Who?" Calsgrave asked.

"Ah." Glasket looked like she'd swallowed a lemon. "A mutual acquaintance, Ms. Calsgrave. I think I understand now."

"Well, *I* don't." Calsgrave tried to brush the dusting of blue glitter off her pantlegs, then realized she no longer wore the gloves to protect herself and sighed. "This is impossible to get rid of. Why am *I* the one who had to go investigating in the greenhouse anyway? Isn't that part of *your* job?" As soon as she said it, the witch clapped a hand over her mouth. "I'm so sorry."

"Well, now we know what happened." Glasket gestured at Amanda. "Miss Coulier cultivated what was Dreamscape while sharing her thoughts and feelings no one else was supposed to hear. Now, anyone who touches the flowers loses their verbal inhibitions completely and says what they're thinking."

"It's pretty freeing," Calsgrave said with a chuckle. It died immediately under the principal's intense gaze. "Right. But not appropriate at a school."

"Miss Coulier?"

Amanda wrinkled her nose. "Yeah?"

"I can't hold this honest mistake against you, and I won't. I *will* hold you responsible for rectifying it. I suggest you get to work on an antidote for this…Dreamscape dust. Preferably now."

"Okay, but I don't—"

"Oh, it's all right here." Calsgrave flipped to the next page in the giant encyclopedia. "Everything you need to reverse the effects. Only we don't have any of those things at the school. Should probably put that on the list of things for you to grow next, right?"

Glasket grabbed her cell phone from her desk and made a call.

"Fortunately, we're incredibly close to a kemana that does carry those ingredients. Hi, Mr. Frederick. Yes, everything's fine. No, I know, the field will be back under control very soon. I'm sorry to inconvenience you on a Saturday night, but Miss Coulier needs to take an important trip to the kemana for me. Do you mind? Great. Thank you."

When she hung up, her lips pressed together so tightly they almost disappeared as she reached into a desk drawer and pulled out a small black handbag with a zipper. She handed this to Amanda and nodded. "To pay for whatever you need. Potions and supplies only, of course. Mr. Frederick will meet you behind the girls' dorm as usual, Miss Coulier. Please don't keep him waiting. I'd like to deliver this to everyone affected as quickly as possible."

"Yeah, okay. I'll go right now." Amanda spun to head for the office door, then stopped. "I'm sorry. I really didn't mean to—"

"Don't apologize." Glasket barely managed a small smile. "Just fix it."

With the black bag of money in her hands, Amanda hurried out of the principal's office and raced down the main building's stairs. *Better make this fast. I hope nobody spits out something they'll never be able to live down.*

Shep was all smiles and nods when he met her behind the dorm, and they headed out for a last-minute, unscheduled trip to the kemana. "Don't you worry yourself on my account for one second, girl. Understand? It's part of my job."

"On a weekend, though?"

"Sure. I'm the driver. Boat captain. Whatever I need to be whenever Dean Glasket needs me to be it. Don't worry 'bout that list of ingredients, neither. She sent me a picture of the whole list, so I got it right here in my pocket." He patted his back pocket where she assumed he kept his phone.

"Well, even if it's your job, thanks anyway."

"You bet." Shep removed his hat and scratched his thinning hair with one hand while the other gripped the throttle control stick of the airboat to keep them steady on the river. "Though, she ain't said what exactly happened out there in the field. Fancy dance party y'all were havin', and *poof*. Things got goofy."

"It's a...strong reaction to a new kind of plant in the greenhouse." Amanda shrugged. "One I accidentally grew without knowing what it does."

Shep chuckled. "That's how we learn, ain't it? Accidents 'n mistakes 'n it's all worth knowledge s'long as we keep from grinding ourselves down in the gutter over it. We'll get these supplies, girl. Sure. Then you got your antidote, and folks can all move on together."

"I hope so."

# CHAPTER TWENTY-EIGHT

Getting to the Hidden Market Apothecary was easy enough. With Shep reading off the antidote ingredients list, the Light Elf running the shop this late on a Saturday night quickly found everything they needed. He even threw in mixing up the ingredients to make the antidote right then and there and filled a hundred and fifty small vials full of single doses. Then he bundled up all the items in layers of tissue paper and stuck them snugly into a box before sliding that aside on the counter. "We'll call it three hundred even for everything."

"Wow. Okay." Amanda unzipped the black handbag and counted out Principal Glasket's money to pay the apothecary owner. "I'm really glad you had all this stuff."

"Uh-huh. I bet you are." The Light Elf squinted at her over a tiny smile. "You're one of them students up at that new Academy a few miles upriver, ain'tcha?"

"Yeah."

"Runnin' errands for Dean Glasket herself," Shep added, readjusting his belt and puffing out his scrawny chest in pride. "Reckon it's hard to run a school on her lonesome. We're happy to be of help."

"Right." The Wood Elf chuckled, took Amanda's money, and slid the box toward her. "No jostlin' these things. Understand? You get 'em mixed up, and they're more likely 'n not to blow up in your face before you can use 'em for…whatever pickle you got yourself in at that school, miss. Take care."

"Thanks." Amanda grabbed the box and tucked the handbag under her arm, feeling ridiculous with both of them in tow. "It's gonna be a long night handing this out to everyone who needs it."

Shep held open the door for her and grinned. "Well, like I said, I'm only the driver. Wouldn't even dream of steppin' in to try my hand at mixin' potions. Or deliverin' 'em. Come to think of it, I ain't never touched some of the stuff in that there box. Ain't fixin' to start tonight, neither."

"That's okay. You've already helped a lot by getting me down here to—"

A dark blue light shimmered in the air in front of her, and Amanda froze when Teo materialized out of nowhere. His upper lip stuck against his huge protruding eyeteeth when he growled low, "You need to come with me."

"What? Why? It's *Saturday*."

The Kilomea grunted. "Let's go."

"Now, wait a minute." Shep stepped forward. "Miss Amanda ain't down here to do whatever her business is with Ms. Jade. That's Tuesdays and Fridays. We're here on official school business and—"

Rolling his eyes, Teo snapped his fingers, and all three of them materialized inside Adalynn Jade's circular study. Shep sputtered and clapped a hand to his head as he gazed around. "Well, I never… Where's the door?"

"No door." Teo nodded at a hard-looking wooden chair behind the wizard. "Take a seat."

Amanda handed the handbag and the box of antidote to Shep, then glared up at Teo. "What's going on?"

"That's exactly what *I'd* like to know," Adalynn said from the other side of the room.

When the shifter girl spun, she almost charged toward the woman to give her a piece of her mind. She froze when she saw Summer tied to a second wooden chair with coils of white rope, a gag in her mouth and wrapped tightly around the back of her head. "What the hell?"

"Yes." Adalynn gestured at Summer as the girl struggled against the ropes. "I'm going to ask if you had any idea she was here, Amanda. Part of me hopes you don't *have* an answer. Because then you and I would have a serious problem."

"I don't know why she's here! You're the one who has her all tied up." Amanda ran across the study, and no one tried to stop her when she untied the gag muffling Summer's shouts of protest. "This is insane."

"This is how I deal with spies." Adalynn's nostrils flared as she watched Summer struggling. "Even amateurs."

"What do you mean? She's not a spy. She's my friend."

The gag fell from Summer's mouth, and the witch seethed at Adalynn. "You're the worst kind of magical for anyone to get involved with!"

"Oh, yes. Do tell me more." Adalynn rolled her eyes.

"Amanda, listen to me." Summer struggled against the ropes around her wrists as Amanda quickly tugged at the knots. Then the ropes fell to the floor. "You have to get away from this psycho bitch. She's trying to steer you down the wrong path. Get you into all kinds of screwed-up trouble—"

Adalynn's high, lilting laugh filled the room. "Is that so?"

"I know what you're up to!" Summer leapt from the chair and lunged toward Adalynn. "You have no idea who you're messing with. She's a *shifter*!"

"I know." When Summer's hand came down toward Adalynn's face, the woman caught the girl's wrist easily enough and tossed her aside. "You're out of your mind."

"Amanda, don't listen to her. I know I'm not crazy. I'm not. But she's gonna do something awful to you. You can't let this psycho get her claws into your head and start controlling you. She'll do it. She wants you dead!"

"Whoa, wait a minute." Amanda reached for her friend to try calming the other girl down. "Are you okay?"

"No!" Summer whirled around to snarl at the shifter girl. "I can't *stop* it!"

She raised both of her hands, and Amanda saw the coating of blue, glittering flower dust streaking across the witch's palms. "Oh, crap. Summer."

"I know you think I'm crazy and I don't care about you, but *you're* crazy if you think anyone who kidnaps teenagers and hides away in a room without any doors is good for you or even *safe*. She's hiding something!"

Amanda wrinkled her nose. "Did you touch the flowers at the dance?"

"What?" Summer backed away while shooting hateful glances at Adalynn and Teo standing guard beside the silent Shep in the chair. "What flowers?"

"The blue ones. Look at your hands."

"That's the stupidest thing I've ever heard. It's a bunch of glitter. You're being an idiot. Did you hear anything I said?"

"Yeah, I did." Amanda stepped between her raging friend and Adalynn Jade. "We had an issue with some Dreamscape flowers at the school. That's why I'm here. I got the antidote for this whole thing. *Summer's* here because...I don't know. Whatever she's told you, she's not thinking that clearly about it."

"What do you mean?" Adalynn's eyes widened as she looked down at Summer's blue-dusted hands.

"I mean, the flowers make it to so anyone who touches them can't keep their secrets to themselves anymore."

They both seemed to realize what it meant at the same time when Adalynn glanced at her hand—the same one she'd used to catch Summer's dust-coated swing at her face. Yes, there were streaks of blue sparkles across her palm too.

Adalynn backed away from the shifter girl. "Teo—"

"What are you?" Amanda shouted. "That's all I wanna know. Tell me what you are!"

It was a long shot, but that was the first question that popped into her head. *Now or never, I guess.*

"Amanda, this—" Adalynn clamped her mouth shut and gritted her teeth. The flush creeping up into her cheeks quickly darkened. "I won't…"

"Tell me. What's the big deal, huh? Why the secret?"

"I'm a Saithe, Amanda. Another Oriceran, like the rest of us in this room, only there are very few of my kind on Earth. No, you can't *smell* me because Saithe can block our scent and our magical trail at will." Adalynn's hand flew to her mouth, but she stopped it before her fingers could touch her lips and opted for ruffling her wispy bangs instead. "We…"

Her hand was trembling.

"Yeah, there's obviously more." Amanda folded her arms and fought back a smirk. She'd probably pay for this one later, but she didn't care. "Spit it out."

"We've had a partnership with shifters since the very beginning. On Oriceran and now on Earth too, for however—" The woman's teeth clicked loudly together, but she couldn't stop herself from continuing. "For however many of us there are on this planet. That's why I have the connections I do with The Coalition and how I'm especially suited to helping you with that transition—"

"What the hell is she *talking* about?" Summer hissed.

"Shit!" Adalynn looked startled by her outburst—either the volume of her shout or the fact that she'd finally lost control and cussed against her own rules.

On the other side of the room, Teo chuckled and folded his arms.

"Okay, hold on." Amanda raised both her hands for Adalynn and Summer to wait there, and they glared at each other while the shifter girl raced toward Shep. "I need two of those."

"Sure. Sure." He opened the box but refused to take out any of the vials himself. "Did I miss somethin', girl?"

"Yeah, probably." She raced back toward Adalynn and handed her a vial. "Here. Summer, you should take one of these too."

"Gross. That looks like someone puked in a vial."

"Drink it."

Adalynn didn't need any extra prompting. She snatched the tiny vial out of Amanda's hand, opened it, and drained the whole thing. A shudder rippled through her when she swallowed, then she patted her short hair and took a deep breath. "That was quite the underhanded—"

"That was me taking advantage of a situation out of my control." Amanda spread her arms and used all her willpower to keep the smile off her face. "Guess I was finally patient enough for long enough."

Adalynn tossed the empty vial into the open drawer of her desk, and the woman slammed it shut again before pointing at the shifter girl. "Don't ever bring this up again. Anything that's happened tonight, and anything you've heard. You and your friend can go. We'll no longer be meeting in the kemana."

"Awesome." Amanda grabbed Summer's wrist as the black-haired witch smacked her lips and scowled at the taste of the antidote.

"Jesus Christ, what *is* this stuff?"

"I don't know. Tell me your deepest darkest secret, and we'll see."

Summer jerked her hand out of Amanda's grasp and scowled at her. "Why the hell would I tell you something like that?"

"Well, the fact that you wouldn't means the antidote works."

"Teo, please see them out." Adalynn lowered herself stiffly into her chair and stared at the surface of her desk.

"Now, just one minute," Shep started as he stood. "Where you and Miss Amanda do and don't meet ain't up to you to decide on your own. Dean Glasket oughtta—"

Teo snapped his fingers, and the next thing they knew, Amanda, Summer, and Shep were standing on the surface of the island beside the wooden outhouse on top of the Everglades kemana.

"Well, stick me through and call me a barbequed hog." Shep glanced around. "How in tarnation did he do that?"

"Teleportation." Amanda grabbed the box of antidote vials from him and shrugged. "I guess we're not gonna be coming down here anymore. Thanks for doing it anyway."

"Okay, shifter girl." Summer folded her arms. "You better tell me what the hell happened. And why we're not dead."

"Adalynn doesn't wanna kill us. She wants to help *me*. Which I probably would've told you eventually if you hadn't gotten so pissed at me for not playing rule-breaker with you." Amanda stomped across the island toward the Academy's moored airboat.

Summer scoffed and glanced at Shep, but the wizard lifted both hands in surrender and shrugged. "I'm only the driver."

"You're not making any sense. Amanda!"

"I don't have to make sense. You almost got yourself in serious trouble."

"Oh, yeah? What about *you*?" Both girls stomped up onto the airboat, and Shep shuffled after them. He didn't try to insert himself into the conversation as he untied the rope around the tree stump and hopped onto the airboat to get the propeller started. "You were meeting that crazy...whatever she is twice a week to, what? Be her slave?"

"Saithe," Amanda muttered.

"What?"

"That's what she is." A slow smile crept across the shifter girl's lips. "Ever heard of a Saithe?"

"Until tonight, no. And I don't care."

Shep steered them back upriver toward the kemana, pretending to ignore the entire conversation as the girls sat on the deck.

"I kind of think you do, though."

Summer snorted. "You're delusional."

"Maybe. *I* wasn't the one spouting off conspiracy theories about Adalynn Jade trying to turn me into some kind of criminal shifter slave or...whatever you thought she was doing to me."

The witch slapped the back of her hand against Amanda's arm and looked out over the swamp around them. "Shut up. That was... I couldn't help it."

"Yeah, I know. Maybe I should've let you keep talking for a while without the antidote."

"Well, it's too late now."

"Yep." Amanda grinned. "You're welcome."

---

The Academy's campus hadn't settled down that much by the time they made it back from the airboat dock. Shep saluted the girls and took his leave, probably to go back to wherever he lived on the school grounds and stay away from this newest bout of mischief. The other students, however, still roamed around the grounds, shouting at each other or muttering their secrets to themselves. No one seemed to notice Amanda and Summer booking it toward the main building and Principal Glasket's office.

They didn't make it halfway up the stairs before Glasket came racing down to join them. "Did you get it?"

"Yeah, it's all in the box. We should have more than enough." Amanda handed her the black handbag still mostly full of cash. "I thought you'd want to—"

"I trust you, Miss Coulier. Now it's time for you to deliver these to the dorms and wherever else your fellow students may be at this hour."

Summer snorted as they all headed briskly down the staircase again. "Hiding up in your office, huh?"

"I most certainly was not *hiding*—" Glasket cleared her throat. "I believe Miss Flannerty may need one of these antidotes as well."

"Naw, I already got one."

The principal stared at her, then gestured toward the front of the building. "Then please be quick about delivering them to those who've been affected by the Dreamscape. If I had to guess, I'd say that's everyone at this point. Oh, and I'll take some to the other teachers."

Amanda didn't move fast enough for Glasket, who reached into the box of vials and grabbed a handful. "Come back to my office when you're finished. Hopefully, this'll do what we need it to do."

Then the principal stalked off toward the back of the main building, her low heels clicking urgently against the floor.

Summer hissed out a laugh and stuck a thumb over her shoulder toward Glasket. "*She's* got somethin' up her skirt, huh?"

"Yeah." Amanda shot her a sidelong glance and hurried for the front doors. "Maybe it's the fact that you're still talking like you didn't get an antidote at all."

"What? Hey, come on." Summer raced after her. Then they were both outside, heading toward the closest group of students huddling together in the grass and sharing their secrets. "Wait a minute, shifter girl. Hey. *Amanda.*"

"What?" She stopped and turned to frown at the witch. "What do you want?"

"I... Shit. I only wanna help."

"Really? Because I'm not sure how following me to the kemana and getting caught and trying to convince me Adalynn Jade's trying to kill me is all that helpful."

"Okay, *that* was the blue flower dust talking." Summer scratched the shaved side of her head and shrugged. "Which apparently was like some dark fear I had or whatever. I get it. I was worried about you. Whatever that lady's into, or whatever she'd told you, I wouldn't be so convinced it's all good stuff. And, you know…going *completely* criminal isn't the right way for you to go."

Amanda stared at her friend and readjusted the box of vials in her arms. "I know. So *you* know, she's not a mob boss. If that's what you were wondering."

"Maybe a little, yeah."

"Okay, look. She's helping me connect to some other shifters who…can maybe help me figure out how to do this whole school and eventually be a bounty hunter as a shifter thing. No, she hasn't made me do anything illegal, either."

"Right. I get it. I just… I mean, I guess you could've told me that sooner."

"Maybe don't be a jerk next time."

Summer choked back a laugh. "Sure. I'll try. I know you can take care of yourself, shifter girl. I was…worried. I guess."

"Well, thanks." They both stared at the box in Amanda's arms. "We should get these out to everybody."

"Yeah, totally. I'll help."

# CHAPTER TWENTY-NINE

By the last week of the semester—which was shortened to allow all the students to only take *one* final per day—the students had finally forgotten about what had happened with the Dreamscape dust and the chaotic night of Spring Fling. Or at least they'd all stopped talking about it. An unspoken agreement went through the school, students and teachers included, that everything said that night before they received the antidote would be completely wiped out of memory.

It helped that they still had the last few Louper matches of the season to look forward to although the Florida Gators came in second-to-last on the roster. LeFor didn't seem remotely put off by it, and the school still threw the team and the student body a party the week before finals to celebrate their first Louper season. "We'll get 'em next year! I can feel it!"

"I bet he can't even feel his hand with how hard he's grabbing that mic," Jackson muttered.

Amanda and her friends chuckled and headed for the massive spread on the banquet tables and the giant cake shaped like an alligator—complete with a fondant VR headset across its frosting-scaled eyes.

That was the last bit of celebration they had before it was time to buckle down and focus on their finals.

Ms. Calsgrave told Amanda she'd pass her for the year with the required credits for Illusions class, which she'd earned with her second semester spent in the greenhouse. "You grew an entire row of a plant that's pretty impossible to grow, from what I understand. However unintentionally you did it."

"Thanks, Ms. Calsgrave."

The witch studied the greenhouse and raised an eyebrow. "We'll work on a better labeling system for the seeds when you come back next year. Are you *sure* you got rid of all the grubs?"

"Yeah. I dusted this place pretty thoroughly." Amanda pointed at the plastic tote filled with salt. "They're all in there. Want me to—"

"Nope. No. I'll get rid of it myself. You go focus on the rest of your finals, huh?"

That was exactly what Amanda did. She turned in her History of Oriceran report that was basically a bunch of speculation about what other races existed on Oriceran and might have made their way to Earth without anyone knowing about it. She *really* wanted to write up something about the Saithe but had a feeling Ms. Ralthorn would have no idea what she was talking about and would fail her. She passed with a B.

Mr. LeFor wanted them to write an essay about how they would improve their robot projects, knowing what they knew now, and that was easy enough to pump out four pages of what she figured the Augmented Technology teacher wanted to hear.

Their Alchemy final for Mrs. Zimmer consisted of nothing more than being *willing* to attempt using the crushed grub-skin powder on a tiny lockbox their teacher had imbued with various wards. None of the freshmen succeeded in opening the thing—although Alex walked away from his attempt with a singed shirt and a blush that deepened every time Zimmer said his name.

"Get ready for next year," the teacher called after them as the students raced from the room. "That's when the *real* fun starts! Have a good summer!"

---

Whether it had been designed that way or came about through sheer luck, their last final of the week was for Petrov and his impossible obstacle course.

As the freshmen gathered on the training field first thing in the morning on their last day of school, Amanda glared at the obstacle course.

"This is never gonna happen," Grace said beside her. "How are any of us supposed to pass this class and our finals if we couldn't finish the thing?"

"Hey." Amanda grinned at her friend. "Remember what you said about tearing it down?"

"It's the last day of school, Amanda. We can't do that."

"Well…not the way *you* were thinking, maybe. I'm sick of being tossed off that thing. I have an idea." She turned and scanned the field, but Mr. Petrov was apparently running late for his last final of the semester. "Okay. Before he gets here, tell our team what's happening."

Grace shook her head. "What's happening?"

"Come here, and I'll *tell* you." Amanda whispered her plan into her friend's ear, fighting the whole time to keep from laughing when the blonde witch kept leaning away from her and staring at her in disbelief.

"Are you *sure*?"

"Yeah, it's worth a shot. Let everybody know."

Word went around through the freshman class in under five minutes, and while at least half of them shot Amanda weird looks, no one argued with the plan. Some of them—like Jackson and Summer—burst out laughing and shot Amanda a thumbs-up when they heard it.

The whispers died instantly once Petrov finally showed up on the training field with a mug of coffee in hand. "All right, kids. You know the deal. Looks like I won't be passing anybody this semester, but hey. There's always next year, when you get to start over with the *new* freshmen. What are you smirking at, Brunsen?"

"Nothing." Tommy clasped his hands behind his back and shook his head, but he couldn't wipe the smile off his face.

"Whatever. First team! You're up! Maybe one of you will finish this thing." Petrov sat in his folding chair in front of the training building door and sipped his coffee. With a quick wave of his hand, he conjured the floating timer in the air and pointed at it. "Go!"

Amanda was the first to take off, as her plan dictated. *This time, I'm not holding back.*

The other five students in her team held back and watched.

"Oh, come on." Petrov rolled his eyes and shook his head. "What's the point if you're gonna freeze up? Go!"

All the other students were watching Amanda at this point.

The second she made it up the rope ladder at the beginning of the course, she snarled and shifted, darting out of the way when the first magical gun blast launched her way.

Petrov snorted coffee from his nose and groaned as he tried to keep it all from spilling into his lap.

Shouting encouragement, the rest of her team raced toward the obstacle course and got to work climbing the rope ladder.

Amanda couldn't have been better suited for this obstacle course as the small gray wolf darted away from bright-orange blasts. It got even better when she clawed her way up one of the short wooden posts holding up this end of the monkey bars and leapt up on top of the bars instead of trying to swing across. The magitech weapons swiveled on their limited heads and shot off bright orange blasts at her, but the shifter girl was too quick. She grabbed the first in her jaws and with a quick shake of her head, wrenched it from its setting and tossed it over the side of the course.

The second one got batted aside by a swift paw until it aimed directly at the third gadget-gun and blew it off its mount. The gadget whined as it dropped to the grass below, throwing sparks and spewing random bursts of orange magic.

The freshmen cheered—even the ones still on the ground waiting for their turn to run the course.

Behind Amanda, the rest of her team swung easily across the monkey bars without getting blasted by devices once she'd launched the last gun off its mount and it landed in the grass at Petrov's feet.

She belly-crawled beneath the wall of crackling purple light covering the suspended bridge, then stopped at the thin ledge before the final platform and waited for the rest of her team to catch up. The trickiest part was getting Corey across the bridge, but fortunately, Tommy managed to slam the Kilomea down onto the wooden slats in time to avoid both of them getting caught in the magical charge. Then the entire team was across and standing on the final platform. They spread out, taking their time to make sure they had the right footing on the platform before the wooden panels slid away from each other and left a giant hole in the center. Because this time, they didn't have to avoid being shot off the course.

Amanda crouched on the edge of the final platform and snarled when the wall of brilliant white light that looked so much like Adalynn Jade's magic flared in front of them.

*It's not her magic. I'm finishing this course.*

She leapt through the shimmering white wall and landed on all fours in the grass on the other side.

Her teammates roared in encouragement and leapt after her one right after the other. The rest of the freshman class exploded in cheers and laughter, mostly at the sight of the destroyed magic-blasting gadgets that had plagued them for an entire year.

The rest of Amanda's team jostled each other and patted each other on the back, grinning at the small gray wolf sitting back on her haunches and panting.

Petrov stared at the dismantled gadgets littering the grass and slowly stood from his lawn chair. "Quiet!"

The cheers cut off instantly although a few kids still laughed and pushed each other around in their excitement.

"Listen up." Petrov scowled at the team who'd finally beaten his impossible course. "*That's* how you use the skills you already have. And teamwork, for what it's worth. Coulier."

Amanda stood from her haunches, her sides heaving and her tongue hanging out of her mouth.

The teacher snorted. "Go put your clothes back on. The rest of you can get outta here. Looks like you're all passing the class after all because I don't have an obstacle course anymore."

The freshmen cheered and jumped around again, and someone took up chanting, "Shifter girl! Shifter girl!"

Amanda had to ignore all of them as she picked up her clothes in her wolf's jaws. Petrov smirked at her and opened the door to the training building to give her space to shift and get dressed again in private. "Way to use your head, Coulier. Maybe next time, don't destroy my gear."

He closed the door behind her, and she grinned as she shifted back and quickly tugged on her clothes.

*Maybe next time they'll cheer my* name *instead of shifter girl. I guess it works for now.*

---

The school threw another huge party with a giant feast for lunch, celebrating the end of the Academy of Necessary Magic's first successful year. Amanda lost count of how many times she had to listen to the story of her as a wolf tearing down Petrov's obstacle course, but she wasn't tired of hearing it. Not yet, anyway.

Jackson tried to make a toast to her for the fifth time, and the other kids groaned and waved him off. Still, they kept talking about the shifter girl who'd been able to beat the course because she could be a wolf too.

Amanda's smile faded a little when she heard the crunch of tires on gravel, and she slipped away from the celebration to go check out the entrance to the campus. *That's a familiar engine.*

Sure enough, Sheila's bright red shape rolled down the gravel road between the Academy's front gates. Amanda grinned and broke into a run before Johnny stepped out and shut the door behind him.

"Johnny! Hey!" She waved furiously with her arm stretched over her head even though there was no one else around on this side of the school grounds. She stopped when the passenger-side door of the dwarf's red Jeep opened, and it wasn't Lisa Breyer getting out.

It was Fiona Damascus.

"Hey, kid." Johnny sniffed and hooked his thumbs through his belt loops as he walked toward the shifter girl.

"You're early." Amanda tried to smile, but she couldn't stop staring at the redheaded shifter woman who'd gotten out of Johnny's Jeep. *Why is she riding around with him?*

"Yeah, well, figured I might as well come and congratulate you for a year at…school. Or whatever." Johnny stopped and frowned at Fiona. "And I got more stake in this than I wanted. Y'all have met?"

"Yep." Amanda blinked. "Why are you—"

"We had to change a few things about our arrangement with Ms. Jade," Fiona said with a smile. "I heard what happened with the flowers. Or at least as much as she wanted to tell me."

"Okay…" The shifter girl glanced back and forth between Fiona and Johnny, who scowled at everything. "What does that have to do with Johnny?"

"Yeah, I ain't a fan of this whole setup either, kid. Trust me.

But I ain't fixin' to get in the way of your trainin' and whatever else you need to do to…be yourself. Or whatnot. So. I'm takin' you home. You and this…Fiona can start gettin' to work doin' whatever it is she thinks is so important for you to start right now."

"Oh, don't say it like it's such an inconvenience, Johnny." Fiona grinned at him. "We'll stay out of your hair."

"Uh-huh. All summer long, too." He nodded at Amanda. "Your bags packed?"

"Well, no. I thought you were coming tomorrow."

"You got a problem leavin' today?"

Amanda paused, then threw herself at the dwarf and wrapped her arms around him. He stiffened, then gently patted her back. "Nope. I can be ready in, like, ten minutes."

"All right. Then I'll come with ya." Shooting a warning glance over his shoulder at Fiona, who stayed put beside Sheila, he took off toward the central field and the dorm buildings beyond with the shifter girl at his side. "Between you and me, kid, it was a helluva surprise to be gettin' a call from Adalynn Jade. She's the one suggested I made some room for you and that redhead shifter to get started on…whatever."

"You listened to her and did what she said?" Amanda laughed. "That doesn't sound like you."

"Yeah, it normally don't, huh?" Johnny chuckled and rubbed his mouth and thick red beard. "Adalynn's an old friend. From way back when I ain't fixin' to remember much. I trust her. Reckon she's got your best interests in mind too, so it's a done deal on my end."

"An old friend?" Amanda peered up at the dwarf with a sly smile. "Figures."

"Oh, yeah? What's that supposed to mean?"

"I don't know. Now I get to spend my summer learning from some shifters who apparently really know their stuff."

"Uh-huh." Johnny smirked and playfully nudged her shoulder.

"I heard they do somethin' or other with magic, too. Should be interestin.'"

Amanda barked out a laugh. "Oh, yeah."

Classes continue in the third semester. Will Amanda figure out her talent? Bounty hunter training continues in *CURSE IN THE GLADES*

Get sneak peeks, exclusive giveaways, behind the scenes content, and more. PLUS you'll be notified of special **one day only fan pricing** on new releases.

Sign up today to get free stories.

Visit: https://marthacarr.com/read-free-stories/

There are a few things we're all supposed to do as grownups, but we put off until we have kids. One of them is getting a will. I waited till last week.

It's not smart to wait. So, don't use me as your role model on this one.

I have a grown child and should have done it sooner but for all the years he was growing up I didn't have much to leave him. The Offspring is fond of pointing out that I hit it big as an author *after* he was out of the house and he didn't get to enjoy any of it. I just smile and say nothing. He responds with, "Uh huh," in a knowing way. It's our thing. And I've found as the parent of a 33-year-old, saying very little with a slight smile is always the right choice.

Anyway, I finally got around to doing a will and all the parts that go with it. I thought about doing a will eleven years ago when I was diagnosed with terminal cancer (another and longer story), but I was trying to stay alive and didn't want to make dying easier. Crazy thinking, but again, I didn't really have anything to leave anyway.

But here's what I've learned. It's not all about distribution of assets. There's a lot more that will get you thinking about your life as a whole. May even get you to tweak a few things or even change course.

First there's a financial power of attorney and a health power of attorney. The first one will get you to ask yourself who you would trust with what you've squirreled away. That one may be easy, but if it's not, it's an interesting note to yourself that there isn't anyone you trust that much. I have a few, which is just about the right amount. A mentor once taught me that we have rings of people around us. The most outer one is strangers, then acquaintances, then friends, and then that most inner circle where only a few get to enter. However, a lot of us mistake acquaintances for friends and friends for our inner circle. We then get surprised when they don't reciprocate. In the end, most of the people we know are acquaintances, about ten people are in the friend category at most, and only a few are in the inner circle. That was a great lesson to learn and making a will clarified it all over again.

That last one, the health POA in Texas can even come with a longer questionnaire called, Your Way that really spells out your wishes if you can't speak for yourself and asks you to write about your life, knowing this won't be read till you're close to checking out.

It even spells out a definition of what's a friend and how to choose. Apparently, a lot of us don't really know. We collect people like jellybeans and then are surprised when a lot of them are sour.

Anyway, the questionnaire ran me through a long list of questions about the last days, and death and specifically asks for comments about how I felt on each of those topics. No answers are wrong – it's really about what you want. Knowing this would actually be used if needed made me really think about my answers. I wrote that I'm not afraid of death, it's just the next adventure and if I can't participate in life anymore, I'd rather go and see what's just over that distant hill.

The questionnaire then ends with '*at the end I want people to know...*' Wow, what a question. Here's what I said. I have had a great time and it's only gotten better. I'm glad I pursued my dreams and stuck around long enough to see them come to fruition. I made it as a writer and got to try my hand at being a journalist, a national columnist, a non-fiction author, and a fiction author. But even better were the people who've been in my life, especially the Offspring. Being his Mom was the most challenging and best job ever. To do it well I had to keep growing.

In life I did my best to be of service and to listen more than talk and to love without judgment. It's been a blast.

Now that it's done, I can get back to living and pushing the envelope as far as it will go, with my circle of friends around me. More adventures to follow.

Thank you for not only reading this story, but here to these author notes in the back.

I will admit I don't personally have a good will and since I don't want to talk about MY will at the moment, I'll talk about character wills.

I considered talking about James Brownstone's will (another character series here in the Oriceran Universe), but figured it might get complicated with the whole Shay, Allison, new baby boy etc.

Because of the complications with Brownstone (and even worse with Bethany Anne from the Kurtherian Gambit series) I decided to work on a will for Skharr DeathEater in the sword & sorcery barbarian helmed Skharr DeathEater series .

The only close kin he shows (so far) in the series is Horse... his, uh, *horse*.

Skharr would make sure Horse had his freedom, or a good group of mares to be with if Skharr suffered a sword through the guts, a head cut off (hard to come back from that one. Not much to be done with a health potion.)

Now, in the stories so far Skharr has been making a capable

Battle-Axe for reasons known only to him. We know he is making it for his clan, the DeathEaters. The exact why is vague.

Should he die before the Axe is delivered, the Axe would be bequeathed to Ghurn DeathEater, present leader of the clan, or whoever holds that position, as it has been known to change somewhat frequently.

Any gifts from the God Theros, Skharr would bequeath back to the Temple, figuring they would know who should get them.

If Skharr had a bow with him, it would go to the best archer in the DeathEaters clan who could both pull the weight and hit the middle of a target at sixty paces.

The money in his account with the guild would be paid to Sera Ferat to help pay for any of Horse's needs should he show up. If Horse did not show up, then to pay for those Sera employs. Same person for his swords, as she would know who best deserves any sword he would carry.

However, he would request he be buried with his personal axe or axes.

As many times as he has had to fight spiritual beings, he might need them in the afterlife.

I hope you have a fantastic week (or weekend) ahead of you!

Ad Aeternitatem,

Michael Anderle

**Solve a murder, save her mother, and stop the apocalypse?**

What would you do when elves ask you to investigate a prince's murder and you didn't even know elves, or magic, was real?

Meet Leira Berens, Austin homicide detective who's good at what she does – track down the bad guys and lock them away.

Which is why the elves want her to solve this murder – fast. It's not just about tracking down the killer and bringing them to justice. It's about saving the world!

If you're looking for a heroine who prefers fighting to flirting, check out The Leira Chronicles today!

# OTHER SERIES IN THE ORICERAN UNIVERSE

# BOOKS BY MICHAEL ANDERLE

**Sign up for the LMBPN** email list to be notified of new releases and special deals!

**https://lmbpn.com/email/**

For a complete list of books by Michael Anderle, please visit:

**www.lmbpn.com/ma-books/**

## CONNECT WITH THE AUTHORS

**Martha Carr Social**

Website: http://www.marthacarr.com

Facebook: https://www.facebook.com/groups/MarthaCarrFans/

**Michael Anderle Social**

Website: http://lmbpn.com

Email List: http://lmbpn.com/email/

**Social Media:**

https://www.facebook.com/LMBPNPublishing

https://twitter.com/MichaelAnderle

https://www.instagram.com/lmbpn_publishing/

https://www.bookbub.com/authors/michael-anderle